Dying

Famous

JOEY

Just for a second, Joey holds the anti-freeze in his mouth. It's disgusting. Bitter. Rank. Rancid. He tries to swallow but can't. His mouth is rebelling, refusing to allow access for such a noxious substance; as if it were trying to protect the body in which it lives.

With an effort of will Joey finally swallows. The anti-freeze barrels down his oesophagus - a lethal chemical missile, primed to explode in his stomach and unleash waves of poison which will fuck his kidneys, his liver, his brain.

Oh no, no, no....what has he done? Hah! This is what happens when you're stupid enough to get drugged up just before you appear on "the nation's favourite chat show" and then mouth off, live and on air terrible stuff about the Queen of England. How could he have said what he said?..it was obscene, inappropriate and so not #MeToo. It was a career killer. A Joey killer.

The anti-freeze arrives, detonates, in Joey's stomach. It burns and throws out waves of nausea. Joey gags but holds it down. That's it. The first step on the road to the grave. He thinks of his mum; he is a boy and she is holding him in her arms. She is firm and solid, she is comfort and love and she smells of sausages and fry ups. Do his boys think the same about him when he holds them? Is he firm and solid, comfort and love? Does he smell of sausages? He hopes so. Joey realises that his mind is panicking – understanding that its death warrant has just been signed – and throwing out random image after random image: mum and dad, growing up in Doncaster, the boys, Katy, friends he hasn't seen in years, arriving in London poor and ragged, countless flashes of countless photoshoots, catwalks, himself in magazine spreads and standing unnaturally tall on billboards. Contracts. Contacts. Fame. Notoriety. Wealth. Celebrity. And like the total idiot he is, he's only gone and blown it all.

Joey stares down at the bottle of anti-freeze in his hands. Maybe he should just swallow it all down and end the whole sorry, sad show of his life in one go? But, no – that's not the plan. Just a little bit every day. Enough to kill him, but not quickly. This is his last and most demanding role so he needs to follow through and get things right. For once.

As soon as Andy mentioned dealing with the viciously negative 'foul-mouthed attack on Her Royal Highness' fall-out with a pretend cancer scam, Joey saw what he had to do. He had to go along with Andy's plan - only more so. Joey wasn't going to pretend to be dying. He was going to die. He was going to die as 'brave and beloved' Joey, 'struggling against a terrible odds' only to 'tragically lose his fight against a killer disease'. He was going to choose his time and place to die.

Joey was going to go out on top.

THE PRODUCER

This afternoon is one of The Producer's Fun Days, he is going to have a bit of R and R. And why the hell not? He deserves it. He's built up a huge media empire over the last few years and if he wants to have some fun, who's to tell him no? No-one. No one would dare. People don't say no to The Producer. Not ever. He can make you, or he can break you – the Producer decides who and who will not be a celebrity. And nowadays everyone wants to be a celebrity, right? Look at America – elected a celebrity to be president, for fuck's sake!

And if it so happens that The Producer's 'Fun Day' involves humiliating and sexually abusing impressionable, maybe even vulnerable, young women then so what? A man in his position, a man of his wealth and power, can do exactly as he wants and get away with it. He knows his victims won't say a thing. Even after he has humiliated and abused them they'll still not tell anyone. Instead they'll keep their mouths shut hoping, just hoping, that The Producer may yet smile upon them and usher them into the world of celebrity – a place where their dreams could come true, a place where they could be the next Kim Kardashian or even a Donald Trump! Even if one of his victims did decide to share their story he has more than enough contacts and influence through his stable of global and national stars, television shows and franchises to control what the media says.

Oh, these 'wannabes', these aspiring stars, they want it. They want it oh so badly. They're his to play with, his to build up and knock down, his to use, his to abuse. He owns them. Body and soul.

SHELLEY

As the car cruises comfortably and quietly through the West End traffic on the way to the restaurant to meet Andrew, that obnoxious faggot, Shelley peers out of the tinted windows, checking out the ordinary, little people, scuttling around the streets. Look at them. Pathetic! Living their hum-drum, dull lives, just finished work, going back to the wives and snotty no-hoper kids, dashing for a bit of shopping in some cheap clothing chain store. Horrible, horrible! Thinking of such miserable, drab ordinariness, she shivers inwardly.

Bored by the sad, ordinary, little people, Shelley's attention wanders, focusing on her Prada handbag and, more specifically, the large rock of crack cocaine hidden it. Christ, she loves her crack does Shelley, fantastic stuff! Okay, so maybe the next day you might feel a bit down and a bit paranoid, but nothing that can't be smoothed out with a few drinks. Or some more crack. And the hit, wow, the hit! Once felt never forgotten! She knows of course that she shouldn't really be smoking it, what with her being famous, rich and beautiful and in a responsible position due to her influence over the young people of the world - but the public just doesn't realise that being famous, rich and beautiful is very hard work! Every day is filled with questions. What should I wear? Am I slim enough? How's my make-up today? Have I got the right handbag for this or that occasion? Who should I be *seen* to be speaking to? Which party do I go to and which should I snub? Where should I be this afternoon to stand the best chance of being papped? These are all difficult and complex questions. Being a celeb is a demanding business, not everybody can handle it. Her lifestyle involves a lot of a pressure, and the crack is Shelley's way of relaxing, of dealing with the stress she endures every day. She deserves it. She is *entitled* to it.

Briefly Shelley considers getting her driver to make a stop so she can smoke a quick rock before she meets Andrew. But, she reconsiders – where would she find somewhere private enough on a busy day in the West End of London for a smoke? Plus she needs to keep a clear head; she needs something from Andrew and, faggot or no faggot, he is *very, very* smart. She needs to be on top of her game to make sure she gets what she wants from him.

JANEY

The limo speeds away from Heathrow and Janey is delighted with the way things went. What a fucking entrance! The moment she stepped into the arrivals lounge it had been total chaos: screaming fans, paparazzi, cameras, microphones, journalists, police, security. All there for her, Janey Jax. She's a *real* star. Rivals come, rivals go and still she stays at the top. Numero. Uno. No-one comes even slightly close – not even Madonna. And look at that Missy Go Go. Where is she now? Nowhere.

Of course, she could have flown over in the private jet, but with a world tour about to kick off she needed an entrance with maximum impact - at least that's what Charlie had advised and, as always, Charlie had been right.

The day's events have left her tired, though. So tired. People forget that she's not a young girl any more. She may still look like she's in her twenties but, in reality, she's far removed from that happy decade. Nowadays it takes hard work to keep looking as good as she does. Hard work and fresh, young flesh. Very young flesh. She hopes Charlie won't have any problems sourcing what she needs here in England. But, no, she shouldn't worry. Charlie is very capable. He knows what she wants, and he is bound to her. By blood. He is her creature.

ANDREW

Ahah! You're here, good! Welcome to my world - the weird, dysfunctional world of celebrity – a world of fakes and freaks, liars and cheats, and I include myself in that little list. Anyway, I'm glad you've decided to join me on this journey into Celebrity Land. Please be aware though, you're in for a bumpy ride, so, fasten that proverbial seatbelt. Right, come on, stop hanging around out there like a spare tool, Shelley's arrived at the restaurant so come in and join us!

What a hideous, pointless, nasty human being. That's my exact line of thought as I sit here in what is arguably one of the best restaurants in the country. It's certainly one of the most expensive. Across the table from me is Shelley Bright. I should be at least vaguely pleased with myself, after all Shelley is one of the most beautiful and admired women in the country, christened "England's Sweetheart" by my mates in the trashy tabloids and glossy celeb mags. To the rest of the world Shelley is a chart-topping singer, television star, famous beauty, fashion icon. To me the woman is a total…well, I won't repeat myself - please see above.

As I chew on my ridiculously expensive Kobe steak I try to look interested and engaged as Shelley drawls on, in her grating accent, which is half Essex and half south

London council estate, about her handbag collection. Apparently she's got nearly a hundred of the bloody things, worth far north of three hundred thousand quid. She sees no contradiction in such grotesquely conspicuous consumption of over-priced bags with her role as a United Nations Goodwill Ambassador. But that's a very celeb thing. These people are not like ordinary folk. Their toweringly titanic egos dictate to them that they are simply not bound by the same rules of decent, normal behaviour as other people. I think Shelley, like many other celebrities (and lots of bankers, financiers and industrialists - but that's another story for another day), is actually a borderline psychopath. Not a goggle-eyed, axe-wielding psychopath but someone who displays psychopathic traits such as an inability to feel empathy, compassion, or guilt.

Shelley is talking. Still talking. About sodding handbags. Gucci, Prada, Chanel, Versace. She has the lot. God bless her. I am *so* pleased for her. I look closely at Shelley as she witters on. Now I am gay as gay can be, I wasn't so much hit with the lavender stick as I was bludgeoned by it, but even I can see that Shelley is an extraordinarily beautiful woman. Tall, slim, great tits, long and glossy blonde hair cascading over elegant shoulders, framing a face with luminous blue eyes, high cheekbones, luscious cupid's bow lips and that famous, finely structured nose that is neither too big nor too small. And yet despite all this beauty there is a problem.

Look closely, that's it, get right in there. Look into her eyes. Sure they are the brightest blue but they are peculiarly empty, devoid of life or even emotion. There is nothing going on. The wheel is turning but the hamster is well and truly dead. In fact, Shelley reminds me of one those velveteen covered, plastic nodding dog toys that people used to stick on the dashboards of Ford Escorts. Poor Shelley, she has everything needed to be a celebrity: good looks, ruthless ambition, the readiness to betray anyone or anything in a single heartbeat and a vast, ever hungry ego. Apart from that, though, she's shallow, empty and as thick as a prison wall. Shelley is about money and fame. And that's it. If you scratch her outer veneer of celebrity glamour, if you peel it back and look beneath, you'll find nothing but a gaping, black space with the wind whistling through it.

*But who am I, anyway, to so bitchily take the piss out of "England's Sweetheart?" Well, this is definitely the first time we've met (don't take this the wrong way, but I do move in somewhat more elevated circles than you), and you won't hear my name mentioned on the tele or see it in those crappy celeb gossip magazines that you buy almost religiously from Tesco every week. Despite my deliberately low profile, I'm intimately involved in the celebrity world. I'm one of celebrity's backroom boys. In fact I'm **the** backroom boy. I am Andrew Manning, celebrity agent extraordinaire. I've spent twenty years working with the rich and famous. I* *specialise in stars in trouble, I'm the guy celebs come to when they've screwed up, when they've been caught taking drugs, sleeping with the wrong girl (or boy), when they've been discovered cheating, lying or stealing, when they have a messy divorce to deal with or when they need something doing that's a little bit (or quite a lot) outside the bounds of the law. If you're famous and you're in the shit then I'm your man – people in the business call me The King of Scandal!*

Apart from that...I am average looking (though with the glossy sheen that only money and very expensive dentistry can achieve), I am short, I have a receding hairline, I am a happy, proud and (given the chance) proselytising homosexual, I am in my forties, I am ridiculously wealthy, I am a fixer, I am a press agent, I am a re-packager and reviver of damaged celebrity. I know where all the bodies are buried. I know who did what to whom. I am a powerful and feared man. Mess with me and I'll fuck you up. Big time.

That's about as much as I'm going to tell you about me – for now. It's a pleasure to make your acquaintance. I hope you stick around, I'm sure we can have fun together.

Enough introductions, let's get back to the restaurant, where Shelley has (finally and mercifully) moved on from talking incessantly about handbags. At last I'm going to find out what this ghastly woman wants from me.

"So, Andrew, I got, like, a little problem you could help me with, innit. It's Jack, like, it's all that gay stuff, I just can't take it no more. I is a woman, I need to be loved, innit. I just can't stay in no pretend marriage one moment longer!"

Jack is Jack Brierley, her very wealthy and extremely famous (and secretly gay) Premier League footballer husband. Jack and Shelley live in an outrageously opulent mansion in Cheshire. Their marriage four years ago (all put together by yours truly, thanks very much) was the celeb event of the year. Jack needed a wife to smother (the all too true) rumours about his sexuality and Shelley wanted a high profile and (very) rich husband. Ah, a celebrity match made in heaven!

I look at Shelley more closely. I ponder exactly what she is going to ask me, and reply, "Shelley, love, hold on a moment, let's just rewind here. Why are you so squeamish all of a sudden? You knew Jack was gay when you married him and you know he's been fiddling around with other football luvies and God knows who else since day one, so why's all this become a problem now?"

Shelley seems momentarily nonplussed by my remarks, then gathers herself and comes back with, "Andrew, I is really not sure that you should speak to me like that, I thinks it's a bit rude, innit."

"Oh, for goodness sake, spare me... *rude* is what I do! It's one of the reasons I'm good at my job, it's a sign of my willingness to get down in there in the shit and sort out the kind of problems people like you get yourselves into. If my business had a motto, it'd be 'I get my hands dirty and yours stay clean,' so you'll have to grant me the odd act of rudeness, I'm afraid. Now, cut the wailing and gnashing of teeth about the horror of having a gay husband and tell me exactly what's going on and what you want me to do for you."

Shelley's quite right, I am rude. And, by the way, my use of bad language is appalling. I'm not sure why I swear so much, but I do – God knows why. Consider yourself warned and I hope you're not going to prove to be uptight and easily shocked. If, however, you are a sensitive soul then you might as well fuck off now. Oops, sorry, there I go again...

Truth be told, I'm already pretty sure that I know what Shelley wants. I'm almost certain it'll have something to do with her on-going, and so far unsuccessful, attempt to break the American market.

And waddaya know...here we go..."Well, like, it's not that I don't love Jack, even if he is a quee...sorry, gay, innit. It's cos me and my management, well, we reckon I can be, like, dead big in America, innit, but, like, no-one knows Jack in the States and, like I really, really want to make it out there..."

Now I know *exactly* where this conversation is going and I start singing Tammy Wynette's D.I.V.O.R.C.E. in my head.

"....and you see, my management have got me all fixed up over there with DJ Extasy and he is, like, just sooo famous in America, innit, and he says he'll be my boyfriend so we can get some really good press and, like, those Swedish guys have written me some great songs, innit, and, like, Jack won't be no help breaking me in the American market and I mean, like, I don't see why he should stand in my way, it's cos I got the right to fully express myself as, like, a woman and a star, innit?..."

"Okay, okay...slow down. Let's just be honest here, Shelley, you have a marriage of convenience with Jack and now you're looking for a divorce of convenience so you can enter into a new relationship of convenience to further your career and earn even more money than you already do. Oh, and I'm guessing you're also looking for Jack to take the blame for the divorce and to pay you off with a nice, juicy settlement. Would that be about right by any chance?"

Shelley looks a trifle petulant, but nods in silent agreement.

"And how, exactly, might we go about achieving your wishes? Any ideas?"

"Well, I thought we could..." Shelley mumbles, averting her glance away from me, the end of her sentence so quiet as to be inaudible. Not that I need to hear what she's saying to know what's on her mind, I just want to make her squirm a bit, so I reply, "I'm sorry, I missed that, what did you say?"

"I thought we could…." Shelley's lips move but still no sound.

"And again…" I press, leaning forward and cupping my right hand behind my ear.

"Oh, shit, fuck… blackmail, blackmail. I thought we could blackmail him! There, is you happy now that I is saying the word?"

"It's not a question of being happy, I just want to make sure we're both singing from the same script."

I lean back in my seat, look at Shelley, again I see a dead hamster in my mind, tumbling around lifelessly inside a spinning wheel, and I think about how I might deal with her request. Quickly I come to a decision. "Alright, this is what we'll do. Jack's weak point is, obviously, his sexuality. We'll put together a little scenario in which he'll come into a contact with an attractive guy in a controlled environment, that being one in which we can covertly film. Based on Jack's taste we'll select our guy carefully to ensure that he'll give into temptation, we'll get a nice movie made of the action, and, bish bosh, you get your divorce. And when it comes to your juicy settlement…no problem. Just show Jack the mini cinematic classic we have of him going at it hammer and tongs with another bloke. You'll get whatever you ask. Jack knows what happens to fags in football." This is ironic, to my mind. Trust me, there are lots and lots of gay footballers. God knows I've rescued enough of them from the shit over the years! I mean, let's be honest, what kind of a man likes running around in tight shorts with fit young men for ninety minutes, and then get naked and jump in a bath with them afterwards? A gay man, that's who - it's bloody obvious!

Across the table, I can see Shelley is listening intently. She looks very excited by the idea of a divorce and a big pay out: good grief, could that be a spark of life in her eyes? Surely not!

"That all sounds great, like, but you forgot one thing, innit."

"What's that, Shelley?"

"I got my public profile to think of ain't I? It's like what you said, innit, you gotta make sure he's the one what takes the blame for the divorce."

"Already factored that in, piece of piss, we just find some long-legged blonde with big tits and bung her some cash to be the third party. That way you can be SHATTERED SHELLEY WEEPS IN PUBLIC AS AFFAIR WITH BLONDE BIMBO REVEALED and Jack will be BONKING BRIERLEY BANGS BUSTY BLONDE. You're a cruelly wronged "England's Sweetheart" and Jack's a red blooded heterosexual male...you're happy and Jack builds on his macho, shagging, lads together, hetero reputation - though at the cost of a huge divorce settlement to you."

"Oh, Andrew, you is a genius, innit, in a, like, twisted way, and I still think you is rude, but, yeh, like, you is genius. Will it cost a lot?"

"Well, obviously. You know I don't come cheap, but you also know I always deliver."

"Okay, so will you set it all up like?"

"Yep, don't worry, I need to think about exactly where we do the job, and I'll need some stuff from you - Jack's movements, the kind of guys he likes - but let me think things through and we'll meet again to finalise everything."

Shelley looks very happy. Like the cat that got the cream. She's delighted, and genuinely happy at the prospect of completely fucking over her husband. Bless her.

Right. At this point I think I should level with you. You've been listening in on me for a while now. I'm guessing you think I'm a bit of a shitbag, ready to slag off the people who fund my lifestyle, prepared to blackmail one of my own kind to line my pockets. So, here's the deal. Your opinion (even though I appreciate the sincerity of its offer) is simply an irrelevance to me. That's to say, I don't care what you think. I'm not like you.

I've never wanted two kids and a mortgage and a nine to five job, not even if I had been unlucky enough to have been born straight. I've always wanted more: more money, more power, more independence. I may well despise most celebrities and lots of them are truly disgusting people, but given the lifestyle working with them gives me, I'll put up with the rough that comes with the smooth. Sorry, I'm unapologetic about what I am and what I do so if you and me are going to get along, you're just going to have to accept that. As the divine Gloria once said, "I am what I am." Like me. Don't like me. I really don't give a damn.

Meanwhile, back in the restaurant, the delightful and scintillating Shelley, who's confident that she's now got what she wanted, has moved the conversation back to the pressing subject of handbags. And then make up. And from there she segues almost seamlessly to the subjects of fashion, expensive fragrances, Vertu phones and other bling. You know, all the important and meaningful things in life.

And still Shelley talks. On and on. Spouting a load of non-stop, total crap. I distract myself by looking at a cute young waiter over the other side of the restaurant. Briefly, I toy with the idea of slipping him my number. Then I remember that, though very rich, I'm probably old enough to be his dad and not exactly sex on legs. Anyway, my gorgeous Johnny is waiting for me back home in Primrose Hill.

When I've had absolutely as much as I can bear of Shelley, and feel myself sinking beneath a sea of utterly pointless pointlessness I, politely, call a halt to proceedings by citing a heavy workload. We stand, say our goodbyes and air kiss. I tell Shelley we'll meet again to put the finishing touches to our plan for Jack's demise as her husband. Outside the restaurant she has a car waiting for her. She asks if I would like a lift, but the idea of spending any more time with this hideous woman makes me feel queasy so I decline.

SHELLEY

Shelley's chauffeur opens the door to her car, allowing her to step in and relax into the comfortable leather back seat. She is extremely pleased that Andrew has declined the offer of a lift. She snaps out an address in Holland Park to her now seated driver, imperiously waving a "forward" motion with one immaculately manicured hand.

That fucking gay wanker, Andrew. She fucking hates him. Smart-arse, shit stabbing, gay bastard with his clever words and his turd-burgling ways. King of Scandal? Hah, bollocks, hideous bum bandit, more like. Bloody queers, she's fucking sick of them. For God's sake, it's bad enough being married to one, let alone having to pay shed loads of money to one to get rid of the other!

Nope, there'll be no more poofs for Shelley. She can't remember the last time she had a proper shag. Doesn't Andrew realise how hard it's been for her, married to bloody Jack? Okay, the marriage did wonders for her career, but at the cost of having to live with some bloody shirt lifter. She has needs, she's a special person who should be treated right, and that bloody Jack got a good deal out of the marriage too. Nobody whispers about him being a fag anymore. She saved his career, and now it's only right that she should be allowed to move on and that she should get a huge divorce settlement for pretend wife fucking services rendered. Who the fuck is Andrew to look down his nose at her?

Oh, but enough of Andrew! Shelley's thoughts shift again to that tightly wrapped cellophane package in her handbag. She opens the bag, for the seventh or eighth time today, just to check that the package is still there. She feels a stab of relief and excitement when she sees that indeed it is: when she gets to Anthea's place they're going to have such fun together!

Oh yes, Shelley has her needs...

ANDREW

After Shelley glides away in her chauffeur driven car I decide, it being a mild October night, to walk back home to Primrose Hill. Two minutes from the restaurant and I'll be on Charing Cross Road, from there I can walk to my house in less than forty minutes. Actually, I like to walk. I find its repetitive, mechanical pace very calming and it helps me think, which is good, because at the moment I have a lot of stuff on my mind.

Let me tell you why my thoughts are so busy, trust me, you'll find it interesting.

Tomorrow I have a meeting at with Charlie Gold. Like me, he is (amongst other things) another one of celebrity's back room boys. Charlie is American, loud, brash, obnoxious, fantastically and morbidly obese and *(this is the bit you're going to like)* lawyer and special advisor to Janey Jax. Yup, that's right, *that* Janey Jax, America's number one pop star, damn it, the *world's* number one pop star. For twenty five years she's been up there at the top of the celebrity tree, hugely loved and admired, stunningly sexy, pushing fifty (at least!) but still looking like a woman in her twenties (how *do* these people keep looking so young?). Janey is a phenomenon, stars just don't come any bigger than her. She makes poor old Shelley look like a nobody. Everything about

Janey is Huge with a capital aitch! And there's the worry. Presumably whatever problem or request Charlie is going to put before me on her behalf is going to be as larger than life as the woman herself.

I see you're excited now. You think you might get to meet Janey Jax, don't you? Let's talk about that later: if you knew Janey as well as I do then I'm not entirely sure that you'd really, really want to spend time with her.

My mind full of thoughts of Charlie and Janey, I don't notice the geography of North London sliding by as I walk: Hampstead Road, Mornington Crescent, Arlington Road, Regents Park Road. Before I know it I'm in Primrose Hill and home. Home is Chalcot Square. Gorgeous house, darling. All five floors of a beautiful, Victorian townhouse in one of the most expensive parts of London.

Forgive me for boasting, but I'm proud of this place. It's one of my rewards for nearly twenty years of worshipping at the Altar of Celebrity. Or should that be prostituting myself at…?

Standing outside my enviable home *(sorry, I'll shut up about it now)*, I fumble around in my trouser pockets for my front door keys. Locating them, I quickly unlock the door and enter the house, walking down the hallway towards the back of the property to the kitchen.

Sitting there at the kitchen table drinking a cup of tea is my Johnny. God, I love this man. What a fucking star, a solid piece of diamond, foul-mouthed working class trash from Deptford (as opposed to me, lower middle-class, foul-mouthed trash). Twenty years we've been together. Yep, twenty years!

"Awright, darling, how you doing!" shouts my beautiful Johnny. Honestly, all these years mixing with the rich and famous and he still sounds like a Deptford boy!

He's been with me all the way has Johnny. We met in a Tandy store in Manchester. He was working behind the counter, sent up there from the Deptford branch to fill in for the local manager who'd been caught with his hands in the till. I was there looking for a three-way plug extension. We clicked immediately we saw each other. At that time I was a reporter for a local Manchester rag. But I was ambitious and smart and I soon landed myself a job with a national paper in London where, in a short and intense period, I quickly charmed, bribed, threatened and blackmailed my way to the position I really wanted: Entertainments Editor. I made good use of that position. I spent the time building contact upon contact, listening to the gossip people let slip, storing away fact and hearsay in my head, figuring out how the dynamics of power in the world of celebrity operated. Along the way I threw a few minor league stars to the wolves but I rapidly learnt that it was much more fun saving celebrities from being torn to pieces by the media than it was being part of the savaging. Much more profitable too! And so I, Andrew Manning, fixer to the (oops, gone a bit wonky) stars and The King of Scandal, was born.

There, now you know a little bit more about me...as long as I'm telling the truth, that is. Believe me. Don't believe me. Makes no difference to me. I would say that we meet up over drinks one night so that you could tell me a bit about yourself, except that I already know all about you.

Back in my kitchen, Johnny has stood up, walked over to me and enfolded me in his huge arms squeezing me up against his solid pecs. He's a very big man is Johnny, pushing six foot four and built like that Jack Reacher character from those Lee Child novels. Love those books! And, unlike me, he's a big time gym bunny.

"Oooph," I gasp "lemme go, you're squeezing too bloody hard!"

"Sorry, luv," he releases his grip, which is a relief, "so you got any work you need me to do, bin a bit quiet recently, annit?"

"Well, it's maybe been quite for you, I've been working my arse off as usual. As it happens, though, I do actually have two jobs for you. One's a standard scare 'em off, the other a much more interesting blackmail operation, which I *so* know you're going to love!"

As I talk, Johnny wanders over to the other side of the kitchen and knocks me up a cup of tea, with milk, strong, three sugars. He returns, hands me the drink and says, "hmm, a scare'em and a blackmail, eh? Sounds like it could be fun, what they all about, then?"

At this point I should tell you that Johnny, as well as being the other half, works with me in the business. He's joined in that by Kerry and Griselda, my lovely, talented girls, who are based in the Mayfair office. They're great - you'll meet them later…anyway, back to Johnny. What attracted me to him all those years ago, when he was standing behind that counter at Tandy (besides that fact that he is one is fucking handsome devil) was his sheer physical size and an air that he carried of rough, brutal masculinity with a simmering undertone of aggression. Okay, okay, so I like it a bit rough! So what…we all have our little foibles, don't we? Anyway, those kind of attributes can come in very useful in my line of business. Truth be told, Johnny is a man who relishes violence, not that he goes out seeking it - just that if you decided (foolishly) to start something then he would most definitely finish it and you would be spending a not inconsiderable length of time in hospital.

"Right, well, first up is that vile old queen Michael Reilly. Again! Disgusting man, peddling his repulsive Uncle Tom gay stereotype – 'look at me I'm gay but don't worry, I'm harmless because I'm a camp lisping fool' - fucking idiot!"

As you can probably tell, I can't stand the guy. I think he's utterly creepy. I mean, honestly! Generations of gay men have fought for the right to be treated equally and taken seriously and this idiot goes and sells us all down the river with his camp twat act for a few shekels of silver. What an arsehole! That said, he is a paying customer so I'll take his money and do the job. Here's the story. Unlike the great British public, I know that Michael, rather than a camp and harmless chat show host and comedian, is actually a sleazy old git. Anyway, turns out that he's been paying a twenty one year old rentboy not just for sex, but for dirty, golden showers, piss sex. Said rentboy is now looking to blackmail said piss-fiend. A story as old as time…

I relay all this to Johnny and he looks at me with a look of mock disgust on that ever so handsome face and says, "urgh, too much information…that guy just can't keep it in his pants, can he?"

"No, he can't, and paying someone to piss on him is definitely contrary to his silly and harmless gay act. What I need you to do is deal with the rentboy. He's asking Michael for money, that or he goes to the tabloids about Michael's love of water sports. Of course, our sleazy friend could just pay the boy off but, as we know, if he gets paid once he'll want to be paid again and again. So, Johnny, your job is to arrange a meet with the guy, like you were just a regular punter, and then scare him shitless to make sure he leaves Michael alone and keeps his mouth firmly shut. Call Griselda at the office tomorrow and she'll give you all the details you need to set up a meet with our entrepreneurial little hustler."

"Awright, Andy," says Johnny with a distinct gleam in his eyes, "leave it wiv me, I'll make sure he never says another word about Michael."

"Good man. But listen, don't go too far. You can slap the guy around a little bit if needs be but no "death by buggery" this time. That last incident was just *too* much. If I didn't happen to know every top copper who's taking back handers from the press then you could have gone down!"

"Okay, yeh, but I din't actually kill him did I? I mean, I were maybe a bit excessive…"

"A bit excessive! Johnny, love, you put him in intensive care for a month, the poor sod still can't walk properly to this day!"

* * * * *

Later that night, over a nice bottle of Rioja (or two), I tell Johnny about the other job I have for him. The Jack Brierley blackmail job. He's very excited that Jack is the target (he just loves his legs, apparently). I tell Johnny that I've decided to get Jack where he feels his most comfortable and unthreatened: in his own home. It's a simple matter of Shelley letting Johnny into the house when Jack's out training so he can get a couple of cameras in there. When Jack returns Shelley will find an excuse to absent the marital home for the evening. On her way out of the Brierley mansion she'll 'accidentally' leave the gates to the driveway open, allowing our specially chosen bait to come knocking on Jack's door. And that's it! Let the seduction commence!

Right, well, that's enough for me and you're looking a bit tired. Let's call it a night and get some sleep. We'll talk again tomorrow, don't worry I still have lots to tell you! What do you mean, what's my back story? Are you some kind of fucking Hollywood screenwriter all of a sudden? I may or may not have a "back story" but I'm not going to tell you either way. You cheeky fucking nosey twat. Remember - you're only here to observe, although you can comment if I specifically ask you to do so. Do not ask too many questions, and do not stray into areas of my life where you're not welcome. I will tell you only what I want to tell you.

THE PRODUCER

Today's victim, today's 'Fun Day', for The Producer, is called Sharise. Sharise is from Manchester. She's nineteen, she lives with her mum, and she works in a bar. Like all The Producer's victims, she really, really wants to be famous. Sharise is a pretty girl: tall, slim, high cheek bones, jet black hair, deep green eyes that are full of life and still brim-full with the hope of youth. Great tits and ass, too. The Producer thinks she looks a bit like a dark-haired Shelley Bright. He fucked Shelley once, when she was young and needed favours to get ahead in her career. Fucked her pussy and did her up the arse then came in her face, right here, in this office.

After one of The Producer's PA's has ushered in Sharise. He pushes a clever little button on the underside of his desk that locks his office door and closes the blinds. This is for his own privacy and also acts as a signal to his staff that he is absolutely not to be disturbed. He's got important work to do: shattering somebody's dreams, stealing their innocence and corrupting their body.

"Sharise, welcome, come in, please, I saw the little film clip you sent us, lovely, very nice, you're a very pretty girl - maybe there's something we can do with you."

"Oh really!" squeaks Sharise. She is excited that her dream might be about to come true, but a bit put out that there is nowhere to sit in The Producer's office. "I really, really want this, I'll do anything to get famous! It's all I've ever wanted, it's my dream!"

"Okay, that's great…now stop shuffling, love…just stand there in the circle on the carpet." Sharise looks down at the office floor, she notices there is indeed a circle woven into the thick, luxurious carpet that covers the floor of The Producer's office. It is about five feet from his desk. She positions herself there, in the circle, as instructed.

"Well, love, here's the good news. Besides being a very pretty girl you're obviously enthusiastic and committed, that's good, I like that. The bad news is that your voice is a heap of shit, you just can't sing, love, you're hopeless, bloody awful."

Sharise's mouth drops open, her peachy complexion reddens. She looks lost, confused and distraught; her parade has been well and truly rained on.

"But hold on in there, all is not lost. With a lot of work you could be in with a chance, but that will require a lot of effort on my part, and commitment and personal sacrifice on your part. Above all, Sharise, we need to trust each other and you absolutely must do what I say at all times." Sharise nods eagerly, she's been knocked down, now she is being built back up. She's ready to play her part.

"Trust and commitment," continues The Producer, "that's what this is about, that's what I need from you.

Now, look, your best feature is your body, that's what we can work with - but I need to see more of it to know exactly what I'm going to do with you, how I'm going to, erm, market you. Will you take off your knickers for me?"

"My knickers, sir?" queries a surprised and disbelieving Sharise.

"Yes, your knickers, love. Trust and commitment, remember? Let's not fall at the first at the first hurdle shall we, dear?"

"No sir, yes sir," Sharise coyly reaches up under her skirt and slides her knickers down her smooth, shapely legs.

Now The Producer has a raging hard on. She is ready to play. Good girl.

"Hmm, yes, that's very good but now I need a little bit more commitment from you. Are you ready to lift up your skirt and show me your pussy?"

Sharise looks genuinely shocked by the obscenity that has come from The Producer's mouth, and at the obscenity of his suggestion. The Producer sees her discomfort and his dick gets even harder.

"Sharise, do you really, really want this enough to do what you're told? Come on, love, this is all about you trusting me and you being committed to being a star. Show me you have that commitment – show me you're ready for the lights, the cameras, the fame, the money!"

Sharise struggles with her embarrassment and fear. Makes a decision. She really, really wants it. So she lifts up her dress.

Bingo! The Producer's got her, she's all his. His dick is so hard that it's straining against his trousers, trying to burst out.

The Producer gets up from behind his desk and walks up to Sharise, standing just in front of her. "Lovely pussy you got there, darling, I can definitely do something with that. I'm just going to put a couple of fingers up there, that's okay isn't it, love?"

Through gritted teeth and with eyes closed Sharise says just one word "yes", and tears begin to slide down her pretty, young face (seeing these almost causes The Producer to blow his load in his pants right there and then).

As The Producer feels around inside Sharise with his fingers, his other hand unzips his fly and frees his erection. "Lovely, lovely, you got lovely lips too, beautiful, now, love, trust and commitment, remember, I want you go down on your knees and use those lovely lips to suck my dick...okay?"

Sharise (trusting and committed) drops to her knees. The Producer pushes his erection into her warm, young mouth. "Oh yes, that's superb, I just know we can work together... yeh...now, do you trust me not to come in your mouth?" Sharise looks up and (mouth full) nods her head slightly to show The Producer that she does indeed trust him. "Oh, you silly, silly girl," says The Producer and shoots a massive load down her throat.

SHELLEY

Finally, the slow and tedious drive through London's crawling traffic is over and Shelley arrives at Anthea's house in Holland Park. She always stays there when she's in London. She and Anthea are Best Friends Forever. They've known each other since way back, from when they were in "Girls Gone Wild." There were four girls in the (quite successful at the time) band but Shelley only ever really liked Anthea. Chardonnay and Alicia were dumb bitches - and where the fuck are they now? Fucking sad skanks. Losers. They hadn't been smart, but Anthea and Shelley had been. Shelley had used the band as a base from which to start her solo career, Anthea had exploited her celebrity and good looks to grab herself an extremely ugly but ridiculously rich banker. Christ, Shelley can feel nothing but admiration for the way she played that prick! Led him by the fucking nose, married him, stuck with him for a couple of years then divorced him, taking almost everything he had. Honestly, men can be such gullible dickheads - show them a bit of tit and a glimpse of snatch and, in no time at all, you can have them behaving like well-trained dogs!

Once inside Anthea's house (she has her own key, that's how BFF she and Anthea are), she makes straight for the beautiful living room and throws herself into a gorgeous sofa, dropping her Prada bag onto a gorgeous coffee table which rests on a gorgeous carpet. Shelley *really* likes Anthea's place. She makes her mind up that she too will buy a home in Holland Park when the divorce money comes through from Jack faggotpants.

Yes, the divorce settlement...more money, more success...what a wonderful day it's been! It's going to be so great when Anthea gets back from her latest shopping trip. Shelley can't wait to tell her what's about to happen to Jack, how she's about to blackmail him into a *huge* pay out. Hah, she is *so* going to screw him! Nobody fucks with Shelley!

Shelley muses happily for some minutes about her upcoming freedom from Jack and her fabulous future career in America. But then her thoughts stray, unstoppably, to that package nestled comfortably in the Prada bag. She takes it out, rolls it around in her hands - a greedy and needing expression on her face. Using her sharp finger nails she quickly tears at and then unwraps the cellophane from the package, to reveal a substantial, round rock of crack cocaine. She places the rock of crack on Anthea's gorgeous coffee table. Taking a nail file from her handbag she begins to chip away at the off-white coloured lump, which has a texture somewhere between wax and brittle plastic. Expertly she detaches smaller rocks from the main block, each new rock just the right size for a single good hit when smoked. There's loads of crack here, enough to last her and Anthea a couple of nights - if they don't go too mad! As well as

BFFs, she and Anthea are also BDBs, Best Drug Buddies.

Once again Shelley considers the possibility that she really shouldn't be involved with drugs and of course she has been in trouble with the crack before, resulting in some fairly unpleasant media coverage. But, fuck it, she had dealt with it. Although she did have to involve that hideous queer, Andrew. But that's all in the past. She's much more careful now, more discreet, she'll never be caught again. "Never say never," says a little voice somewhere in the back of Shelley's head…but she chooses to ignore it.

Shelley wonders if she should smoke a quick rock before Anthea gets back? Why the hell
not!

ANDREW

The morning of the day after my meet with Shelley, I wake at six thirty, happy and refreshed. I throw on a dressing gown, pop to the loo and go downstairs to the kitchen where the delightful Rosa has coffee and breakfast ready and waiting for me. Rosa's our lady, she lives in and, basically, runs the house and keeps me and Johnny fed and watered. Lovely girl, Rosa, I adore her, couldn't do without her. She's an ethnic Russian from Georgia. She worked as engineer there but she and her family had to flee due to some bizarre inter-ethnic tensions. Eventually, Rosa ended up in London. Her husband is in Israel (for reasons often explained and never understood) and there's a grown up daughter in Spain. I think it's only because of the fact that Rosa's engineering qualification is not valid here that she's ended up working for me. Personally, I'm pretty sure she's far more intelligent than I am.

She's certainly brighter than you! I mean, don't get me wrong, you seem a nice enough person, but you're definitely not the sharpest tool in the box, are you? Oh, don't look so offended, I'm sorry, I'm just pulling your leg, okay? Apologies, my sense of humour is a bit OTT at times - go on, give me a smile...oh, for fucks sake. Get over it. Don't get over it.

"Morning, meester Manning, how are you today?"

"Good, Rosa…and all the better, my love, for seeing you."

You see, I can be a charmer when I want, didn't expect that did you? And I see you're smiling again. Good. I'm glad. I'd hate to fall out with you this early in our trip together. I promise to play nice from now on.

"Oh, meester Manning, you are sweet man, thank you much. I have question. Today I order from computer shop, you want anything special?"

Rosa's referring to our online account with everybody's favourite upscale supermarket. She can't pronounce the name so always says "computer shop" instead. "I'll just leave that to your good judgement, thanks, Rosa, although…yes, there's a list of wine on the bureau in the living room, could you order that in?"

"Of course meester Manning. Must not forget that, this house is like machine that have engine that work with wine not petrol!"

"Hah! You're not wrong there." And indeed she's not, we do love a drink do me and Johnny.

I finish up my coffee and breakfast and go back upstairs to shave, shower and dress. As I'm meeting Charlie Gold today I go for one of the Givenchy suits - the nice purple-blue one - and I think I'll wear the lilac Yves Saint Laurent shirt and matching tie. Nice Church's brown brogues to finish it all off. Super. Well smart. Proper.

Dressed and ready to go, I decide to take the tube to the office. Northern Line from Chalk Farm, Central Line from Tottenham Court Road. Johnny's not even awake yet (lazy git!), but I call goodbye to Rosa on my way out. I cross Chalcot Square, into Berkley Road, right into Regents Park Road and across the bridge to get to the underground.

A few minutes later and I'm down in the tube, waiting for the next train. It's crowded with people, the morning rush. Men and women dispersing themselves around the city. Off to work as lawyers, cleaners, surveyors, bankers (aka wankers), concierges, maids, chefs, journalists, street cleaners, traffic wardens, pushers, whores, muggers, fraudsters (aka bankers). All of London squeezed into one tube station. Just up the platform a pretty young black girl takes a bottle of perfume out of her handbag and directs two sprays, one to either side of her neck. Some of the fine perfume mist that didn't land on target drifts down towards me. It smells warm, rich and sultry. For a few seconds the smell excites something in my brain and the prosaic is transformed into something exotic and exciting. God, I love this city!

Eventually I arrive at Bond Street. It's a quick walk to the offices from here, Oxford Street, left into Duke

Street, into Mayfair and right into George Yard, bit further on and I'm there.

"Offices in Mayfair, hah!" I hear you say, "he's up his own arse, that one," I hear you say. Not true. I'd prefer to not have the expense of a place in Mayfair myself, but it's what the clients expect, and in this business, darling, expectation and image are pretty much everything.

Stepping through the doors of my expensively-priced workplace I see that, although it's still early, both Kerry and Griselda are in and working. Bless them. I do love my girls! Kerry, a slim, pretty girl and Griselda, a huge, hunky, brooding, unfeasibly ugly lesbian.

Oh, for goodness sake, relax and take your PC hat off, snowflake! I'm not being horrible about Griselda because she's a lesbian. She's not brooding and unfeasibly ugly because she's a lesbian, she's just…brooding and unfeasibly ugly…

Kerry's job is to keep work flowing smoothly and to keep an eye on the finances. Griselda is my little investigations whizz. She's a phenomenally good hacker and has the search out and destroy instincts of a hungry ferret with a bug up its ass, as our American friends might say. She also keeps a check on all our surveillance work. Some of this we do directly for clients in the course of our work for them, but most of it we do for various media outlets.

Bet you thought, as sweetly naïve as you obviously are, that the media didn't do stuff like that anymore?

Yeh, right! They've just changed the *way* they do it. They pass the work to people like me. I in turn pass it on to one of a number of private investigators we work with, and they in turn pass it on to another party. All helps to muddy the chain of responsibility and if it all goes tits up the guys up at the top can (almost) legitimately say "weren't me guv, don't know a thing about it, wasn't there, wasn't aware." Plausible deniability I believe they call it. I like the surveillance work. It's lucrative, relatively easy and during the course of it many other useful nuggets of information that interest an inveterate scandal hound like me get flushed out of the undergrowth.

Before going upstairs (my offices are set within a small converted mews house - Kerry and Griselda work downstairs and I work upstairs) I give the girls a cheery greeting and ask, "Griselda, give me ten minutes to sort myself out then pop up to my office and let's have a quick review of who we've got our eyes on at the mo, and Kerry can you see if you can get Shelley Bright in here sometime this afternoon, I'm sure she's in London today. And both of you...remember that Charlie Gold will be here soon, so best behaviour!"

"Of course, boss," says lovely Kerry, "ugh!" grunts the less than lovely Griselda.

I spend a happy half hour with Griselda as she gives me a rundown of who we're currently surveilling.

What's that? You want to know who's on the list? Sorry, I can't give away any names. All I'll say is that our list currently features: a prominent film star, two much-loved soap stars, two members of a fantastically successful boy band, a famous and beautiful super model, an ageing rock legend, a top Hollywood executive and...oh...actually, you know what...I'd better stop there. That's all your getting, so stop asking. The only thing I'll say is that all the above are up to no good.

My little surveillance list represents a wonderful tale of human venality, ranging from the everyday to the barely believable. On a personal level, it represents money in my bank account. People, eh? I do love 'em, and the nastier and more twisted they are the better! God bless the innate vileness of the human race and all its perverse, odd and downright weird desires!

Once me and Griselda *(yes, she really is called Griselda and, no, I really am not taking the piss and you understand now what I meant by "unfeasibly ugly" don't you?)* have worked our way down the "dirty laundry list," I congratulate her on her thoroughness and say, "Griselda, do me a favour will you and get someone to keep an eye on Shelley Bright, someone with a nice big telephoto lens would be good."

"Shelley Bright, sure, no problem. What you got in mind for her, boss?" Griselda whistles this remark at me through her two missing front teeth. She's been like this for years. Never bothered with falsies or implants. She's never seen the need. "Ah, well," I reply, "you know better than most people what you can find if you start poking around in other peoples' lives…and I've got a hunch about Shelley."

Actually I have both a hunch and a plan about all matters Shelley related, but nothing you or Griselda need to know about yet: let's just say I may be able to put my own unique spin on the Jack Rigby blackmail job. If it works out I just know you're going to love it…

Just ten minutes after Griselda leaves me, Kerry buzzes from downstairs to let me know that Charlie Gold has arrived: "send him up please, Kerry."

Quick, before Charlie gets up the stairs, I need to tell you something very important about him and Janey. Remember my remarks earlier about celebrity and psychopaths? Charlie and Janey both fit into that category, but not partially. Fully. They're both dangerous people, you need to stay out of their way and leave them to me. I've met Janey before and she scares me. She is cold, calculating and completely dedicated to money and career. She is soulless. She is a woman I believe to be capable of bad things. And, Charlie? I've known him for years and he's no better. Aside from Janey, his other clients are multi-millionaire oligarchs and Mafiosi. These are the kinds of circles he moves in. Charlie is responsible for the deaths of at least two people that I know of. I suspect there are many more. You can understand, then, that I'm a bit nervous about this meeting – exactly what does this fat fucking bastard want from me?

And you? You just sit there quietly and, for fuck's sake, make sure Charlie doesn't see you.

****

The door to my office swings open. And in comes Charlie. Lawyer, special advisor and confidante to Janey Jax. And murderous fat bastard. Charlie is about six foot tall and just as wide. It's hard to tell where his neck ends and his head starts. He's clad in an expensively tailored suit, but he is so obese that, despite its price, it still looks like a tent. His piggy eyes are almost lost in folds of fatty flesh. His nose is large, broad and splayed across his face like a pig's snout and the fat fingers on his shovel sized hands are so covered in extravagant, large diamond and gold rings, that it's almost impossible to see any skin.

"Andy, you old bastard, long time no see!" His voice is heavily accented New York, full of faux bonhomie, bullshit and cuntola and actually I'm thinking not fucking long enough, you fat cunt.

"Charlie, yeh, it's so good to see you!" I get up from my chair, walk round my desk and shake hands with him. My hand, literally, disappears into his huge mitt. His hand feels cold, clammy. It's like touching a dead thing.

"Please, Charlie, sit down," I gesture to a rather nice Charles Eames chair I have in my office. Momentarily I panic: as Charlie lowers his huge bulk into the chair, it creaks ominously under the strain of supporting so much blubber. Happily, it does not break. "So, what brings you here? And how are things with Janey? She's amazing that girl, still as successful as ever, what with a world tour about to start and even a new album coming out soon, I hear."

"Yeh, yeh," replies Charlie, "there's no stopping Janey."

"And how does she stay looking so young, is it, erm, surgery?"

"Looking young, well…that's kinda why I'm here…"

Charlie pauses and instead of finishing his sentence moves the subject on to small talk: who's screwing who, who's up, who's down, the foibles and tribulations of various mutual acquaintances. It's like he wants to talk about anything other than the reason he's here. He's nervous. I know he is. And if a man like Charlie, a man who is ready to kill to get his own way, is nervous then I'm *very* nervous.

He natters on, and I'm feeling more and more antsy, so I decide to find out exactly what he wants: "Charlie, look, it's great to see you, and it's always a pleasure to talk, but perhaps you could let me know why you're really here?"

"Right, okay, well it's like this…" At this point Charlie reaches inside his jacket and extracts a grey, metallic box, it looks like a mobile phone but seems to have a more complex display. He does something with the box, it beeps into electronic life and he puts it on my desk, in between the two of us. For a moment I'm nonplussed. I have no idea what the bloody thing is. Then it hits me, I know what it is, it's one of those handy little devices that can detect electronic bugging devices. "Shit, Charlie!" I exclaim, "what the fuck! I know I can do some dodgy stuff, but bugging my own clients, hey, that's way beneath even me!"

"I know, I know, I'm sorry, it's just that what I have to say is kinda sensitive."

"Okay, now you're worrying me, spill, what's going on here?"

"Right, okay…like you said yourself Janey's looking damn good for her age and, well, there's a reason *why* Janey's looking so good, or at least she thinks there's a reason. Cupla years back she met this Indian Guru and he put her on this special "youth preserving" diet. Well, it's more like a supplement to her diet and she's been on it since she met the guy. It kinda involves stem cells, I think…"

"This is all beginning to sound really strange…what exactly is this "supplement?" And Charlie tells me…

And for a moment I have a sensation of falling, of the ground giving away beneath me, like I'm falling into some strange, perverse, alternate universe. I jump up from my seat and explode: "a human foetus, she eats human fucking foetuses, you are one fucking mad cunt and she's a cunting fucking lunatic!"

A look crosses Charlie's face that I'm fairly sure is the last thing some people have seen, so I rein myself back in, sit back down and take a deep breath, "Charlie, wow, I mean…I'm really not happy with this. I'm sorry but I'm not going to touch it, you need to find someone else to help you with this one."

"Hey, Andy, you've not really let me explain things. Me and Janey have already decided you're the best person for this job as we trust you and we think you're competent. I've told you what Janey wants and just the fact you know about that means you're already involved. Andy, I'm not *offering* you this job, I'm *telling* you that you're going to do it. This is not open to discussion, and you know me well enough to know that if I say you're gonna do it, you're gonna do it. Hey, don't look so pissed, you can still bill us, so what's the big problem?"

As he says this Charlie's piggy little eyes are boring directly into mine, they are dark and glinting with barely suppressed menace.

He's right of course. You just don't turn down Charlie Gold and Janey Jax, especially when it means you might end up as a loose end waiting to be tidied away in what would be the biggest celebrity scandal of the century if it ever became public. I have no choice. I'm not at all comfortable with this, but I have to do it. The bottom line is do value my life and lifestyle more than I wish to preserve my already dubious moral landscape?

Too fucking right I do.

"Well, Charlie, since you put it that way, it will of course be my pleasure to help you and Janey in this matter. You want to run me through the details?"

" Good guy! I knew you'd see things my way! Okay, it goes like this. The Guru has got Janey on one foetus every three months. Up to now I've been sourcing them from, erm, compliant abortion clinics in the States but they need to get to her within a few hours of the abortion. That's why I need a you, Andy - it'd take too long and be too complex to bring them in from the States. As well as getting the foetus to Janey in the shortest possible time you need to ensure it's between twelve and fifteen weeks, definitely no more than fifteen weeks. After that they start to develop proper bones and that makes them no good for the way she likes to eat them."

I know I'm going to hate myself for asking this question, but I just need to know *(and you want to know as well, don't you? Go on admit it, your finding all this talk of foetuses at once repellent and fascinating, aren't you?).*

"So how does she eat the foetuses, Charlie, just out of, err, curiosity? Fricassee with a nice drop of Chardonnay perhaps?"

"Hey, finish it with the sarcasm, already. To be honest she doesn't eat them as such, she drinks them really, I guess. Feeds them raw into a liquidiser, makes them into a puree, then she strains and drinks. That's it."

I feel vaguely sickened. I wish I hadn't asked the question. This is all quite disgusting, but there's no point raising objections now. I'm stuck with this piece of shit job. The best thing I can do now is get it done, and get it done properly.

"When's the first foetus due, Charlie?"

"Well, Janey's here for the next six months, she's finishing off the new album and starting the world tour here, as well as overseeing work on that stately home place she just bought in North-Hamptons-Shire, so actually you'll need to find two foetuses. And she wants the first one seven days from today." Charlie is more relaxed now, he knows he's got me tied into this, but the menace has still not entirely receded from his eyes. "It's good to have you on board, Andy, I know you'll do the job well. Just remember, Janey is an industry in her own right. A lotta people got a lotta money invested in her, including me."

Yeh, thanks a lot, Charlie, like I need to be reminded what's at stake here.

After more discussion about the how and when of delivering foetuses, Charlie asks me what it's all going to cost. I pull a ridiculously large sum of money from the air and Charlie doesn't bat an eyelid. Eventually he lifts his gut-bucket frame from my poor bloody Charles Eames chair and waddles away, apparently to some mansion that Janey has rented on The Bishops Avenue for the duration of her stay here.

What did you, think of Charlie, then? Fat, evil bastard, isn't he? Bet you're glad I told you to stay out of the way aren't you? And what did you think of all that foetus stuff, it's shocking isn't it? I have to say that I'm not comfortable about it. Not at all.

Where am I going to get a foetus from? Ah, well, that's for me to know and you to ponder – needless to say, I think you'll find I can get my hands on pretty much anything I want.

THE PRODUCER

After Sharise fled from his office in tears, The Producer sat down at his desk, lay back in his plush and stupid-expensive office chair and had a right laugh! What a stupid, pathetic slut! Christ, she was up for anything, that one. Little whore. And so dumb. So fucking dumb! Imagine thinking she had any talent besides cock-sucking. Oh, how much he loves these young, stupid, pretty people who are so ready to anything for a shot at fame and celebrity!

In fact, The Producer had enjoyed abusing Sharise so much that he decides he's going to set up another Fun Day. To that end, he begins his Fun Day ritual - which goes something like this. Every month his A&R department receives dozens of submissions from young, wannabe musical stars. The Producer has all these forwarded to himself. He checks each one. Primarily he's searching for good-looking boys and girls, whether they can sing or not is irrelevant, nowadays computers can make even the tone deaf sound like Caruso. The real trouble is that good-looking youngsters are two a penny, there's far more out there than The Producer could ever promote as potential music stars. So he goes through the submissions and automatically bins the fat or ugly boys and girls ("fuglies" as he likes to call them), so that only the best looking ones remain. Then he further refines his selection further by, almost at random, making three piles. One to join the "fuglies" in the bin, one to go his

A&R people to follow up on. And another special, private pile for his own personal delectation: beautiful but probably untalented boys or girls, who will receive a cherished invite to The Producer's office to "discuss their career," to play their own special and unexpected role in his Fun Day.

That's when The Producer really starts to enjoy himself. Exactly how much do they want fame? How far are they ready to go? Do they *really*, *really* want it?

ANDREW

Never call the Queen a Rancid Old Cunt on live television, even if you have snorted some fat lines of coke and downed half a bottle of vodka. If I ever wrote a "how to" manual on celebrity, that would be the first rule. I suppose I should confess that I'm absolutely not a fan of the Royals myself, I can't see the point of them. To me they're an extremely dull bunch of not very intelligent, aristocratic benefit scroungers who get to live free in extremely grand and expensive council houses. And they breed too much. In short, I really can't get my head around the concept that some inbred idiot should be worthy of respect and privilege simply because they were squeezed out of a "royal" vagina. Weird.

This is what's going through my head as I sit at home later that night. I have *mostly* recovered from the horror dropped upon me by Charlie Gold earlier in the day, and I'm having a quiet night in. I'm sitting back, "chilling," as the young people say, digesting both the events of the day and a beautiful meal that Rosa knocked up for me (something Ukrainian or Russian I believe, made with sour plums and chicken) and slowly drinking my way through a lovely chilled bottle of Krug.

Can you have some Krug? Bollocks you can. Have you any idea how much this stuff costs? Anyway, you need to keep a clear head or you'll not keep up with the pace of events, I don't want you losing track of things or saying something you're not supposed to because you're pissed.

What's bought on this line of thought is the plight of one of my clients that I *do* like. To be honest, I not only like - I fancy the fucking pants off him. He's one of those rare celebrities who is a decent, if fundamentally screwed up, human being. And he's gorgeous. Drop dead, top totty bloody gorgeous.

He's straight, unfortunately. But I'm just as prone to flights of fancy as you are, so you'll have to forgive my little fantasy. I mean, it's not like you don't have any fantasies yourself, is it? For example, I know all about that embarrassing incident from last year, at the office party. Talk about misreading the signs, eh? Poor you, you must have nearly died of embarrassment! How do I know about that? That's a silly question, I've told you before that I know all about you, I think you must be forgetting who I am and what I do.

I'm talking about Joey Camps of course. As you already know, it all happened for him eight years back when he was the photogenic winner of TV's favourite reality show, "We're Watching You." From there his good looks won him the role as the face of GK underwear. Suddenly a cute, but basically quite shy, lad from Doncaster found his face and body on television ads and billboards the world over. More modelling work followed, TV appearances, six page spreads in "Hi There" magazine, coffee table books featuring picture after picture of Joey's sculpted body, a line of men's toiletries. Nowadays Joey's fame is global, his smiling face beaming out from posters, televisions, magazines and papers from Birmingham to Beijing. His fame was not even dented by his troubled marriage to the beautiful but flawed Katy Morgan, who died of a drugs overdose just three months after giving birth to twins. If anything this sad incident simply reinforced Joey's fame as it led to a slew of stories about "brave" Joey as a "tragic" single parent.

Oops, I'm wittering on like a silly old queen aren't I? Truth be told you know all this stuff about Joey, it's old news to an avid celeb watcher like yourself. What you really, really want to hear is the juicy stuff, isn't it? You want to know how Joey's gone from international heart throb to www dot joeycampsfight4life dot com.

Let's go back three months.

It's late at night and I get a panicked and distressed phone call from Joey, he's yelling down the phone at me, "Andy, you gotta help me, I'm fucked," he sounds hysterical and on the edge of tears, "I'm so fuckin' fucked, I'm over, finished, I've done meself in!"

"Woah," I say, "slow down, Joey, take a deep breath, tell me what's happened..."

"You bin watching the Paul Hunter show?" The Paul Hunter show *(once again, you know this, I hear you love to watch it),* is the nation biggest chat show, live and primetime every Saturday night.

"Urrh..no, I've been busy with work." In fact, I had been busy doing some rather impressive sexual athletics for a man of my age with a rather gorgeous piece of upmarket rent whom I had just paid and dispatched (to his next punter, I suppose) but Joey doesn't need to know that, *and you, you keep it to yourself.* "Joey...are you pissed, are you pissed *and* coked up?" I'm beginning to get a bad feeling about this, "for Christ's sake, how many times have I told you that substance abuse and live television do NOT go together."

"I just 'ad a cupla lines, well, maybe six, like, and 'alf a bottle of vody, you know me I get a bit nervous, and I guess it got me more than usual cos I 'adn't eaten an' that Paul were bein' a sarcy cunt. You know what 'e's like, snobby twat, an' 'e was makin' out I was this blond bimbo an' a thick northerner an' I got right pissed off. Then 'e started talkin' about the Royals an' then, like, 'e asked me if I 'ad any thoughts on "monarchy versus Republic," the fucking, smartarse dickhead, an' then it just came out an' I said that we should 'ave a republic an' that the Queen is a rancid old cunt…"

Oh, bollocks, cunting buggering shitting arseholes, this is worse than I thought, this is an out and out celebrity car crash death disaster scenario! I smell the acrid whiff of a career in flames. Joey has committed a number of drug and drink related indiscretions over the years, and each time I've called in favours and saved his career, but this, this is in another league!

"Joey, Jesus Christ, what the fuck have you done...where are you now?"

"I'm at 'ome. They cut the cameras after I said the cunt stuff an' I din't want to stick around so I ran outta the studio, threw meself in a cab an' now I'm 'ere..."

"Okay, good, that's at least one thing you did right. This is bad, you know that don't you?"

"I do, Andy, I'm brickin' meself..." he pauses and speaks again, this time sounding calmer but sad and lost, like a little boy who's just lost his favourite toy, or a grown up facing the realisation that everything he's built up over the years is about to turn to shit. "It's over for me, ain't it Andy? I've screwed it all up, ain't I? I've totally fucked up everythin'!"

Like I said, I've a bit of an attachment to Joey, and his tone plucks at my heart *(you see, you think I'm a cynical old bastard but the truth is I do have some finer human feelings)* and I resolve at that point that I'm going to get Joey out of this mess, one way or another I'm going to save his career.

"No, Joey, it'll be fine," I reply, trying to throw him some hope "we can sort this this, we just need a plan. Let's just say your career is in intensive care, but it isn't dead yet! First thing you need to do is to get out of your house because the press are going to be camped outside the place within the hour. Leave the twins with the nanny and tell her that you won't be back until much later and get round here now. We'll need to come up with some excuse pretty quick to explain why you said what you did. The papers are going to eat you alive tomorrow, Joey, it's not going to be pretty so you need to prepare yourself for it."

Fortunately Joey lives up in Belsize Park, a very short trip even by foot from my place, so I only had a few minutes to marshal my thoughts before the doorbell buzzed. I checked the video intercom, confirmed it was Joey and opened the door to him.

And there he was. Tall, slim, blond, languid and impossibly handsome, big blue eyes and moist, sensual lips, broad shouldered, slim hipped. When I first met him he was a boy really, just twenty years old. Eight years on and he's matured into a beautiful man. As always when I see Joey my heart beats just that little bit faster. "Quickly, get in, we need to talk," I say and Joey steps over the threshold, still with his cocky northern swagger, even given present disastrous, career-threatening circumstances.

Moments later we're in my study, having briefly been interrupted by a rather grumpy Johnny who's been disturbed by the doorbell, and being fussed over by an ever solicitous Rosa, still awake and happy to look after us even at this hour, bless her. I quickly send them both away, for in the few minutes it's taken Joey to get here, I've already formulated a plan *(you'll learn that about me as we continue our journey together, I'm quick and nimble on my feet)* and I need to discuss it with him privately. It's a simple but daring plan, one where nothing can go wrong. At least that's what I thought at the time.

"Andy, thanks so much for lettin' me come round 'ere...you're right, them bastard journalist are gonna fuck me over, I don't know what to say to 'em, what am I gonna do?"

Joey's beautiful, sensuous lips tremble and the big blue eyes moisten over with nascent tears and again I find myself wanting to do something, anything, to help him. I realise, with not a little shock, something I have known but repressed for a long time. I don't just *fancy* Joey Camps. Truth is, I'm really a little bit *in love* with Joey Camps. Perhaps even more than a little bit.

I remember we were both seated on that big, old sofa I have in my study, and I reached out to, comfortingly, touch his shoulder, to show him he's not alone, and suddenly he dissolved into my arms sobbing and I am holding him and being reassuring and, fuck, I'm really, really caring about this guy – really, really wanting him.

This is not good, not good at all. I can feel the barrier of professional distance melting away, the client/agent relationship shattering into something much more personal and messy.

As much to calm myself down as anything, I gently push him away, hoping that restoring some physical distance will restore some professional distance, and tell him "Joey, I can't help you with what's going to be written and said about you tomorrow, it's too late for that, that's already all screwed up, but I can manage the damage medium and long term." He looks at me and nods, a flicker of hope blossoming in his eyes.

"Here's the plan, tomorrow you're going to be the most hated man in Britain so we need to find an excuse for why you said what you said about our, uhm, beloved Queen. And we need it to be an excuse that people will understand, that justifies your actions as a moment of madness caused by stress. It needs to be something that will shift the agenda back in your favour, something that gets the public back on board, something that will save your career and all those lovely sponsorship and advertising deals."

"Okay," nods Joey, "tell me, what we gonna do, 'ow are we gonna find our way out of this bloody mess?"

"You, me old mate, are going to get cancer!"

"Fuck me, cancer, in't that a bit strong an' anyways I'm dead 'ealthy me!"

"Don't panic, Joey, it's going to be Celebrity Cancer, which is to say, it doesn't really exist. You're going to go on a crash diet, so you look pale and drawn. You'll pay regular visits to a nice private hospital I happen to know well. As far as anyone's concerned you'll be there for radiotherapy or some such stuff. In reality, a dodgy doctor friend of mine will be in charge of your 'treatment,' which'll consist of you sitting down and reading a good book for a couple of hours, or playing a game on your iPhone, or whatever it is that you young people get up to nowadays. The press lap up sick celebrity stories, we can make it something like, mmm, testicular cancer, yeh, bollock cancer, that's a good one, it's quite fashionable nowadays. We can even get 'Charitable and Brave Joey' to give his time free to a testicular cancer awareness campaign, that'll make you look good. To start, the public will feel sorry for you, then they'll sympathise with your brave fight against your dreadful illness, they'll worry what will happen to those beautiful twins of yours should the worst happen to you, and by the time you 'get better' in a few months' time, the public will have taken you back into their hearts. We can splash pics and vids of you all over social media - all featuring courageous but ill Joey and push out constant updates about your illness and your state of mind. People will find that really compulsive. They'll be totally gripped! We can even set you up your own fucking website with exclusive daily streaming live updates, 'joeycampsfight4life dot com'! Just imagine the potential of a site like that, the number of hits it's going to get and the amount of advertising revenue it could pull in!"

"You know what, even though I say it myself, this plan is brilliant! The best part is that you only got your cancer diagnosis yesterday, just before you went on the Paul Hunter show. It gives you the perfect excuse for tonight's outburst! Oh, the stress, the worry, the shock, the panic, you didn't know what you were saying, you were worried sick about the twins, you hardly knew where you were, the shock of it all had snatched the ground from beneath your feet. Oh yes, we can have fun with this, save your career and make you a shitload of dosh as well! This whole thing could actually turn out to be a fabulous opportunity!"

"Andy, if you think this'll work, I'll do it mate...but isn't a bit, well, like, cancer, I mean a bit sort of...tasteless?"

"Well, yes, obviously, it's *grossly* tasteless but since when did being a celebrity have anything to do with good taste?"

Joey seems undecided for a few seconds, but then something in his face changes and I know he's made a decision, he's going to go with it, "what about my management?" he asks.

"They're to know nothing about our little game. Let them handle the flow of news, set up the website, talk with sponsors, advertisers and all that shit, but as far as they're concerned your fucking riddled with cancer!"

"Okay" nods Joey, "look, I'm really grateful for this, it ain't the first time you've 'elped me out..." suddenly those beautiful blue eyes seem to cloud over, "but is this enough to really save me cos I'm a serial fuck up, I mean I'm gonna fuck up again, I know I will, an' what excuse do we come up wi'then? An' I really, really want this, the fame, the money, the 'ouse, the cars. I want to make sure I leave summat for me kids an' there's no way I'm goin' back to flippin' bloody burgers!"

"Hush, hush, Joey," I say, again placing a calming hand on his shoulder, "this *will* work and you *will* learn from it and you will *not* fuck up again. You'll see, six months from now the public will love you even more than they did before tonight's slip up, your "treatment" will have worked, you'll have conquered your 'cancer' and everything will be back to normal!"

Joey looks me straight in the eye, for some reason he seems suddenly infinitely sad and says "let's do it, Andy, let's make me ill..."

In retrospect of course, I really should have paid more attention to that look of sadness and Joey's comments about how much he really, really wanted fame: and the remark about the kids...how the fuck did I miss that? I guess it's like I said, at the time it seemed such a simple plan.

What do you mean, you thought Joey's cancer was real? For God's sake, I know I said you were naïve but now your just being plain silly! Use your brain. Don't use your brain. I'm not here to think for you. Just don't believe everything you're told, things are rarely as they seem. Cuntola. It's all fucking cuntola. A huge, great stinking pile of cuntola, put there to amuse, titillate, confuse, scare – all to distract you from thinking about how shit the world really, really is.

JOEY

That night he called the Queen a rancid cunt, well that was it. Joey Camps went from being adored celeb to serial fuck up and scumbag. It was all the fault of that twat Paul Hunter. Joey's there on Hunter's chat show, he's already seen the questions Hunter's going to throw at him in the interview, all easy soft-ball stuff and he's already learned his answers word for word. So even though he's flying on half a bottle of vody and some seriously fat lines of coke, Joey is confident that this will be a nice, easy interview. All he needs to do is parrot his rehearsed responses and look pretty.

And then, suddenly, Hunter goes right off the fucking script, starts asking Joey questions out of the blue. Joey is thrown, he knows Hunter is needling him. Hunter is a fat, public school educated prick. At least Joey's worked to get where he is, not been employed by some other smug, upper middle class cunt because they both went to the same school where they used to bum each other in the fucking dorms. It's very obvious to Joey that Hunter is getting off on patronising and belittling somebody he sees as a working class twat, and he really doesn't know how to deal with the situation.

Then Hunter starts going on about the fucking Queen. For chrissake, exactly how is the fucking Queen relevant to his life? Why is she so fucking special, anyway? As far as Joey can see she's no more than a rather doddery, sour-faced old dear who's head of a family of pointless people who all live a life of privileged luxury for fuck knows what fucking reason. So when Hunter asks him "republic or monarchy," that's it, Joey has had enough and before he knows it his brain is switched off but his mouth is motoring and forming the words "the Queen's a rancid old cunt."

Bang. Smash. Wallop That's it. Game fucking over. Signing off. The end.

Hunter is looking at Joey, his mouth is hanging open, he can't believe what Joey has just said.

Joey can't believe what Joey just said.

For a few seconds you can, literally, hear a pin drop in that studio. Audience, crew, host, other interviewees all shocked into silence.

Then all chaos breaks loose. A member of the audience boos, then another and another, the producer yells to the camera crew to stop filming. Hunter looks at Joey with a smug smile on his face and says, "you've finished yourself, you idiot boy."

Joey wants to say something back to Hunter, to apologise to everybody for the words that just spilled from his lips, but the boos from the audience are now so loud that he's not sure he could make himself heard and he's in a state of shock, anyway. Fuck, what has he done?

He jumps from his seat, with the audience's disapproval ringing in his ears, he runs from the studio, out into a long anonymous corridor, down the corridor to a fire exit, setting of an alarm as he barges a fire door open. He flees down two flights of stairs, out of the studio building and into the street where he is lucky enough to be able to hail a black cab almost immediately.

Once in the cab he asks the driver to take him to Belsize Park. After a few minutes Joey notices the cab driver looking surreptitiously at him in the cab's mirror - "ere," he says, "sorry to bug you, feller, but are you that Joey Camps bloke?"

Joey captures the driver's glance in the mirror and replies "me mate, no mate, me, I'm nobody."

And that, Joey realizes, that is what he now really is. Nobody. What a fuck up, him and his big fucking mouth, him and his fucking love of booze and coke, what a fool, what a total prize fucking prick. Joey can't see a way back from this, just saying the word cunt on live television would be bad for his career, but using that word in conjunction with the words "rancid," "old" and "Queen," well, that's it, boyo. Career fucking over. No more photo shoots, no more spreads in "Hiya" magazine, no more interviews, no more television appearances, opening ceremonies or lucrative sponsorship and advertising work and he guesses his own exclusive line of fragrances will end up in the remainder bin at ninety nine pence a bottle. It's back to obscurity for Joey Camps, back to Doncaster, back to flipping burgers, and the house will have to go, and the cars, and the expensive watches, the beautiful clothes, the exotic holidays and the nanny for the twins...everything gone, three fucking words and one moment of stupidity and he's over.

There's only one hope, he must get back home and call Andrew, if anybody can salvage anything from this nightmare, it'll be Andrew.

ANDREW

The day after the foetus deal I'm back in the office, catching up on calls and doing some paperwork. Shelley Bright had been due to turn up after Charlie had left yesterday, but she turned out to be a no-show. Why so unreliable all of a sudden, I wonder? I buzz Kerry and ask her if she's managed to get hold of Shelley again. She has indeed (efficient as always, bless her) and Shelley has "like, totally promised, innit" to call into the office early in the afternoon. Good. That gives me time to deal with some other pressing issues. I put a call through to my dodgy doctor friend and arrange a meet. Absolutely everyone in my position should know a dodgy doctor. They're indispensable for so many things, from helping clients keep up their addiction to prescription drugs, through to diagnosing and treating Celebrity Cancer to getting your hands on freshly aborted foetuses.

No, I won't ask him to give you a prescription for some Oxycodone! Sit down and shut up, you're beginning to annoy me now! What you doing taking that shit anyway, don't you realise how addictive it is? You need to sort out that little habit of yours or it'll really screw up your life.

I don't tell the good doctor exactly what I want him to do but I intimate there's a big wedge in it for him.

That sparks his interest and he says he'll bump a couple of appointments and be at my office "within the hour." Money talks, people mumble.

Whilst I'm waiting for the doc, Kerry passes me up a call from Rocco Norton's management.

Now for goodness sake, stop sulking and forget about the Oxycodone, there's some interesting stuff coming up now so pay attention. Oh, for fucks sake. Sulk. Don't sulk.

Rocco is, of course, Rocco from Rocco And The Band, America's greatest rock outfit. He is loud, brash, espouser of all sorts of cuddly left wing ideals, feed the starving, forgive the debt, always hanging round with politicians and even crawling around the fucking Pope for fuck's sake.

Trouble is, it seems that his left wing ideals don't match the reality of his own behaviour. A heavyweight American paper has investigated Rocco And The Band's finances and done a front page special on them. Turns out that Rocco and his fellow band members avoid paying their fair share of taxes by hiding vast amounts of their income in various tax havens using a string of shady holding companies. Nice one Rocco! I guess he believes in helping the world's poor and huddled masses, but only with your money, not his own.

This kind of thing isn't for me. I do crisis management where there are disputable facts that can be manipulated. I work and thrive in the emotional and factual grey areas that make up celebrities' often confused and chaotic lives. If Rocco's management had come to me *before* publication of the figures, then perhaps I could have applied some pressure or done a deal to stop them being printed. Now, I'm afraid, it's all too late. Rocco has been caught bang to rights in a whirl of indisputable facts. There's no wriggle room in this for me, numbers is numbers, and that's that. I politely inform his management to seek help elsewhere. I suppose I could have offered to help manage the fall-out from all this but, as it happens, I think Rocco is a cunting hypocrite and I quite like the idea of seeing him exposed as such.

You're disappointed? You thought Rocco was one of the good guys? Please, do me a favour...are you serious? Fuck me, you really are an innocent abroad, aren't you?

An hour passes and my doctor friend duly, and punctually, arrives. I'll give the good doctor one thing, when I inform him of my requirement for two foetuses, he doesn't even bat an eyelid, any moral questions or concerns about that Hippocratic Oath nonsense already anaesthetised by the amount of money I'm offering him. This doesn't surprise me, some of the most greedy and unscrupulous people I've ever met are doctors. He knows what I want now, when I need it by and he has the contacts and necessary amorality to confidentially and quickly deliver what I've asked of him. He'll never know who the ultimate client for the foetuses is, and he's savvy and streetwise enough not to even ask why I need them, let alone who they might be for.

You're still conflicted about this foetus thing, aren't you? It appals you and disgusts you. But...on the other hand, there's that dark place in your mind, the one where you don't want to go but can't stay away from...and it's telling you "let's keep looking, let's see where all this is going." And you can't resist it, can you?

After the doc left, the next visitor to my office that day is Shelley Bright, God bless her and all her stupid-minded emptiness. Not.

Oh, you're glad Shelley's back are you? You find her funny? Hmm, that's not way I would describe her, but if she brings a smile to your face, then, hey, go ahead, knock yourself out.

"Hiya, Andy, love!" trills Shelley as she lets herself into my office, having been directed upstairs by Kerry.

"Hullo, Shelley, darling," I reply, all inscrutable insincerity and shit-eating grin.

"So then, you ready to, like, fix my Jack problem now?"

"Of course, there's just a couple of details I need to run past you first. For example, one thing I don't know is what kind of guys Jack goes for, and that's crucial to our plan, we need to make sure he succumbs to temptation so we can get our film made."

"That's easy, innit!" replies Shelley, "I've caught him at it, like, haven't I, twice, and in our bloody house and all, the dirty git! Oooh, it makes me flesh crawl, innit! And my bloody Jack, like, he was only taking it up the arse, weren't he! Bloody horrible…oh sorry Andy…"

I decid to ignore Shelley's unconscious, knee jerk homophobia. I'm surprised that Jack should have been so indiscrete as to shit on his own doorstep and get caught at it by Shelley, but it does show that Jack's easy to lead and prone to indiscretion.

"…anyway, they was, like, big black guys, innit. Dead handsome they were, I remember thinking what a, like, total waste it was that they was gay. One of them were…."

Shelley goes on to give me the name of one of the guys that she saw doing Jack up the arse, and, in fact, he's another prominent Premier League and international football star.

Yeh, right, like I'm going to tell you his name, dream on. That name stays with me, and me alone, you can hold your breath and stamp your feet as much as you like, I'm not sharing.

So, Jack Rigby is not only a gay, it seems he also loves up it the bum, he's a screaming Martha. How sweet. Bless.

"That's great, Shelley, that's solid gold info, now I know exactly how to get Jack to do something silly. This is how things are going to work…"

I ask Shelley to pay me a healthy sum of money on account and I explain how we're going to set Jack up in his own home, the last place he'd expect any problems. Johnny will be in charge of the job and she and he need to arrange a meet at the Brierley mansion the next time that Jack is out training, playing a game or whatever, so that Johnny can plant two tiny, remote controlled cameras, one in the main living area and one in whichever bedroom Jack uses (I'm betting this particular odd couple don't share a marital bed).

All Shelley has to do after that is to make sure Jack is in the house alone for the evening. That's when our man will visit him. I know who to use for this job, a young guy called Kelvin, a stunningly handsome young, gay, black man who, I know, is trying to build a film and television career for himself (not too much success yet, poor love). He knows me and what I do, and he knows he needs to bank a few favours (he'll also like the big wad cash that comes with the job).

And that was that, Shelley's divorce sorted. I got the loathsome woman out of my office quickly as I could, and got on with other business.

* * * * *

Later that day, back home, and being at a bit of a loose end, I surf on to joeycampsfight4life dot com to catch Joey's latest update in his struggle against his 'cancer'. As I predicted the site has been a tremendous success, as indeed has my whole cancer campaign. All the sponsorship deals that Joey lost at the time of the Queen debacle have now been reinstated and a long list of advertisers are promoting on the site heavily. Best of all, the great British public has fallen back in love with him. It's enthralled by the gutsy young man's struggle against a deadly disease, his determination to conquer it for the sake of his kids and his simple gratitude for the support of his loving and loyal fans. Blah,blah,blah. Cuntola, cuntola, cuntola. In tabloid terms Joey has, in the space of just three months, gone from EVIL, TWISTED SCUMBAG CAMPS ATTACKS OUR BELOVED QUEEN to BRITAINS BRAVEST DAD IN HEROIC STRUGGLE WITH CANCER, WE'RE BACKING JOEY.

As things seem to have been running so smoothly with my cancer scam, I've not bothered to check Joey's website for a while and I'm disturbed and a bit shocked by what I see. As the daily update streams onto my iPad I notice Joey looks awful. Thin, pale, drawn, lips dry and cracked, black circles under the eyes. That beautiful blond hair looks lank and greasy. Now him looking pale and thin I understand, I would put that down to the crash diet that was part of the original plan, but at this stage in said plan we should be thinking about giving the public the good news that Joey's treatment is working, that he's on the mend. There's no way we can do that now - he looks like shit!

What's going on with that boy?

My mind drifts back to my earlier appointment with Doctor Dodgy. He did mention Joey, in fact. Said that he thought he was playing the role of being ill all too well, but my mind was full of gay Premier League footballers, the hideous Shelley, Charlie Gold and foetuses and liquidisers and I didn't pay his remark much attention. Maybe I should have?

The more I think about Joey, the more nervous I become. The doc's remark about him playing the role too well keeps coming back to me, repeating in my mind, and so does something Joey said on the night of the "rancid old cunt" incident, I remember he started going on about how "I really, really want this." I'm beginning to wonder exactly how *much* he really, really wants it, and if he's perhaps playing a completely different game to the one I originally set in motion.

What do you think? Have I missed something? Is he up to something that I'm not aware of? Listen, I need you to do me a favour. Run what I've told you about Joey back through your mind and let me know your thoughts,

I need some extra input. Come on. Talk to me, we need to figure out what's happening here.

Next day, after a night of fitful sleep, I'm sitting in my kitchen, enjoying a lovely breakfast of waffles that the darling Rosa has made for me, and drinking my way through my third cup of coffee when Johnny comes bumbling into the kitchen, looking a bit worse for wear. "So how did it go with our young hooker then, Johnny?" I ask, eager to catch up on the news of Johnny's visit to Michael Reilly's prostitute friend. "Uhh..good, good...'" replies Johnny as he sits down at the table, facing me, but looking at Rosa as she brings him over his own plate of waffles and a large, steaming coffee. He looks down at the plate of food Rosa places before him and then looks up at her with a big, boyish, playful grin (make no mistake, my Johnny may be a bit of a thug, but he can be just *so* charming when he wants to be) and says, "oh, Rosa, sweetheart, you're a proper lifesaver, you are!"

"I know this, now you eat your food and shut up. I go now read my papers so you give me some peace!" Rosa says this with mock severity, determined to give the impression that she is unaffected by Johnny's doleful eyes and winsome charm, I, for one, am not fooled.

Johnny's gaze follows Rosa from the kitchen for a few seconds, then he turns to me, grins widely and tells me "yeh, it went well wiv the rent, he won't be saying a word to no-one 'bout Michael, nah, not a fucking word!"

"Erm, okay, great, but please tell me that this never doesn't involve never as in never due to death by buggery?"

"Nah, leave it out, as it happens I were quite restrained, weren't I."

"Okay, that's good! So, tell me how it all went down."

Johnny looks at me smiles and explains, "it all went smooth as silk, sweetheart. Griselda had all his details for me, so I ring him up and book a session wiv him like I were a regular punter and I go round his place. Lived in this block of council flats near Old Street, din'he, eleventh floor like. Anyway, I'm in his flat and we chat a bit and then, just as he thinks I'm gonna give him money and do the business, well, instead I give him a good slap in the face and before he knew it he was hanging from his balcony by his feet. So I tell him, I tell him 'you make one fucking sound, you little shit, and I'll fucking drop you' and he says nothing just sorta nods, whimpers and pisses himself, literally pisses himself...made me fucking laugh I can tell you.."

"Johnny...too much detail, already," I interrupt, "cut to the chase, is he going to keep his mouth shut?"

"Corse he is sweetheart, I let him hang over the balcony for a cupla minutes, then I gets him back in the flat and I tell him that I'm best mates wiv Michael and what wiv Michael being on the telly and all that he don't want his private life airing in public and if that should happen, well, I'd have to assume that he was the one what was spreading the muck and I'd have to come back and kill him. Don't worry, Andy, he was fucking petrified!"

"And you're absolutely sure of that, yeh?"

"Totally, sweetheart, no worries, job done, sorted."

I reach across and squeeze his arm, I've no doubt what he says is right, the little scrot won't say a word: my Johnny can be a very, very scary man.

"Good stuff," I say, "tell me, though, you look pretty hung-over and I didn't hear you come in last night. Did you, er, have a late one and celebrate the successful outcome of your job?"

"Yeah, that's right, did the job, felt good, so I went down The Dungeon."

"Oh, you cheap, dirty whore!" The Dungeon is a notorious rough gay sex club down in Vauxhall, knowing Johnny's appetites I'm guessing he had a very busy night indeed!

I suppose this is an appropriate point to tell you about me and Johnny's sex life. Put bluntly, we don't have one. At least not with each other - that all stopped about five years ago. Does happen in long term relationships, I'm afraid. We do screw around though. Have done since we first got together. Like gay men everywhere, we just don't do monogamy. It's never affected our relationship, though. We've always known that whoever we go off with for a night, we'll always be right back with each other by morning. If you have any gay friends who say they are entirely faithful to their partners, then don't believe them. They're telling porkies. But, hey, don't you look so smug, you think hetties are that different? By God, I could tell you some stories that would set you straight on that (no pun intended)!

Me and Johnny spend the next half hour together, stringing out our breakfast, chatting like old friends, and I take the opportunity to tell him that tomorrow he needs to get himself up to Shelley's place in Cheshire. Shelley's already let me know that Jack will be out training, leaving her there on her own. Perfect timing for Johnny to pop up, install our little cameras and put my blackmail plan into operation. I tell him to pick up the equipment from Griselda later that day, and to listen carefully to any instructions she gives, we don't want any fuck ups.

After we finish our chat I wander upstairs to my bedroom. I'm not going into the office today, I have some important things I need to do. I definitely need to visit Joey to find out what on earth is going on with him, but first I have to make my weekly addition to my Little Black Book Of Infamy. Actually, that's just what I call it, it's in fact a movie rather than a book. A movie featuring me, just me, talking to camera. I do it once a week every week. It's an insurance policy, if you like. I sit down, and recount everything that has happened during the course of the last seven days. I describe exactly what I'm doing for my clients, how much they're paying me, and, most importantly, I name all the fuckers. The recording then goes into a safety deposit box somewhere in London, only me, Johnny and a very exclusive and costly firm of solicitors know the location.

I'm not telling you where it is, so don't ask, and be warned that you too will be getting a mention. I'm certain that, now we've spent time together, we are going to remain friends, but you never know. People are strange creatures and it's always better to be safe than sorry, that's what I say.

And if you think my little "insurance policy" is a little underhand, well, more fool you. You don't know how shallow, vicious and dangerous the world of celebrity is. Don't believe me? Fair enough – but I suggest you wait until we've spent a bit more time together before you judge me.

Nobody knows for sure that I make these little films, that I'm sitting on a tinderbox comprised of years and years of scandal and shoddy, often criminal, behaviour. However, I have been *very* careful, via the odd artfully misplaced comment (when I've supposedly had far too much to drink) to make sure that lots of people *think* they exist.

As I sit in front of my little camera and unburden my soul of the weight of all the dreadful things that *those* people require of me, I'm careful to look scandalised when I describe my client's troubles and requests to sort them out, shocked when I discuss the amount of money they're prepared to pay and horrified when describing the things they make do for them. Usually my outrage is cuntola. But not always. Definitely not always.

JOHNNY

Johnny loves Andy. Unquestionably, absolutely. Furiously. He is the only man for him, always has been, always will be. He will live and die, stand or fall with him. There's nothing he wouldn't do to protect him and their life together. Nothing.

And what a life that's been! Johnny has gone from working in Tandy that day (many years back now) that Andy handed him a three way plug extension, to living a life of wealth and privilege. Andy has lifted him up, made him special, somebody who wants for nothing. Somebody who can do absolutely what the fuck he likes without reference to anyone. He knows that he owes everything to Andy, and Johnny is a man who always honours his debts. Be they good ones, or bad ones.

The fact there is no longer a physical side to their relationship is irrelevant to Johnny. Let's be honest, Andy has always been no more than an average looking guy - no Adonis by any stretch of the imagination! But the physical thing was never what attracted Johnny to him. It was his sharp intelligence, the dry sense of humour, the ambition, the readiness to stick his neck out to almost ridiculous proportions, his lack of fear, his skill in getting people to open up to him. Andy has an incredible ability to listen to people and store everything, absolutely *everything*, that they say in some kind of huge database in his brain for checking, cross-referencing and possible future use. And most of all, Johnny has always been blown away by Andy's almost psychic talent to see right through people to the nub of their being, see their hopes, their ambitions, their venality, their insecurities, their lies.

All that...all that is what makes Andy such a smart bastard, a fizzing brew of heady intellect, a bloke who throws out ideas like a Catherine wheel throws out sparks. That's the attraction to Johnny.

He has absolute confidence and faith in Andy and his abilities.

And yet, and yet, Johnny is worried. There's something at the back of his mind, a black cloud that is simultaneously indistinct and vaguely threatening, which just won't go away. He feels niggled and uncertain. He's worried about Andy and he's worried for himself, well, *by* himself, to be honest. The truth is that when he told Andy about his night with the piece of rent that was trying to blackmail Michael Reilly he was, to be frank, less than honest about the sequence of events or the amount of force used.

Johnny has always known that he has a, how to put it, predilection for violence and over the years in his work for Andy it's come in useful...there are lots of bad and stupid people in this line of business who occasionally need a short, sharp shock to remind them of the error of their ways. Recently, though, that predilection for violence has become more a thirst, almost a compulsion, something that he can feel building up in him day by day, until it's like an explosion waiting and needing to happen.

Take the rentboy for example. Johnny didn't just slap him about, he beat the shit out of him. The poor sod was begging through a mouthful of broken teeth to be left alone. He had to gag him for fear that the neighbours would hear his moans and screams. The worst thing was the way hitting the guy made him feel. He really, really enjoyed it. It gave him a feeling of power and a burning desire for yet more aggression and more violence At some point, Johnny is aware that he lost the plot completely, he seemed to lose track of where, even who, he was. When normal reality reasserted itself, he found himself kneeling astride the prone body of the rentboy, with his hands clasped tightly around the guy's neck. He had throttled him unconscious. Maybe even killed him. Fearful for what he might have done, Johnny ran to fetch a pan of cold water and threw it in the rent's face. He was distinctly relieved to see the hooker splutter his way back to life.

Johnny has certainly warned the guy off, he'll not trouble Michael anymore and he won't ever breathe a word of what happened to him. But he's well aware that the level of violence used was completely unnecessary and over the top. Where the fuck did all it all come from? And it didn't end there, only went and popped some guy one for looking at him the wrong way in the toilets at The Dungeon, didn't he?

Johnny's disturbed by this recent turn of events. Yeh, sure, he's always been a bit handy, never one to back away from a fight and not one to be scared of violence. Last night, though, he acted like some kind of out of control psycho. Maybe he's always had tendencies that way and only now have they risen to the surface? He doesn't know exactly what's going on but he thinks it's probably not good. And if he wasn't unsettled enough by the rage that seems to have taken root inside him, then there's bloody Andy for him to worry about!

Sometime after Johnny had told Andy his (heavily edited) account of him and the rentboy, Andy sits Johnny down and says he has something to ask of him and it's a bit strange. Well, he and Andy have done lots of weird stuff together over the years so he's not too worried about what Andy may have to say. But then he comes out with the foetus stuff, and how that mad fucking bitch Janey Jax wants to eat one to keep herself looking young. Fucking vampire. To make matters worse, Andy says he only trusts Johnny to deal with such a sensitive issue and has chosen him to pick up and deliver this package of biological delights. The foetus thing is bad enough but Johnny knows that where Janey Jax goes that evil bastard Charlie Gold will be slithering close behind. That makes all sorts of alarm bells ring with him. Besides being a fat bastard, Charlie is a dangerous man. A killer.

Then there's Joey Camps and Andy's cancer scam. Andy told him about that some time ago, and it seems to have been going on for months. Faking cancer is typical of the kind of daring and brilliant plan that Andy would come up with. But it's risky, very risky. If anything goes wrong, if the truth gets out, then things will rebound catastrophically, not only on Joey but Andy as well.

There's too many things going on for Johnny's taste, too many things in the air, both with him and Andy, too much possibility for the unexpected to happen. He doesn't like surprises, not at all, so he hopes he's mistaken, he hopes everything will be okay. But that black cloud at the back of his mind…it just doesn't want to disperse.

ANDREW

Later that day, I'm on my way to Joey's place in Belsize Park. It's a quick walk, Primrose Hill Road, over Adelaide Road, across Englands Lane, past The Washington on your right, straight on into Belsize Park

Gardens and second right into Glenilla Road, where Joey lives.

I see you're coming with me. Hmm, okay. Have to say I wasn't very impressed by your thoughts on the Joey matter. I'm not sure the phrase "no idea" counts as meaningful input. Still, never mind, I suppose you're new to all this. By the way, do you absolutely have to wear that particular top, do you not think it's a bit too, well, bright? You've obviously never done a Colour Me Beautiful course, have you?

As I approach Joey's place I see it's well staked out by paparazzi. It's been that way since the start of his 'cancer'. I pass through the paps unmolested, I get a few nods of recognition, but none of them snap me, they know that's a no-no. *Don't worry, they won't take any pictures of you. To them you're a nobody. Especially in that top.*

The door is opened by Joey's mother, which I find odd as his parents (despite Joey's oft repeated offer to buy them a London home) live up in Doncaster, so it's a long way for her to come. Joey's mum says "come in, luv," and within seconds of closing the door behind me, and before I've even had a chance to say hello, she looks at me teary-eyed and says, "oh, Andy, 'es not doin' well, you know, I came 'ere on a visit last week an' I've not left since. Me poor lad, 'e's so ill, 'e needs someone 'ere for them babies and someone 'ere for 'im so I ain't goin' nowhere 'til we get 'im better."

Now this surprises me on many levels. I've known Missus Joey for almost as long as I've known Joey. To me, she's always seemed a solid, steady person, certainly not given to shows of overt emotion. I don't get it. Why should he be so ill that he needs his mum here? He shouldn't be ill at all!

What the fuck is that boy up to, what is going here?

There is sudden noise and chatter, I look up the stairs and I see a camera crew descending. This means that Joey must have just done his daily video diary for joeycampsfight4life dot com, and the many satellite TV channels across the world that have also signed up to run the daily updates on Joey's "brave struggle" against "this cruel disease". Once the crew has congregated in the hallway, his mum opens the front door for them to leave and looks at them with disdain bordering on outright hatred. "An' stop 'im doin' that will you, Andy, it's just 'int right, 'im living in front 'a camera like that, it's got no dignity."

I briefly consider mentioning that selling one's dignity can be highly profitable: witness silly amounts of money joeycampsfight4life and the video diary are bringing in, but decide it would be particularly tactless. Instead I switch to my default mode and lie, "of course, Mabel, you're absolutely right. I'll see what I can do, but you know Joey, when he sets his mind on something it's bloody hard to shift him!"

"Aye," she smiles, "'e were always a stubborn bugger. You' ave a try tho,' an' that doctor of 'is Andy, I don't think 'es 'elpin 'cos Joey's right sick now, you'll see what I'm sayin' when you're up there. I just dunno what's gonna 'appen wi' 'im!" As she says this one of her small, feminine hands goes to her face, squeezes her bottom lip, a shadow crosses her features and small tears well up in her eyes. "I think we're gonna lose 'im, Andy, oh them poor bloody kids, first their ma an' then their da...." Now the tears flow freely and poor Mabel is pressed up against me and I'm hugging her, making shushing noises of comfort whilst her tears soak into the jacket of my suit (Saville Row today). "Don't you worry about a thing," I assert in what I hope is my best calming voice, "it's all going to be fine, I'll go and talk to him now, see how he is, cheer him up a bit, and I promise you that the doctor is doing everything possible. There's really nothing to worry about, Mabel, nothing at all, trust me."

After a couple of minutes of hugging and shushing I manage to reassure Mabel a little bit and she stops crying. I give her a peck on the cheek and she goes off to see to the twins. I start walking upstairs to Joey's room. I want to sprint up those bloody steps and shout, "what the fuck are you doing" at him, but given the state Mabel is in I think a display of outward composure is called for.

For a few seconds I stand outside his room, I take a deep breath, let myself in quietly and close the door behind me.

Shock number one.

Joey is in bed, propped up with pillows. He's thin, pale, he seems to be losing his hair, his eyes are bloodshot, his lips cracked and dry, his complexion is yellowish and dull. Like he looked on joeycampsfight4life, but up close and personal - Christ, he looks even worse. I'm no doctor, but to me Joey looks a very sick man. Any ideas I may have had about announcing his return to health are most definitely out of the window!

I'm gutted to see him looking this way. Okay, I have real affection for Joey, but all that aside, he's just a really sweet guy, a bit immature and irresponsible at times perhaps, but there's no malice in him (most of my clients have malice in bucket loads so it's a refreshing change to work with someone that doesn't).

I get over the initial shock of his appearance and slowly and deliberately put one foot in front of the other. I walk up to his bed, sit on the edge and reach out to clasp one of his hands in both of mine. His hand has no strength, it lies limp, sweaty and unresponsive in my grasp. "Joey," I say, urgently and insistently, "what the cuntola is going on here? You're supposed to be fucking pretending to be fucking ill. We're paying that bloody doctor a small fucking fortune to treat you for imaginary cancer and here's you come down with something that looks pretty fucking real to me!"

He fixes me with a weak gaze and says, quietly, "oh, it's nothing, Andy, I just gotta bit o'flu, that's all.."

"Bollocks, I may be many things but I'm not an idiot and you, my son, are spinning me a line. I'll ask once more, what is going on and if you don't tell me the truth I'm phoning an ambulance for you right now!"

Joey coughs. Looks directly at me. And I see once again that pool of infinite sadness in his eyes. The same one that was there the first time we discussed his "cancer."

I don't know about you, but that look scares me. It's the look of a man who has one foot in this world, and one in the next. No, I can't tell you what's wrong with him, I'm not being stroppy or secretive, I simply don't know.

"Okay, yeh, there is summat up, I guess I knew we'd 'ave to 'ave this discussion."

"Andy, mate, I'm dyin'."

Shit, fuck, that's given us something to think about hasn't it. This doesn't look good. I bet you didn't expect this in a humble tale of everyday celebrity, did you? I certainly fucking didn't.

Shock number 2.

"What the…" I almost recoil back from Joey in shock, "…what do you mean? You can't be fucking dying! That's ridiculous! All this, it's…it's just a silly game, nothing more than a little bit of clever media manipulation to get your career back on track and make some good money on the way. It's not supposed to be about you *actually* dying, for God's sake, stop talking such total crap!"

"No, I'm dyin' an' I'm dyin' for real. I bin poisoning meself 'aven't I…every day for the last six weeks I bin drinkin' anti-freeze. It's got ethylene glycol in it, right poisonous stuff it is…looked it up on the net din't I. I 'ave just a little bit every day, not enough to kill me right away but enough to cause more an' more damage to me heart, me kidneys, me brain, me blood. I'm totally fucked. Even if I stopped now the damage 'as gone too far, this ain't summat I can come back from, it's too late."

"And next week I'm gonna finish it, I'm gonna take shit loads of paracetamol. Wi' what I'm gonna take a normal 'ealthy bloke might last three or four days, knackered like I am I reckon I'll be gone in one or two.."

Suddenly Joey is wracked by coughing and retching, he indicates a bowl by the side of the bed, I pass it to him. He vomits into it and the stench is fowl.

Now I'm an excellent judge of people and, watching Joey vomiting into that bowl, I realise with a cold shiver down my spine that I know one hundred per cent that what he has told me is the truth. The truth, the whole truth and nothing but the fucking truth. The question is why? I am seized by horror, by panic, by regret, by a massive sense of impending loss. I want to grab the kid, slap him and scream "why?" Instead I take the reeking bowl of vomit into Joey's en suite and flush the contents down the loo. There is blood in the vomit, a lot of blood.

So, Joey is dying. Having established that fact, we have to decide where on earth we go from here? Well, where I go from here, I think you're probably a bit out of your depth on this one, best if you restrict yourself to simply observing. Please, stop asking me questions and just shut up for a few minutes. I have to be calm and I have to think. There must be a way out of this.

I return to Joey's bedside and sit back beside him, he smiles weakly at me, "I know that look, Andy, you're checkin' all the angles, measurin' stuff up, lookin' for a solution or a way out but there ain't one 'ere mate, it's a done deal, I'm a dead man."

"Jesus Christ, I don't know what to say to you…why, why on God's earth have you done this? I told you we could sort your problems and look how well it's gone so far, the press is back on your side, the money's pouring in and the public has fallen back in love with you!"

"Cos I'd only fuck it all up all over again, you already 'elped me outta the shit more than once. I'm a total gobshite. You know me, I'd go an' get pissed or coked up, like I do, say summat else stupid an', mate, there's a limit to 'ow many times you can get cancer. You woulda got me through this, yeh, I know that, 'cos you're bloody good at your job, but what about the next time an' then the next time?"

"Hey, hey, now you're just being silly."

"I wish I were, Andy. At the end of the day, I'm just a working class tosser from Doncaster, an' like people say, you can take the boy outta Doncaster, but you can't take Doncaster outta the boy…I would lose everythin' at some time or other, the whole fuckin' shooting match, the 'ouse, the cars, the money, me an' them poor bloody kids woulda ended up back at me ma's or in some shitty council house, an' I'd be back to cookin' burgers if I could even get a fuckin' job. An' me kids, me poor bloody kids! They'd end up in some shitty school wi' nowt ahead of 'em but a lifetime of shitty zero 'ours contract jobs. I got outta all that crap and I can't go back to what I were an' I won't do it to the twins. Andy, you gotta understand, if I end it all now I go out as someone, as brave Joey, who fought against cancer an' lost and me kids get to live wi' me ma an' da in a lovely house, in a good area wi' good schools an' wi' a shit load of money left to 'em. That's what I want, Andy, please don't stand in me way, in fact I need you to 'elp me.."

"No way, this is complete madness, you just don't need to do this, I'm not going to just stand around and let you poison yourself to death!"

"Listen to me, please, an' remember, I'm all messed up inside already, I've passed the point of survivin' this. Get your doc to gimme some tests or summat an' 'e'll tell you I'm already dead! Please, please have a think on everythin' I've said an' at least listen to what I'm gonna ask an' then go away an' consider stuff before you say yes or no."

Because of my feelings for him and because both intuition and Joey's awful appearance tell me that he is indeed a very sick, no, a *dying* man, I decide to hear him out and I say, "all right, I still think this is all completely insane but go on, tell me, what do you want from me?"

"It's simple, Andy. I done really well with the website and interviews an' all that an' what wi' the money I got saved already the kids an' me ma and da'll be right well off, but there's no 'arm in 'aving more so I've done this deal, an' I've sold the rights to me death. TV, pictures, internet, everythin'. When I die there'll be cameras 'ere to film it all an' it'll all be broadcast live, a live celebrity death, just imagine 'ow many people'll watch that...."

"Woah, woah, let's back up here a bit, this all news to me! Who the fuck have you sold rights to your own death to?" Despite the awfulness of the situation and the deep unhappiness I feel, my professional pride is slightly dented by the news that Joey has been off negotiating deals on his own initiative.

Let's be honest, a celebrity death, live on telly, that's a bloody good idea. I should have thought of that one. What do you mean you wouldn't watch it? Bollocks, that kind of thing would be just so up your street. You'd be there with your mug of drinking chocolate and your packet of Digestive biscuits, absolutely glued to the screen, you wouldn't miss a second of it. Oh come on, don't deny it, I know you, remember.

Shock number three.

"Charlie Gold, two million quid for all rights."

"Charlie fucking Gold! You've done a deal with that fucking cunting arsehole! Joey, I know you're ill so forgive me, but you must be fucking mad, that man makes me look like a fucking teddy bear. Jesus Christ, if he finds out this whole cancer thing is a scam he'll have us by the balls! Oh fuck, what have you done!"

"Don't worry, that Charlie's just as taken in wi' your cancer idea as everybody else. The only difference wi' 'im is that I had to sell 'im the 'ole celebrity live death idea so I've told 'im that me cancer hasn't responded to treatment and that I'm gonna die, that I've only got days left, which ain't far from the truth anyway."

"Oh, no, no… this is all too fucked up, it needs to stop. Look, I'll call you an ambulance now, we'll get you to a hospital. Whatever you've done to yourself I'm sure it can be fixed! We can tell the public that your cancer is…I dunno…worse than was first thought and you've had to be admitted to a specialist clinic, then we can get whatever you've done to yourself sorted and we'll be back on track with the plan and we can move it on to you recovering…"

I spew all this out, surprised at how desperate I sound. But it's all piss in the wind because I *know* that Joey is dying. Full stop. No amount of judiciously applied pressure, no clever illness scams, no "mea culpa" press interviews, no backhanders in brown paper bags, no threats nor blackmail - nothing is going to help Joey now. Nothing. Because not even I can help him swerve the Grim Reaper.

Joey watches me, strangely serene, as I rant. With what seems a huge effort on his part, he puts his hands on my shoulders and pulls himself up towards me and says, "good old Andy, you've always done your best for me mate, I know that an' I know that this is 'ard for you," Joey pauses for breath as if the simple act of speaking were almost too much for him, "but, you 'ave to understand me, it's over for me, I'm finished, an' nought's gonna change that. When the day comes, Andy, the day that I go, please keep me ma an' the twins away. I don't want them involved in this dying live on tele stuff. An' after I'm dead I need you to make sure that Charlie Gold keeps 'is end of our deal an' I need you see that that doctor friend of yours gets a death certificate all written up proper an' official. I can't 'ave 'em doin' an autopsy on me body an' finding it full of bloody anti-freeze 'cos then we'd both be in the shit!"

I look at that once beautiful face, ruined by pain, sickness and sorrow and now streamed with tears. Gently, I lift Joey's hands from my shoulders and I lay him back slowly, resting his head on to the pillows of the bed. "Joey, look, I'm not going to give you a yes or a no now, but I will think about what you've said." As I say this I know inside that I seriously am going to consider helping him. Madness though all this is, I'm simply too fond of the guy to simply dismiss his wishes out of hand.

All right, so I didn't need to tell you that, you knew already that I'd maybe help him because I fancy him. Do you really need to state the bloody obvious? Go on then, clever clogs, pat yourself on the back for your incredible insight (not) and then shut up because what comes up next is important and a touch problematic. Stop fidgeting and pay attention. Christ, what is it with you? It's like I'm being followed around by a seven year old child! Pull yourself together, for fucks sake!

Before I leave, Joey has one more thing to ask of me. He wants me to quickly scan through Charlie Gold's contract for the televised death, make sure it's kosher. He directs me to a wall safe, well hidden away behind a typically Joey, and terrible, "Limited Edition" framed print *(though, to be fair, I guess it has a kind of kitsch, post-modern, ironic appeal. What do you think?)* and tells me the combination. I open it and inside is not only Charlie Gold's contract but also a plastic bottle of fucking anti-freeze (exhibit number one, your honour) and two large packets of paracetamol. When I see these it dawns on me that Joey hasn't told me everything. There's a remorseless logic here: he said to me he's going to kill himself with a paracetamol overdose. No way. Not possible. Not with the state he's in. Even just a few days on from here he's going to be too ill to leave his bed. That means somebody is going to have to get those paracetamol out of the wall safe, crush them up and spoon them into a dying man's mouth.

And seeing as the only cunt who knows about Joey's mad plan is me...

Brilliant. Just fucking brilliant. Cunty fucking cuntola with gold fucking knobs on. So Joey doesn't just want me to help with the arrangements for his death. He also wants me to administer the final blow to his existence! This I am really going to have to think about. This is all quite serious. Let's be honest, I've done shitloads of dodgy stuff in my time and I've spent years now bending (okay, breaking) the law without worry for the consequences because I'm rich and because all sorts of people owe me all sorts of favours. But helping someone to die? Killing them? Nope. This is all new to me. And what about you? I think you maybe need to reconsider your position here, are you absolutely sure you want to be involved in this? Don't feel obliged to stick around, I'd quite understand if you want to bow out

of things now, after all, you signed up for a bit of fun -
not this fucking nightmare.

JOEY

After Andy leaves, Joey sleeps fitfully for a short while. He wakes and, boy, does he feel bad! Really bad, fuck, he's damaged his body. His stomach is on fire, and the pain in his lower back and under his rib cage bears testament to damage to his liver and kidneys. And then there's the shortness of breath, the pain in his head, the disorientation, the confusion and today his ticker has been beating in an ominously irregular pattern. Joey knows with certainty that his regular anti-freeze intake has, as planned, damaged his body beyond recovery. In a way this a good day: he understands on an instinctive and intellectual level that he is dying. It's too late to change his mind, too late to back out. His end is inevitable. The only choice he has to make now is to die slowly and in great pain or end it all relatively quickly with an overdose. That choice is a no brainer to Joey.

And his end will all be caught live and on camera by Charlie Gold's guys. The first live on television and internet celebrity death, netting his estate a cool two mil in one hit. He's proud that he came up with the live death idea, not bad for a working class lad from the north. Andy himself couldn't have come up with anything better!

But his self-administered death hasn't been an easy thing for him. He doesn't want to say goodbye forever to the twins, his mum and dad, his friends, his life. He thinks back to the last time he held his lovely, beautiful boys. He hugged them both close, revelling in the feel of their warm little bodies, and to him they smelt of sunshine, flowers and warm soil. They smelt of life. When he thinks of leaving them behind he lies there in that bed of pain and cries and cries, but he needs to do this. The money from the Charlie Gold deal and the large amount of cash that's come in since news of his 'cancer', plus what he's earned over the years, should set the twins and his mum and dad up for life, and he won't be around anymore to fuck it up for them. He'll leave this world as famous and beloved 'tragic Joey' and not 'fuck up Joey'.

He wonders if Andy understood him, his need to go out on top, to leave a positive legacy for the twins. He hopes so, because without him his plan won't work. Only Andy is smart and manipulative enough to separate a mother and her dying son, only he has the clout to ensure that Charlie Gold, the fat fucking bastard, keeps to his promises.

Joey wishes now that he'd told Andy everything. He didn't of course. He bottled it. The bit about needing Andy to feed him mashed up paracetamol, that tiny detail, went unsaid. That was silly of him, it's a question he has to ask and soon. He should have got out it out of the way when Andy was here. Now it's just going to play on his mind. Will Andy help him kill himself, or not? Joey reassures himself with the thought that he knows Andy, he knows the depths of his cynicism and his remorselessly practical view of life, and he's aware that somewhere in Andy's heart, a torch burns for Joey Camps.

ANDREW

I woke up a bit later than usual this morning and found my Johnny already gone, off to Cheshire for the Jack Rigby job. I have an appalling hangover and quickly decide not go into the office. There's nothing going on that girls can't handle or that can't be done by phone or email. And I need a bit of quiet to decide exactly what the fuck to do about Joey.

The reason for my hideously bad hangover is that I had an extended and very drunken dinner last night at a nice Italian place in Primrose Hill.

It's not the sort of place you'd go to, out of your league in terms of prices I'm afraid. Maybe I'll take you there one day, my treat. I'm sure you'd enjoy it and the food's great, but I guess we should get through this little journey of ours first, eh? Speaking of which, I'm glad to see that you're still with me, you've obviously decided that you do want to continue with things despite the unexpected turn of events with young Joey. Well, that's okay with me, as long as you're completely sure, long as you know what you might be getting into. Stay. Don't stay. Your call.

My dinner date was Harry Ketchum, the artist. Harry's not a client, he's a friend and I always enjoy his company. Harry's made himself a multi, multi-millionaire by flogging 'sculptures' and 'pictures' created from his own and other peoples' faeces. Harry would forgive my quotation marks applied to his work, he freely admits he's a 'crap' artist (and winner of 'The Turder Prize', as he likes to joke), but what he *is* good at is marketing. In fact he's a marketing genius, he's created his own brand and, what's more, his own market. In the process of doing that he has, literally, turned shit into dosh. Nowadays he doesn't even create his own work, he employs a small army of people at his studios in Wales, shitting and painting and turning (turding?) out a steady stream of highly prized Ketchum artworks. Remember that large, diamond-encrusted turd that recently sold at auction for an eight figure sum? That was another Ketchum 'masterpiece'.

You got to admire the guy, and he's such an amusing bloke! Complete pisshead though, as my own banging head and dry mouth (resulting from my vain attempt to match Harry drink for drink) testify. Not even Rosa's specially requested greasy bacon, eggs and extra coffee have helped shift this particular hangover.

However, hungover or not, I need to come up with a plan to deal with all matters Joey related. Things are reaching a critical point. I don't think his mum is going to let stuff lie much longer. All it takes is for her to panic and ring up an ambulance and everything will go horribly, horribly tits up. Even a blind, deaf, dumb and completely incompetent doctor would figure out pretty quickly that Joey's not got cancer. And then, boy, the shit'll hit the fan big time and me and Joey'll have a lot of questions to answer. As much as I'm a devious, slippery and resourceful character, this time there'd be no saving Joey or me. The great British public would see the whole cancer scam as the grotesque, tasteless and perverse confidence trick that it is, not to mention the legal shit that would ensue from all the tie-ins Joey's got going with advertisers and sponsors (and Charlie bloody Gold).

A telephone conversation with Doctor Dodgy confirms what Joey said about the effects of his anti-freeze intake. It seems the doctor was going to call me if I didn't call him as he was so mystified by the lad's condition that he decided to run some blood tests on him. He reckons he's in a slow but inevitable state of multiple organ failure, that even immediate and intensive treatment wouldn't help. Joey is going to die and he's going to die soon.

That makes things easier to some extent. But let's remember here that Joey doesn't only want me to organise stuff *around* his death, stuff like his mum and Charlie Gold. He also wants me to be the person who gives him a fatal overdose. *Okay, fair enough, he's not said that yet, but to me it's as obvious as the rather large four hundred pound gorilla sitting over there in the corner.* And so I come back to that question again – how far am I prepared to go to help Joey kill himself? Admittedly I've not found it yet, but there has to be a moral red line somewhere that I'm not prepared to cross. Hasn't there?

Joey's right, I am fond of him but I do have to admit that he *is* a serial fuck up. His celebrity lifespan will always be limited by his inability to take the whole fame thing seriously and his inability to behave properly. In reality, calling the Queen a rancid old cunt should have finished him already, it's only my exceptionally brilliant celebrity cancer plan that's saved him.

And then without the fame, without the money, what is there for him and his kids? Fuck all, really. That old post-war consensus of redistribution of income (albeit limited) and a commitment to social justice (limited, again) went out of the window in the eighties. Somewhere along the line the bankers and the corporate classes and, well, people like me, reversed up the arses of the politicians and started pulling all the strings. We rolled back unionisation, we destroyed the working class by exporting their jobs and insourcing cheap labour and we undermined what social mobility there was by utterly devaluing the education system. We kept you lot quiet by stuffing your mouths with benefits or easy credit and by feeding you the dream of celebrity. You can be famous, you can be wealthy, you can escape your shitty, dull, drab life, and you don't even have to work for it, you just have to want it enough. To really, really want it. And just to reinforce that point, every now and then we select some barely talented but viciously ambitious non-entity like Shelley Bright and use every trick in the marketer's handbook to speed them up the ladder of fame.

Whilst you are distracted by the antics of characters such as Shelley, and by your own dreams of celebrity, me and my kind are siphoning ever more power and wealth upwards to ourselves. Slamming more and more windows of opportunity in your life shut - and making sure they stay shut. I don't know if you'll believe any of this, but I place it here in the genuine hope that it might spark in you some understanding of your woefully disadvantaged position in life. Please don't think that the politicians can help you. We own them body and soul. They work for us, not you. Don't think for a moment that elections represent a genuinely democratic choice, rather see them for what they actually are – a pantomime financed by the wealthy with a script written by guys like me; a reshuffling of pig snouts around the trough. Don't you see, people like you should be dragging people like me out into the streets and kicking us to death. People like you should be invading the City of London, pulling the bankers and hedge fund managers out of their plush offices and hanging them from lamp posts. Do it. Don't do it. But if you don't do it, you are so, so fucked.

I don't want to see Joey losing all he has. I don't want to see his body smashed and broken on the altar of celebrity. I don't want to see him being torn limb from limb by the tabloid wolf pack. I don't want him to be remembered as a fuck up. I don't want to see his kids struggling in life. I don't want to see him dying slowly and painfully of a bodged overdose attempt. Joey is special to me. I will give him everything that he wants, but not necessarily in the way he wants it.

Decision made, I feel a bit black, a bit empty. However, my mood soon picks up after a rather attractive young bicycle courier arrives at the house to deliver a small package for me. Inside are some rather interesting pictures of Shelley Bright. I study them closely and think, Andy, you clever sod, proved right again!

I see you're looking surprised. I bet you thought that I didn't have a conscience, let alone a social conscience. Well, let that be a lesson to you, a lesson not to make assumptions and to remember that I have the capacity to surprise you when you least expect me to do so.

JOHNNY

Johnny is parked up, sitting in a rental car in a quiet little lay-by, about a quarter mile from Shelley and Jack's place. Johnny himself is a bike man but he had too much equipment to bring with him today for the bike to be an option. He's spent the best part of the day with Shelley in the Rigby mansion, planting and testing two top of the range spy cameras. High tech and efficient, the cameras film in HD and record digital quality sound. Shelley and Jack's extravagant living area and Jack's bedroom (separate bedrooms for these two, notes Johnny) are now wired and ready to broadcast!

Now it's just a question of waiting. Jack should be back from training soon, and when he arrives home Johnny will ring Shelley, posing as a distraught friend who needs immediate help. She'll make her excuses and leave the house to attend to the distressed "friend" and very soon after that a handsome young black man will enter the grounds of Jack Brierley's home through the gate that Shelley has "accidentally" left open on her way out.

Johnny checks his laptop to check the pictures being relayed from Shelley's place, nothing happening, could be a long wait. He thinks about Shelley and decides Andy is right about her. She is fucking brain dead. Pretty but thick as two (no, three) short planks, and not remotely likeable.

Still, what the hell, this whole blackmail thing gives him the chance to watch at all-round macho man and Premier League hero (and sexy fucker) Jack Rigby taking it up the arse! How good is that! This is just the kind of thing that happens when you throw your life in with Andy Manning - you get a bloody exciting ride with some pretty amazing opportunities on the way.

His attention is grabbed as his mobile beeps the arrival of a text message. It's Kelvin, the sexy young guy who will be the other star of the upcoming live sex show, as long as all goes to plan, that is. Kelvin's letting him know that he's in position and ready. Johnny texts him back to say wait for now, nothing happening yet. Shouldn't be too long though, or at least he hopes it won't be too long. Shelley and Jack's mansion stands isolated in the Cheshire countryside and Johnny supposes it's all very pretty but rural landscapes are just not him and he's already been sitting in the bloody car with nothing to do but look at bloody grass and trees for two hours now!

Johnny tries to pass time by fantasising about the sex act he hopes he's about to see. Maybe that Kelvin's got a massive knob? Imagine a big, fat monster cock being squeezed up Jack's tight footballer arse! A picture of this delightful image forms in his head and gives him a huge hard on. He wonders if he's got time to bang out a quick one before Jack turns up? On balance, he decides it's wouldn't be professional and he should keep his mind on the job; a decision justified only a few minutes later when muffled sound from his laptop alerts him to the fact that Jack has finally arrived home. The sound becomes clearer as Jack enters the living area and becomes visible to the camera. From somewhere out of shot Shelley calls out a greeting and as Jack puts down his kit bag, Shelley, too, appears on camera. Jack lowers his lithe and athletic body into a stupidly large leather sofa, kicking up his training shoed feet on to an expensive looking, long and low glass table.

Johnny observes and listens to Shelley and Jack talking. Their conversation is mundane, trivial, at times petulant and bitchy. Johnny realises that there's not a lot of love at all there, if any, on either side. Anyway, time to get the ball rolling. As planned, Johnny puts a call through to Shelley's mobile, it's on that expensive glass table and he watches as she picks it up and answers. He says nothing, letting her do all the talking. With dramatic gestures, raised eyebrows and silent pauses she says "India, how are you darling...oh no, really, oh god..... I'm so sorry, that's dreadful, innit...yes, yes of course you need support....I'll be there for you, love...which A and E are you going to...right I'll leave, like, straight away, see you in twenty mins!"

Shelley hangs up, and Johnny hears her explaining to Jack that her dear friend India is on her way to hospital with a badly gashed arm (having slipped and put it through the kitchen window whilst polishing surfaces, apparently, if somewhat unfeasibly, India being another footballer's wife) and she has promised to help her and is leaving for A and E immediately, and Jack shouldn't wait up as things like this can take hours and she doesn't expect to be back until very late. As Shelley tells Jack of India's misfortune and her impending departure, he looks up at her untroubled and indifferent, to Johnny his face simply says "I don't care, in fact I'm glad to be rid of you for a few hours." It's obvious to him now that Shelley and Jack are not only *not* in love, they don't even *like* each other.

Some minutes later and Shelley has gathered all her stuff together (handbag, lippy, mobile, keys, bank cards, cash, crack pipe and a small rock of crack for a quick hit, just to keep her going) and has left the house. Johnny texts Kelvin and tells him the job is on: get up to the house and do your thang, girl!

For a short while Johnny watches as Jack picks up the TV remote, flicks through channels, scratches his balls, sticks a finger up his nose (not a very good look). Then he looks peeved as the doorbell rings. He gets up and moments later there are, once again, muffled sounds off camera. Kelvin and Jack enter the living area together and Kelvin is saying, "I'm sorry to come up your drive like this, it's just that my car's broken down right outside your gate and I couldn't see any other place to go, you're way out in the countryside here! It's good of you to let me use your phone, mate, dunno know what I've done with my mobile, I must've left it at home. Hey, a question, are you Jack Rigby? You are, aren't you! I think you're great, you're a top player, mate! By the way, you mind if I just take off this shirt? It's covered in oil and I can feel it starting to stick to me." Without waiting for an answer, Kelvin peels off his white (and carefully oil-stained) t-shirt, revealing a sculpted six-pack and a great pair of pecs - smooth, dark skin glistening seductively in the light.

Jack's eyes are almost bulging out of his head and as he accepts Kelvin's invitation to "feel how firm" his pecs are. Johnny can see that Jack wants it bad. There was no point putting that extra camera in Jack's bedroom because the horny fucker is going to do it right there and then. He wants Kelvin's dick inside him, and he wants it inside him now! This is going to be great fun. And as Jack Rigby, Premier League footballer, all round proper bloke and one of the lads, sinks to his knees in front of Kelvin's large and erect penis, Johnny decides that it's definitely time to bang one out!

ANDREW

So I guess you're wondering what was in the photos delivered to me yesterday by that cute courier? They're something to do with Shelley Bright - but what? You want to know what the pictures show, don't you? Okay, I'll tell you, but you need a bit of background first. Sitting comfortably? Here we go.

When I first met Shelley to discuss her divorce, she looked slim and beautiful as always, but maybe a little bit *too* slim, not even the thick layer of very expensive foundation she was wearing was enough to completely hide the dark circles around her eyes.

Now, a couple of years back I had to help Shelley with a little problem she had with crack cocaine. Unfortunately she asked for my assistance a little bit too late and by the time I got involved her little drug habit was already big news in the papers. We eventually neutralised any major issues by running a SHELLEY: MY DRUGS HELL campaign. Yes, Shelley did have a drug problem, but it was all down to the pressures of fame, she was getting treatment and making good progress. She realised that she had made a dreadful mistake, she was sorry she had let her fans, friends and family down. Her intention now was to get clean, to stay clean and give some of her time to drugs related charities, where she felt she could have a positive impact in helping to keep kids off drugs. Blah, blah, blah. Nonsense, nonsense, nonsense. All that sanctimonious shit plus me rapping a few journalistic knuckles and calling in some favours limited the damage and even put a positive spin on things.

Taking in to account Shelley's appearance and her past issues with crack, I had a hunch that Shelley's drug problem may have made a come-back and that's why I asked Griselda to have someone with big telephoto lens follow her around, and, bingo what a fucking result! Top job!

The pictures are snapped from some way off but are undeniable in what they show. Oh, the miracle and power of digital photography and the prying paparazzo! The girl in the pictures looks a bit grainy but is obviously Shelley, her head is wreathed in smoke and she's holding to her mouth a glass pipe, obviously a crack pipe, applying a lighter flame to it. Taking into account Shelley's past drug habit, it all adds up to clear and absolute evidence of substance abuse. Marvellous!

Yep, Shelley's back on the crack. I can see the headlines now: SHELLEY IN NEW CRACK CRISIS, SHELLEY'S CRACK TORMENT HELL, SHELLEY: CELEBRITY CRACKHEAD, ONCE A CRACKHEAD, ALWAYS A CRACKHEAD.

Now one bout of crack addiction is careless, but two, that's just plain silly. If these pictures become public, the media will eat Shelley alive, her career will be left a (crack) smoking ruin.

So, now you know what's in the pictures, you want to know what I'm going to do with them, am I right or am I right? Thought so. I suppose that you have been pretty trustworthy up to now. I guess I could tell you. Mmm, nah, you know what, I don't want to spoil the surprise, you'll have to wait and see.

THE PRODUCER

Today is one of The Producer's Fun Days.

Today's wanna be star and victim is Zandra from Chelmsford.

Zandra is a shop assistant but wants to be a famous singer. She's eighteen years old and lives at home with her Mum, who's always telling her she's a great singer, as do her mates down the local when there's a karaoke night, and she knows they're right, she just knows she'll be a singer and a star one day soon because she wants it so much. She's so excited to be here today, to be invited to see someone as important as The Producer. This is a big step, the start of her road to fame. As she's shown into The Producer's office she can barely contain her excitement!

The door closes behind her. Zandra is now in the clutches of The Producer, she has entered his lair and things will never be the same for her again.

She's a pretty girl is Zandra. Yes, very nice indeed. Great tits, nice arse, flush with the freshness of youth, just like in her photos. She is perfect and ripe for corruption. He is so going to do her. She's come to see him as a sweet angel. She'll leave as a skanky whore.

"So, Zandra," greets The Producer, as he reaches under his desk and presses that clever button that silently locks shut the door to his office and closes the blinds, "you want to be a singer?"

Zandra clenches her hands in front of her, her excitement has abated suddenly and she feels shy and awkward standing in front of the great man himself, a feeling enhanced by the fact that there's nowhere in The Producer's office for her to sit.

"Yes, y-yes" she stutters "I really, really want it and I know I can do it, it's all I want..."

"Good girl, that's what I like to hear. Now stop twitching will you, love. Just stand in the circle in the carpet, yes that's right, the one in front of my desk, that is the only circle in the office, isn't it, dear? It's not like you have lots to choose from..." Oh good grief, this one's even more stupid than usual. Christ, why are these people allowed to keep breeding?

"Good girl, Zandra...but here's the deal, I've heard your demo tape and, to be absolutely honest, you're shit, you can't fucking sing, love, you're hopeless, truly awful."

Poor Zandra, she hears The Producer's words, she blushes red and tears gather in her eyes. She wasn't expecting this, she can't believe it. Why is this man being so cruel?

"But don't panic, all is not lost. I hated your demo tape, but I loved your pictures so there is at least something we can work with...I mean your looks, Zandra, we can work with your looks, you're a pretty girl with nice tits and a great ass. The only question in my mind is how much do you want this? I mean are you ready to do whatever it takes to have a chance at fulfilling your dream?"

"I'll do anything, whatever it takes...just tell me what I need to do," replies Zandra, sensing some hope in her position. Steady now, thinks The Producer, she's nearly his. Already he can feel a stirring in his trousers.

"Okay, so if I help you, will you help me?"

"Yes, yes of course!"

"Will you do what I tell you to do?"

"Yes."

"Are you a shy girl?"

"No."

"Good. There's no place in this business for shy girls, now I want you to prove to me that you aren't one by taking your blouse off."

Zandra thinks for a few seconds, she can't go back now, not now she's being offered a shot at the big time, she could be on her way to fame and fortune, to all the things that she really, really deserves.

Zandra unbuttons….and The Producer's penis swells and bulges in his trousers, his dick is now fully and throbbingly erect.

"Take it off now, Zandra," orders The Producer.

Zandra' s blouse drops and pools round her ankles.

"Now prove you're really, really not shy, take off your bra, let's see those lovely tits of yours!"

Zandra hesitates.

"This is your audition, love, come on don't bottle it now, this is your one and only shot at the big time. Come on, Zandra, if you can't do this for me how can I trust you, and how can I work with someone I can't trust, someone I feel isn't committed?"

Zandra unclips her bra and lets it drop, exposing her full and firm young breasts..

Christ, these kids are so easy, he fucking owns them. This girl is his bitch now!

"That's it, darling, that's lovely, now get down on your knees." Zandra kneels down and The Promoter gets up from his desk. As he walks towards her, he sees that she is silently crying and this excites him further, it inspires him to unzip his fly and pull out his pulsing hard on. He stands in front of Zandra, puts a finger under her chin, tilts her head upwards so he's looking down into her eyes, "you're doing very, very well, love. I can see a very bright future for you. Tell me, darling, do you know what a tit wank is?"

ANDREW

That afternoon I decide to leave the office a bit earlier than usual. To be honest, I'm finding it difficult to concentrate as my head is full of thoughts about Joey. *Have I figured out what to do about him yet? I pretty much have a plan (loosely adapted from his own plan), just a couple of points I need to clarify. I know you want to know what I'm going to do, but I'll tell you when I'm ready, when I've got all my ducks in a row. Until then you'll have to be patient.*

I scoop up the pictures of Shelley having fun with crack, which I have spread across my desk, and tuck them safely into my briefcase. Outside the office, I find it's a lovely day, so I decide to walk back to Primrose Hill. *Come on, walk with me, it's not far, and let's be honest, you could do with shifting a few pounds, couldn't you? Oh, stop whingeing. Walk. Don't walk.*

I stroll quickly down Oxford Street, right into Regent Street, over Wigmore Street into Portland Place, right into Park Crescent, then through Regents Park, out near Saint Marks Square and left into Regents Park Road.

That's it, just down the road now and we're done. Look at you, you're exhausted and that wasn't even a long walk. You're not very fit are you? You really should do something about that, after all, you're not a youngster anymore.

I let myself into my house. I soon, and delightedly, discover that my Johnny is there. He calls out to me from the living room where I quickly join him, not even bothering to put down my briefcase. He came back from Cheshire very late last night and I left for the office early this morning, so I've not really had a chance to catch up with him and find out how the Jack Brierley job went. I don't need to bother asking though as Johnny is desperate to let me know all about it!

"Worked like a fucking charm din't it, that Kelvin looked fucking bootiful wiv his clothes off – he had this fucking monster cock and that bloody Jack, well, he were gagging for it, weren't he and they did it there and fucking then. Jack just couldn't get enough, he went all the way, did everything, yeh, he were a real dirty sod!"

Johnny then insists I sit down in front of his laptop to see for myself. I watch the footage, and to be honest, intended blackmail aside, it's a really hot piece of gay porno, particularly at the end when Kelvin dumps a massive money shot onto Jack's eager-looking face. "Yep, Johnny, that's good, real good, it'll get Shelley her divorce, no doubt about that...now I've got something to show you, too."

I extract the pictures of Shelley from my briefcase and hand them over to Johnny. He shuffles through the photos and as he does so a big smile appears on his face. "Fucking stupid cow," he says, "she's back on the crack ain't she, but why you got these, Andy? I bet you've one of your little schemes in your head, aintcha?"

"Well, you didn't really think I would throw one of our own completely to the dogs did you? And that Shelley, she is *so* fucking obnoxious. These pics will just even up the score, Shelley will still get her divorce but she won't get to screw Jack for a big payoff."

"How's that gonna work then?"

"Because we're going to send a copy of Jack's porno shoot to the man himself with the suggestion, as Shelley wants, that the footage can be destroyed if he agrees to a divorce. But… shortly after Jack gets his film, he'll receive another delivery. This time the pictures of Shelley's little crack episode. Now Shelley has something on Jack, and Jack has something on Shelley. They're bound together by a doctrine of mutually assured destruction so they have to play nice and split on equal terms, that's to say no big pay-off for Shelley."

"Ah…ha ha," laughs Johnny, "love it, mate, love it.."

Bing bing! Score team Manning! There you go I've rescued Jack from being completely fucked over by Shelley and shown you again that I have a conscience, haven't I? Told you I was full of surprises!

"Yeh, and it gets better, we'll let Shelley know that *we* know about the pictures. We'll say they were sent to Jack by some nasty little Pap and that while we can't help the fact he already has them, we can make sure that nobody else gets to see them by buying them back from the photographer for the bargain price of a hundred thousand quid. After all, it would have dreadful implications for Shelley's career if they popped up in one of the tabloids…"

Johnny laughs again and pats me firmly on the shoulders, "Andy, you're one twisted, devious bastard!"

Okay. Fair enough. Screwing money out of Shelley, who's already paying me a whopping fee, shows me up in a slightly less charitable light. Do I care? No. And let's not forget here that Shelley is a sorry excuse for a human being, and if you'd had to spend as much time with her as I've had to over the years, you'd want a hundred grand off her as well. Think of it as compensation for having to endure her company and intellectual damage caused by the brain eating stupidity of her conversations.

"I know, I'm really rather proud of myself, I think I've played a blinder here. Listen, burn a DVD of Jack's porno then tomorrow morning get it and the pictures of Shelley up to the office. Give the lot to Kerry so she can make the arrangements to get them to Jack. I'd do it myself but I have to go and see Joey."

"Okay, how's Joey doing?"

And that simple question uncorks a well of grief in my soul and I spill out the whole thing to Johnny. I tell him what Joey's planning to do, that he's been slowly poisoning himself, that in fact he's dying. I tell him about Joey's agreement with Charlie fucking Gold, the proposed televised death scene. I tell him that I am going to help Joey end his life. I tell him all of it. The whole fucking sorry and awful shower of shit that my simple plan has degenerated into. From my raw emotion it must be obvious to Johnny, if he didn't know already, that there's a depth to my relationship with Joey. He reaches out, holds me, hugs me, reassures me, he tells me I can deal with things, that I'll find a way through it all, that

I'm right to give Joey what he wants, that everything will be okay. That's why I love this man.

Sadly, our charming mutual love-in is broken as reality raises its grim head once again in the form of my mobile bleeping the arrival of a text message. It's from the dodgy doc, it says: PACKAGE RDY 2 PICK UP 2MRW 11AM ASK 4 DELIVERY 4 MR WELLS AT RCPTN.

Oh joy, the first fucking foetus is ready for that mad cunt Janey Jax. Plug those liquidisers in, boys!

"Johnny, I'm sorry about this but that's another little job for you tomorrow, foetus delivery I'm afraid, from the doctor's office to that house Janey has rented in The Bishops Avenue."

"Oh shit, can't say I'm over the moon 'bout that Andy...me and you have done some stuff in our time but this is way too weird..."

I think we're all agreed on that, aren't we? This whole foetus thing is too weird. In fact, it's beyond weird, it's bizarre and scary. I have a very bad feeling about this, I can't help thinking that something, somewhere is going to go horribly wrong.

What's that? You want a copy of Jack's sex film. How strange, I really didn't think that porn was your bag, let alone gay porn. Just goes to show, you never can tell. And, no, you can't have a copy...

<u>JOHNNY</u>

The next morning, before Johnny leaves the house, he is careful to make sure that he's packed in his rucksack the DVD and photos relating to Jack and Shelley's indiscretions. He gives Rosa (sweetheart) a kiss, leaves the house and wanders out into Chalcot Square. He's wearing full biker leathers today and feels pretty sexy. He thinks he looks hot. He knows he looks hot!

He scans the square, picks out his beloved Kawasaki ZX10R (an anniversary present from Andy) and as he walks towards it he mentally plans a route down to Andy's office, then to the dodgy doc's, then up to The Bishops Avenue.

Johnny straddles his bike and fires up the engine. Its throbbing hum resonates beneath him. As he steers out into the road he considers what Andy said last night, the stuff he said about Joey. It's obvious to him that he thinks a lot of the boy, certainly more than he should. Does that bother him? No. Not at all. Joey is straight and, not to put too fine a point on it, he's dying. If he did represent any threat at all to his and Andy's relationship it would strictly (and literally) be a short-lived one. Anyway, after twenty years as partners he is absolutely confident of the strength of his and Andy's relationship. They are together, full stop, period, forever and until the end. Johnny loves him as much as now as ever. He'd kill to protect what he and Andy have, not in an abstract sense, but in a tangible hands around the neck and squeezing tightly sense.

After some time weaving through London's always awful traffic, Johnny arrives at the Mayfair office. He parks illegally outside, crosses his fingers he won't get ticketed and enters the building.

Taking his rucksack from his back he sees Griselda and Kerry, Kerry bright as always and Griselda as scary as ever.

"Hey girls…and Griselda, 'ow you doin'" calls out Johnny…

"Johnny, lovely to see you!" comes back Kerry.

"Fuck off, you fag!" comes back Griselda, grinning through her broken teeth.

"Kerry, sweetheart, you look gorgeous, Griselda you look like, well, a lesbian. You ever gonna get a new set of front teeth or what?"

"Only if I can use them to rip you throat out, Johnny, now stop babbling like a dick and tell us what you're doing here, besides getting on my tits."

"Ahh…" Johnny opens his rucksack and pulls out two large envelopes, both bearing Jack Rigby's name: one contains a DVD containing the footage of him being buggered by Kelvin, the other the incriminating pictures of Shelley smoking crack. They're both to be sent by motorcycle courier up to Cheshire, but some time apart. Jack will get his porno DVD this evening, but the pictures of Shelley indulging her crack habit he'll get tomorrow morning. Andrew had insisted on this delivery schedule. Johnny's not sure why, all he can think is that it's some cruel, but no doubt amusing, little twist in his plan and designed to discomfit Shelley in some way.

Having already been pre-warned (of the first delivery at least) by Andrew, Johnny knows that Shelley has made her excuses to be away in London for the next few days, staying with one of her girlfriends and no doubt getting a bit more crack abuse in at the same time.

Whilst Kerry makes the call to get the DVD couriered up to Jack, Johnny chats happily with Griselda. Griselda shows Johnny a picture of her new girlfriend. Fucking hell she's ugly! But because Johnny is a gent, and because he likes Griselda, he praises the girl's looks and says how lucky he thinks Griselda is, whilst at the same time blocking any mental images of her and her latest squeeze getting down to drinking from the furry chalice action.

Johnny hangs around for a few minutes more, still nattering away and, in Andy's absence, takes a call from Jimmy Morley, host of the Jimmy Morley Show, Britain's highest rating day-time TV programme. Jimmy is a regular of Andy's and Johnny and he know each other, so Jimmy spills out all his troubles. Jimmy's a nasty piece of work as far as Johnny is concerned, a horrible bully of a man. His "show" consists of putting defenceless, educationally subnormal people (dredged up from the darkest recesses of Britain's grimmest council estates) up in front of a hostile live audience of abusive, intolerant bigots and lambasting and belittling them for the mistakes and bad choices they've made in their lives. Anyway, turns out Jimmy's made a bad choice of his own. He's only gone and screwed some eighteen year old girl he had on his show a couple of months back. She's now pregnant and (good for her) asking for a lot of money to keep quiet. Johnny promises he'll bring the matter to Andy's attention "urgently," whilst thinking that Jimmy is one sleazy fucking bumhole.

After the chat with Jimmy Morley, Johnny picks up his rucksack, takes leave of the girls and exits the office, to find that his fucking bike has been fucking ticketed. Bastards! He looks around for the offending traffic warden thinking that he can take the ticket and shove it up his or her arse, but, perhaps fortunately, no wardens are to be seen.

He hopes this isn't a bad omen for his foetus collection job, nah, 'corse not.

Johnny has a bit of time to kill, so he sits astride his motorbike and has a nice ciggy. As he sits there he mentally wills some other bastard traffic warden to dare try and ticket him again and then he's off, up to Harley Street and the dodgy doc's place.

Once in Harley Street, Johnny parks his bike (legally this time) and quickly walks the short distance to the doctor's consulting rooms.

As he approaches and enters the building he's unaware of the blue Mini with the cream coloured roof parked across the road, unaware that inside the Mini someone is snapping away with a camera.

At reception, as instructed, Johnny asks for a "delivery for Mister Wells" and is handed a fairly large and well-sealed, insulated box. He guesses that the foetus must be on ice, at least it'll be fresh when it goes into Janey's liquidiser!

He leaves the doctor's with the insulated box under his arm and returns to his Kawasaki. He has to strap the package onto the back of the bike. For a moment he wonders if the foetus might be damaged or bruised during the drive to The Bishops Avenue, but reasons that it's only going to end up liquidised anyway, so what the hell. As he fires his bike into the Harley Street traffic, destination Janey's place, he still hasn't noticed the blue and cream Mini. Oblivious, he passes it by on his way up Harley Street, and he is equally oblivious as the Mini pulls out into the traffic behind him.

A quick drive past Regents Park, into Primrose Hill, Belsize Park and Hampstead and beyond and Johnny finally pulls up outside Janey's rented fuck-off house cum mansion in The Bishops Avenue. Christ, a short-term rental on a place like this must cost a small fortune. As he waits, a security guard approaches the impressive gates to the property which protect a wide driveway that leads up to the house. When asked his business Johnny, as previously told by Andy, repeats the line "delivery for

Mister Wells," and the massive gate swings ponderously open.

He drives his bike slowly up to the house. He's surprised by two things, the lack of paps outside the property (he puts that down to the degree of pressure the likes of Janey and her entourage can bring to bear on editors), and the lack of security once through the gates. The house is situated in the middle of a garden almost large enough to qualify as "grounds" rather than "garden." It's all enclosed by a fairly high wall, but there's a lot of space to cover, lots of trees and bushes for intruders (read paps) to conceal themselves in. Johnny is not impressed, if he was running this gig there'd definitely be more bodies on the ground. Soon Johnny reaches an impressively elegant stairway that leads to the front door of the property. He parks up, unstraps the box containing the foetus from the back of the bike, and climbs the stairs two at a time, eager to get this too strange assignment out of the way. Johnny reaches the top of the stairs and is less than happy as the door of the house opens and Charlie Gold's massive bulk pours out.

"Johnny, how ya doin," says Charlie, sticking out one of his fat paws out for Johnny to shake. "Not bad thanks, mate, yerself?" says Johnny and returns Charlie's handshake. He finds himself repulsed by the cold sliminess of the man's hand. For a moment they look into each other's eyes and they make each other uneasy. Each man is wary of the other man's capacity for violence. They know each other too well. Both parties make a silent pact to keep small talk to a minimum and as Johnny hands the package over to Charlie he simply says "this is what you want, Charlie, mate, and now the job's done I'm on me way.."

"Hey, Johnny, that's a shame, we coulda talked some more over a drink...but, hey, if you're busy, you're busy, what can you do?" The two men nod at each other, relieved to be going their separate ways, and as Charlie slimes his blubberosity back into the house Johnny is down the stairs, on his bike, along the driveway, through the gates and out of there and away from Janey Jax, Charlie Gold and all their dangerous fucking strangeness.

Driving away from Janey's mansion, he once again fails to see the blue and cream Mini, parked just fifty metres down the road. This time the Mini does not pull out to follow Johnny. No need, thinks the occupant, the real story is here, right here.

SHELLEY

Shelley is at Anthea's place in Holland Park. Forewarned by Andrew that Jack would receive his little film that very evening, she decided that staying a few days at Andrea's would be a good idea. By now Jack will have received his dirty little queer, ponce, bum boy, arse bandit, brown hatter, shit stabbing film and he'll know that Shelley has him by the balls. She can't wait to screw him. Over the years she has come to despise and hate Jack and all his faggotry and now she wants to destroy him, financially and emotionally.

Nobody fucks with Shelley!

Shelley's mobile (Vertu, of course) rings. She checks the display. It's Jack.

Shit.

Yes, here we go!

This is it, freedom, America and even more money and fame here she comes!

Shelley answers the call, "hullo, darling," she purrs, all smug self-satisfaction, "what can I do for you..."

"Shelley, you fucking cunt, you bitch, you fucking whore, I ought to break your legs, you devious, twisted, nasty fucking skank," screams Jack down the phone. Shelley holds the mobile away from her ear and allows Jack to rant and scream obscenities before replying quietly and calmly, "Jack, I guess you've, like, seen that dirty film of you and that bloke. Face it, Jack, you is fucked, innit. If this gets out your career is done, and, like, there's no point blaming me, I weren't the one there taking it up the shit-box, were I? This is all dead, like, embarrassing for me, too. What does it say about me as a woman that I can't even keep me feller away from other guys' cocks. It's demeaning, innit. I want a divorce!"

"Yes, Shelley, I know, just like the little note in the package from bloody Andrew Manning says. I should have known that bastard would be involved in this in some way…"

"Now don't be nasty about Andrew, he is the one got the answers here, innit. All you've got to do is give me a divorce. Oh, and I guess I is going to want the house, like, and let's say twelve million quid too, innit. Do all that, like, and Andy will sort you out with some pretty blonde with big tits and then, like, as far as anyone's concerned she's the reason for the divorce and no-one gets to see you caught on a camera with a cock up your bum. And that, Jack, darling, is your best choice, innit, it's that or your movie goes to the press and they'll have such fun, like, outing you as a nancy boy and a shirt lifter!" At this point Jack launches into another four letter tirade, most of it revolving around female genitalia, and Shelley simply hangs up and switches the phone off. Andrew had suggested that only he should speak to Jack after the delivery of the film, but Shelley had insisted that the note enclosed with the DVD should direct Jack to call her. She's not afraid of Jack's pathetic attacks and bad language, and she couldn't resist the opportunity to personally stick the knife into the dirty queer.

Now the conversation with Jack is over, Shelley is ecstatic, she knows, despite all his aggression, that Jack will be terrified of being outed as a homo. She'll leave him to sweat for the night and then she knows that he'll call her tomorrow and he'll agree to everything she wants, what choice does he have? After that, she can leave Andrew to tie all the loose ends together and she can get on with her life. She would say Jack could get on with his life as well, except that she actually doesn't give a shit whether he lives or dies, just as long as he coughs up the money, the divorce and the property.

How fantastic! Shelley is so happy, it's all good as sorted. She's going to get everything she wants and bender boy Jack is on the ropes and totally screwed. Best of all, she's got another fuck off big rock of crack in her Prada bag. What could possibly go wrong?

ANDREW

After Johnny left the house that morning to drop off the pictures and DVD to be delivered to Jack Rigby (and to pick up that bloody foetus), I watched the daily update on joeycampsfight4life dot com and, Christ, that was grim. The poor sod is looking even worse than he was. I make the decision there and then that I can't let Joey suffer anymore. It breaks my heart but he needs to be released from this life, and he needs it to be done quickly

I leave home and make my way to Joey's. There's a light drizzle falling and it's misty, mild and still, London seems cloaked in funereal grey. Not inappropriate, given the current
situation.

As I walk, as always, I think. Joey's own plan for his death is not acceptable to me. For example, I won't let him take a paracetamol overdose. Did my own research on that, it's a horrible way to die, long, drawn out and painful. I need to speak to Doctor Dodgy, I'm sure he can recommend (and supply) something that will allow Joey to quietly and painlessly slip away. I'm also not going to let Joey die in front of a camera and I'm going to make sure he dies with those he loves being present. At the very least I want his mum and dad to be there. *Have you spotted the flaw in my plan yet? Of course you have, you may not be the sharpest tool in the box, but neither are you completely stupid. Charlie Gold. He's the problem.* Joey not dying on film means no lucrative live celebrity death for Charlie and Charlie is a greedy, fat, murderous bastard who loves nothing in life but money, so talking him out of what looks to be a very profitable opportunity is not going to be easy. At this stage, speaking honestly, I have absolutely no idea how I'm going to do that.

So, that'll be that then. That's Joey, over and out. I'll need to talk to his management, let them know that Joey's "cancer" has taken a turn for the worse. That his treatment has failed and the only remaining option now is palliative care. I'll tell them to break the news to the media, to let the public know that "brave and courageous" Joey is only "days" away from death. I guess the hits on joeycampsfight4life dot bloody com will go through the roof, if nothing else.

Shit, whilst I've been thinking about Joey I've gone and fucking welled up, a small tear is rolling down my cheek. No, it's just the wind in in my eyes, I tell myself. Except it's still. Still as the grave.

I see your eyes are dry. That's interesting. You're quite a cold person, aren't you? Tell me, do you find it difficult to form and maintain close relationships? Or is it that Joey's celebrity makes him at once more and less of a person, that he's a kind of bright and engaging cartoon, cut out character. A source of entertainment rather than a real human being. When all this is over, we'll sit down together, me and you, and talk about all this. I'd really like to know your thoughts about how you relate to celebrities, you see, I don't really get to speak to ordinary, proper people very much.

What is going on with me? When the cuntola did I fall in love with this guy? It's just not right, it should not have happened! I try to persuade myself that it's not true, that Joey is just another vain, narcissistic, sociopathic, money-grubbing, fame-loving piece of celebrity trash. But my heart isn't having it. Truth is he's none of those things, he's just a simple northern kid who ended up famous by accident and never really got used to it. At the root of it all, Joey is vulnerable, wide eyed and innocent. I guess that's the basis of my attraction to him, I mean, let's be honest, he's physically beautiful but he's not my usual piece of rough. What he is, is a delightful contrast in the world in which I operate: a daisy in a field of gravel, a diamond in a cess-pool, a shaft of light in a very, very dark place. Poor guy, he was never made for the world of celebrity, and look what it's fucking done to him!

And, Christ, what am I going to do about his mum? As I've no intention of complying with Joey's request to get her out of the picture for his death, I'm going to have to tell her, face to face, that her son is dying. How do you do that? Tell a mother that she is going to lose her son? Language is simply too limited a tool to explain an issue like that.

Shit, there's just too much going on, I mean what is more fucked up, this whole Joey situation or that bloody foetus job? Suddenly the enormity of all the very, very strange things that I have become involved in hits me and, for a few moments, I feel that everything is scooting badly out of control and I have to make a concerted mental effort to hold myself together. I think happy thoughts. Specifically Jack Brierley opening a large envelope stuffed full of pictures of Shelley smoking crack, I imagine the surprise and then delight on his face. The ammunition to fight his avaricious and vicious wife has just dropped into his lap, courtesy of an anonymous well-wisher.

That's better. I can do this, I can get through it all, and get through it all a winner.

My short, self-motivational pep talk and the image of Jack seeing Shelley's crack photos both calms and reassures me. I feel more in control and as I enter Glenilla Road I am mentally prepared for seeing Joey again. Looking towards Joey's house I note the usual throng of paps, but also there's some kind of commotion going on around the front door. I can see some guy who looks like Paul Hunter…wait, actually it *is* Paul Hunter…a camera crew and Joey's mum. Joey's mum is shouting and screaming and pushing at Hunter and the crew, forcing them away from the house and the paps are jostling forward, snapping away with their cameras, what the fuck is happening and what the fuck is Paul Hunter doing here? This looks bad….

Quick, follow me to Joey's, run, fast as you can, run! Come on, lard arse, keep up!

A PASSING AWAY?

Joey's head tosses on the pillow, he seems wracked with pain, he moans. At the side of the bed his mother holds his hand, silently weeping, close by her stand the twins asking for their daddy to be well again, they are uncomprehending, confused, crying. "Joey," comes a voice from the other side of the bed, "how are you now, are you in much pain? Have you any words for your fans?"

Joey looks up and sees his mum, the kids, a camera crew and the bastard, twaty, smug features of Paul Hunter. He's the one asking the questions. Cunt. If it wasn't for Hunter, he wouldn't be in this god-awful situation. Joey remembers how Hunter patronised and needled him that night on his show when he insulted the Queen. Bastard. But even through the sickness and the pain Joey's aware he has a job to do, and if smarming, lying and eating shit with this shitbag is what it takes to get Charlie Gold's money, then that's what he's going to do.

"I ain't good," says Joey in a weak voice, "I think I'm on me way out. I've fought 'ard against this cancer, but it's got the better of me, ain't it. I'm riddled, it's everywhere in me body, it's metastas…metsta…spread. If it weren't for me friends an' the love an' 'elp of me ma 'ere, I don't know what I'd do…"

"Yes, Joey, you've fought incredibly bravely against this terrible disease, you have the respect and love of the entire nation, you certainly have my respect, I feel incredibly honoured to be here to witness your last moments. Just a quick word from the grieving mum now, have you anything to say, mum?" Joey's mum, it seems, has nothing to say. She simply puts a hand to her face to wipe away the streaming tears and shakes her head, too overcome with emotion to speak. "And look at those little twins, the angels, how will they cope without their dad? Poor boys, they've already lost their mother to a tragic but no doubt accidental drugs overdose, and now they're going to lose their dad to this awful, insidious illness. Joey, there can't be a mother in the country who can think about those twins without crying. How do you feel knowing that you'll never see them again?"

Joey coughs, lets out a low moan, "it's the 'ardest thing," he replies.

"I'm sure it is, it must be almost as hard as saying goodbye to all your fans," prompts Paul.

"Yes, of course, me fans, it's thanks to them I kept goin' so long, their love an' support 'as been brilliant..." Joey's voice fades away, for a moment his eyes roll back in his head, then they reappear, but this time they seem less focused than before, less a part of this world.

"Joey, you okay? Are you still with us?

"Yes...for now.."

"How do you feel about your life looking back, now? You've had your ups and downs, things haven't always gone smoothly for you. I refer particularly to those unfortunate comments you made, on my show in fact, about our beloved Queen."

"It's been a fantastic life, I been dead lucky me. I don't regret nothin', 'cept for the times that I let meself an' me fans down. When I said them things about the Queen, that were bad, I mean I'd just 'ad me cancer diagnosis like an' I were outta me 'ead wi' worry, but there were no need for me to say what I said. The Queen's a lovely lady, she is the 'eart and soul of the nation and she don't deserve to 'ave no-one say bad stuff about 'er."

"I'm sure we've all forgiven you for what was simply an unfortunate outburst prompted by stress and grief and if Her Majesty is watching now I'm sure that she's forgiven you too."

"I hope so.....ahhh," Joey's head suddenly bends back on the pillow, his eyes are wide and pained and his mouth open, emitting a continuous, low moan of extreme agony. Mum cries out, the twins plaintively shout "daddy, daddy" the emotional pitch in the room reaches a new intensity.

This is it, we are witnessing the first ever on camera, live celebrity death! Remember this day, it is an important moment in history!

Paul Hunter looks to camera and, his voice cracking with emotion, he implores "Joey, Joey, stay with us, think of the love of your family and of all those millions of adoring fans, we don't want you to go, we want you to live, Joey!"

"It's no good, Paul, mate, I can't fight this thing no more, it's got me beat!"

"Would you have one last message for your adoring fans, Joey?"

"Yes, in the words of the great Freddy Mercury...I still love you...." Joey lets loose one more moan, which turns into a choking, coughing noise and suddenly he goes limp and his tortured body lets loose a final big breath, then he's still. He doesn't seem to be breathing and his bloodshot eyes are open, staring blankly.

Looking grave and almost (he thinks) statesman-like, Hunter looks to camera and in hushed and reverential tones announces, "Ladies and Gentlemen, it is with The

Deepest Regret that I have to report that a Brave, Inspirational and Much Adored young man is no longer with us. This is a Sad Day that will Unite The Nation in a Display of Unanimous Grief. It is with great Humility and Sadness that I announce.....Joey Camps is....... Dead."

The camera zooms in to focus on Joey's face, and holds the shot, off-camera a voice announces "okay, ladies and gentlemen, brilliant, that's a keeper, cut!"

With that, Joey, with great effort, lifts his upper body from his bed and looks around the room: he sees that his mother is no longer his mother, but some lookey-likey old dear in a bad wig, the twins are no longer the twins, but a pair of snotty-nosed Hampstead stage school brats. The camera crew, however are still the camera crew and Paul Hunter is most definitely still a cunt.

And then all hell breaks loose. Johnny's mum careers into the room, all sound and fury, "what are you doin' wi me son, "she screams, "you bloody parasites, you soddin' ghouls, get outta here now...out...out, you robbed the bloody life from me son, you're not gonna rob 'is bloody death an' all you thievin' bastards, bugger the lotta yers!" Amazingly Johnny's mum (not a big lady) grabs the cameraman by the hair and begins to drag him out of the room, he's so surprised that he's no idea what to do so allows himself to be dragged. The rest of the crew decide it would be a good idea to leave, followed by the lookey-likey old dear, who is thinking she's not being bloody paid enough for this. She's closely followed by the stage school brats, now crying for real, and lastly comes Paul Hunter. As he leaves the room Joey's mum aims a kick (given with real feeling) to his fat and wobbly arse shouting, "take that up yer bum you smug southern bastard!" She proceeds to follow the recent occupants of the room out and down the stairs, shouting, screaming and striking out all the way.

ANDREW

I'm down Glenilla Road to Joey's house like a rat up a fucking drain pipe. I dive into the press of paparazzi, I elbow my way through them, calling everyone cunting fucking wanking arseholes as I pass, until I'm through the throng and into the front garden of Joey's house where I find Paul Hunter is trying to remonstrate with

Mabel. She's responding with a torrent of solid northern abuse. I grab Hunter by the arm and spin him round to face me, I put my mouth to his ear and whisper, "Paul, I've no fucking idea what you're doing here but I do have a very good fucking idea of exactly how much nasty personal shit I know about you! If you don't want to find yourself up to the neck in it, you seriously need to fuck right off, now!"

I think this is an appropriate point to say that you might like to bare my comments to Paul in mind. Don't think I haven't noticed the way that you've been looking at me, with that cocky glint in your eye. I know what you're thinking. You've seen my reaction to Joey's plight, seen me dither and wobble a bit and you think I'm not as tough as I make out. You think that maybe, just maybe, you could take me, that you could do this job better than I can. Don't fool yourself, that kind of thinking is a big error on your part. Remember, what you know about me is only what I choose to show you and what I show you may or may not be true. You've no idea what is actually going on with me. Me, on the other hand, I know all about you. Let me be explicit about this so that you fully understand your position. I know what goes on in your head and I know what you get up to. I know all about that thing that you do, your private thing, the one you've tried to keep secret for so long. I know the shame in your heart. Don't push your luck, don't get any smart ideas.

Hunter hears my words and his fake tan goes several shades lighter, he shoots me a look of utter hatred, but nevertheless spins on his heel and walks away from the house followed by the camera crew and, rather oddly, an old dear in a bad wig and a couple of snot-nosed brats.

Now it's just me and Mabel. I take Mabel by the shoulders and lead her back into the house, but not before I notice a big, black people carrier drawing to a halt outside Joey's place. A phalanx of big security geezers in dark suits pile out and carve a path for Hunter and his retinue through the thronging paps. Stranger and stranger.

I gently guide Mabel back through the open front door. Once in the hallway, I close that door decisively on the chaos outside. Mabel walks to the foot of the stairs, sits down heavily and puts her head in her hands. She is sobbing. She drops her hands limply by her sides, lifts her head and says, "my boy is dyin' int' 'e Andrew, tell me the truth.."

"I...I.." I stutter

"Tell me, I know I'm right, I can see it in 'is eyes, I know what death looks like, I seen it before an' that's the look our Joey 'as, 'e 'as the face of death!"

Shit. I was going to have to tell Mabel about Joey, anyway. I guess this is the time to do it, so I improvise, "Mabel, I'm sorry, I'm so sorry I was on my way here to tell you," I go down on one knee next to her and hold her hands, "the treatment...it's failed, the cancer has spread.

The doctor confirms there's nothing else to be done for Joey. The best we can do is to make him more comfortable. You're right, he's lost the battle. We *are* going to lose him and I'm afraid it's only a matter of days before he…leaves us."

I think I'm doing quite well with difficult subject matter so far, don't you? What do you mean, I should tell her what Joey has been doing? Are you mad? Tell her that her own son has set out to kill himself! No, she's never going to know that. If you say anything, I'm warning you, they'll be hell to pay!

I join Mabel on the bottom step. For some minutes we sit there. I hold her close. Her small body is racked with sobs and she lets out little cries, like an animal that's trapped and in agony. She sings a song of a sorrow that is unbridgeable, unbearable and unmeasurable.

Oh, cunting wank bugger fuck shit bollocks and cuntola, why has this happened. Why?

After some time and much reassurance, Mabel is quieter and calmer, so I say, "Mabel, I'm going to go up and see Joey now, and as soon as I leave here I'm on the phone to the doctor. I'll get him round here straightaway to look at Joey and see how we can help him through this in the best way possible. Now why don't you go and see if the twins are okay? They'll be scared by all this commotion and shouting, and they need their gran now more than ever."

Mabel, still crying, the poor love, agrees to go the twins and I am free to go and talk to Joey.

Slowly, almost reluctantly - scared, I guess, of what I'm going to find - I climb the stairs.

I stand in front of the door to Joey's room, I take hold of the door handle. As on my previous visit, I pause, take a mental and physical deep breath, and enter. Shit, I think, things *are* bad. Joey is in his bed (which I'm now thinking of as his death-bed) looking not pale, but grey. His face is sheened in sweat, his hair looks thin and lank and his eyes are bloodshot.

I walk quickly over to him. As I approach my mouth seems to take on a life of its own as I find myself saying, "oh, Joey, Joey, my beautiful Joey, what have we done to you?" I sit on the bed and take his head in my hands, "I am so sorry, so fucking sorry, I should never have let it come to this!"

Joey's bloodshot eyes stare straight into mine, "no, Andy, this ain't ought to do wi' you, it's my choice. The only other person who 'as any blame is that cunt Paul Hunter, you got nowt to be worried about."

Joey's thinking along the same lines as me about Paul Hunter, the guy *is* a cunt. I've already made a mental note to make things difficult for him. I got a lot of embarrassing stuff on him relating to his finances, insider dealing, that kind of stuff. It won't finish him as all his public school chums will rally round, but it will at least make life uncomfortable for him for a while. "Joey," I say "what the fuck was all that about? Who was that woman, those kids? And what was Hunter doing here?"

"Ah, well, Andy...that were me dyin' on camera weren't it. I 'ad that Charlie Gold round 'ere yesterday din't I and 'e says to me 'e wants to film a mock up death 'cos when it came to me really dyin' I might not die, what were his words...oh yeh...telegenically. Charlie said I might just die quiet in the night an' that'd be no good on the tele, or he said I might die in pain screaming an' swearing like an' that'd be no good either, too realistic, 'e reckoned. Then 'e says that I'd get me money soon as the scene were filmed and I thought that were good 'cos at least I'd know before I died that he'd paid up and I wouldn't 'ave to leave it to you to sort out."

"So 'e says to me to get me ma out of the 'ouse for a while an' then 'e could do the mock death scene wi' an interview wi' Paul an' actors for me ma an' the kids an' 'e'd broadcast that when I died instead of the real thing. Me ma, though, she sensed summat were up. I 'ad sent her to Primrose Hill wi' the twins but she came back early, an', well, you saw what 'appened. It's all another fuck up ain't it, Andy? If you were doin' it you woulda made sure me ma were proper outta the way, an' I *woulda* asked you to do it but I know you're not that 'appy 'bout this Charlie Gold thing, an' 'e just sprung it all on me, like, there were no time to think."

"Yeh, Joey, this is a fuck up, but it's Charlie's fuck up not yours. I'm surprised at him. I mean having the death scene in the can I understand, but all this…it seems a bit of a gamble on his part, all a bit slipshod, he should have thought things through more."

At this point our conversation is interrupted by the trilling of Joey's mobile which is by his bed. I look at the display, it shows Charlie's name. "I'll take this Joey!" I say and grab the phone before Joey has a chance to pick it up and announce (with more confidence than I feel), "Charlie, it's Andy, I'm with Joey, he's too ill to talk at the moment, can I help?" Charlie is obviously surprised to hear my voice, "oh, er, okay, Andy, how you doing? So how exactly is Joey, then?" Bastard, he wants to know how ill he is, checking his investment. The sooner the poor kid dies the better as far as Charlie's concerned. "He's bad, Charlie," thinking on my feet now, improvising again, "I've just come from his doctor and it's not good news, the cancer has spread, the treatments have failed, doc reckons he's fading fast and we're looking at a matter of only a few days before…well, you know…"

"Gee, that's too bad," says Charlie with maximum insincerity and I can almost hear the smile in voice, "such a nice kid. Hey, Andy, I got business I need to discuss with the boy so you just hand me over to him now, eh?"

"No can do, like I said, he's too ill to speak. I presume you want to talk about the bodged up death scene?"

"Whaddaya know about that?" demands Charlie sounding surprised, defensive and aggressive. "Who you been talking to?"

"I saw the whole fucking thing, what a total cock up! Joey's mum came back home before she was supposed to and threw Hunter and his little band of freaks out. I suppose once your deathbed interview was in the bag they were all supposed to sneak out the back of the house one by one, so they weren't pictured together. Mabel fucked you there. She threw them all out the front way, all together, including the old girl with the dodgy wig, right in front of the paps. I think it's fair to say that that screws up your pre-filmed death plan. I mean even the thickest journo would look at what you screened, compare it with the photos of what happened today and smell a very large rat, and that's assuming Mabel didn't go to the papers and tell them all about what you'd been up to..."

"This is no fucking business of yours and, hey, we can just film it again, make stuff look a bit different. Now stop fucking around and pass me over to Joey!"

"No, you're not speaking to him, not now, not ever, and you're not filming a death scene again, real or fake!"

" What the...what did you just say? Who the fuck do you think you are, you fucking Limey cocksucker! You don't fucking tell me what to do, I set the fucking rules here! I gotta contract with that fucking kid so he dies when I fucking want him to die!"

Oops. Charlie is very angry. You can feel it, can't you? You can sense the atmosphere. I've told you before that Charlie is a very dangerous man, there are depths to Charlie that not even I understand, and which I do not want to explore. There is an intensely dark side to this man. I know I've told you already, but I'll tell you again, keep out of his way!

I have to be careful with my words now, very careful. "Charlie, Charlie, calm down, relax, I just want to give the boy some dignity, is all. Look, I know you're pissed off and angry with the situation and with me but you blew it today and you're not going to get away with filming another death scene, not now. Think of all those pictures of today's screw up floating around out there, and Joey's mum knows exactly what happened here, she'll be watching anything to do with Joey like a hawk from now on. And then there's that matter of Janey's special request…. I'm sure you'll agree that is a very important matter that we still have to work together on, so we need to keep things nice between us. Why don't you let me come up and see you at Janey's tomorrow afternoon? We can talk all this through and make everything good." Entirely as expected, my hinting at the subject of Janey Jax and her foetus diet seems to give Charlie cause to think and I can hear a sharp intake of breath from the other end of the line, "okay, I hear ya, come here tomorrow and we'll talk. I guess I can let filming Joey slip. One thing, though. Not doing the deal with the kid's gonna lose me a lotta profit, you need to compensate me for that. I'll settle for six hundred thousand of your English pounds in cash, that's a real bargain for you, just a fraction of what I woulda made off the boy. By the way, Andy, I don't like you bringing Janey into our conversation. Any fuck ups in that particular matter, and you know what happens. I say this so we know exactly where we both stand…understood? Don't forget to bring the money with you tomorrow."

"I hear you, let's say see you about two o…" Charlie hangs up, in that annoying way that Americans do, before I can finish the sentence.

Okay, let's you and me take a step back and assess the situation. The good news is that I've got Joey out of having to die in front of a camera. The bad news is that I am now in Charlie's bad books and he wants six hundred thousand quid off me! First, where the fuck did he get that figure from? Second, I'm a very wealthy man (much wealthier than you can imagine), but spunking six hundred grand still hurts. I tell you, Charlie is mad, barking bloody mad! And you, you think this is all quite funny don't you? I'm beginning to wonder exactly who's side you're on. Support me. Don't support me. I don't accept half measures.

After Charlie hangs up on me, I put Joey's phone in my pocket. I'll keep it from now on to ensure he's not harassed further. I see that whilst I've been talking, poor Joey has fallen asleep. I guess today has been hard on him. Still, I need to wake him as there are things that need to be said.

Gently I stroke his face, "Joey, love, wake up mate!" Joey moans, his eyes open. Those eyes that used to be so bright, so lively, now clouded with pain and fear. "Oh, Joey," I say "you really, really have had enough haven't you?"

"Yeh...yeh...it's too much now," whispers Joey through cracked lips, "the pain is constant an' I'm so bloody tired an' I can't do ought, can't even wipe me own bloody arse, can't even eat fuckin' baby food. I want to go now, please help me go, please! This 'as to stop, for me, me ma and me kids. It's too much sufferin' for all of us...I need to ask you one more thing..." I hold one finger up and press it gently to Joey's lips in a hushing motion. The softness of those lips and the intimacy of the gesture send an electric pulse through me. I am going to miss this young man dreadfully. " Hush, it's okay, you don't need to ask me, I know what you're going to say. You want me to help you kill yourself, I already figured that out. I'll do it, I'll help."

"Shoulda known you'd guess what I wanted, you're a right clever bugger, you. I'm really sorry to ask, I just dunno where else I can turn..."

"Then turn to me, Joey. I know what you want me to do and I'm completely on your side, no need for you to worry, I'm going to help you find a way out of this pain...."

"Thank you, thank you…"

"Hush, hush, no more thank yous, they're not necessary, we are where we are, it is what it is. Let me speak to the doctor and we'll make you as comfortable as we can and then we'll find some way for you to…slip away…something quick and easy that isn't going to hurt - which means we're not doing the paracetamol thing. Absolutely not. It's a nasty, painful way to go, and you're not going to die alone and you're not going to die in front of a camera."

"If that's what you think's best I'd be more than 'appy, but what about Charlie?" replies Joey. "An' what about the money? I need it for the kids, all I gotta do is film that death scene again an' then I'll get me two million quid!"

"I've sorted Charlie, don't worry. Look, I'll pay you the two mil myself." Shit, why did I just say that, put myself on the hook for even more money? Further thought will be required here. "But, listen, my price for helping you and paying that money is that we do things *my* way. Do you trust me and do we have a deal?"

"Mate, I'm speechless…covering that two mil, that's bloody good of you, bloody good and, yes, I've always trusted you and, yes, we 'ave a deal. Thank you from the bottom of me 'eart!"

Joey's crying now. And I can understand why. It must be a relief to know someone else is taking responsibility for what is to come and that he'll be able to die in the company of family and friends and not under the cold glare of the camera lens.

"Andy, I know you don't believe this, probably don't want to, but you're not all bad you know. There's a good man in there somewhere."

"Hmm, well, not sure about that myself, but thanks anyway. Look, I need to go. You should spend the rest of the day with your mum and the twins because I'm going to call your management later and let them know that your "cancer" is now untreatable and terminal and that you authorise them to release that information to the media. At that point things'll get busy, there'll be lots of people who'll want to interview you, there could be good money to be made, but that's up to you."

"Okay, I understand."

"You hang in there, Joey. I'll be back soon and we'll talk more. You don't need to worry about a thing now, I've got it all covered." I bend, kiss his damp forehead, turn and walk away. Just as I leave Joey's room, as I'm closing the door behind me, I hear him say in a weak voice "you're a mate, Andy." I keep walking, if I stop now I'll just start fucking crying.

What do you think? Joey said there's a good man in me somewhere. What would you say? Am I a good man, or a bad man? Me, I would say that you'd be best to see how things play out before you make any assumptions either way.

I make my way downstairs to talk to Mabel. I'm still thinking about Joey, and I'm thinking about tomorrow's meeting with Charlie. That's not going to be nice. At that point I didn't know that events would intervene to make things even more difficult.

JOHNNY

The thing that Johnny noticed most that evening when Andy got back from Joey's place, was exactly how angry he was. Johnny's often wondered if Andy has some kind of borderline Tourette's syndrome, he's never known anybody (not even himself) who can swear as much, but tonight it seems that every second word he says is "cunt" or "cunting."

They're in the kitchen, even Rosa (who herself can swear like a trooper, but in Russian) has fled to the scene, "I must do ironing of the clothes," she said and then beat a hasty retreat to the cellar.

"I can't fucking believe this, that fucking cunting arsehole Charlie fucking cunting Gold, filming a fucking mock-up death scene," rants Andy. "What the cuntola was all that about? Cunting amateur! Well, it all went fucking tits up, didn't it, cunting fucking knobhead!"

Johnny listens as Andy explains about Charlie Gold's abortive mock deathbed scene. He is puzzled. He knows Andy almost as well as he knows himself and he can see his anger. He just doesn't entirely understand it. This is not normal behaviour, Andy is cool, calm, calculating. He doesn't do anger, certainly not on this scale. There's something else going on here.

And then Andy starts talking about Joey and Johnny knows exactly what's going on with him.

"That poor fucking kid, all he wanted was to be famous and then when he gets it, poor fucker realizes that it's just not for him. That's the thing with Joey, you see, he's just not, not...not twisted and fuck-up selfish enough to play the fame game. He's too ready to trust people, too honest to live a life of lies, too fucking...fucking...nice! Now the poor sod is going to die. And what for? For fucking celebrity, that's what for! Worthless, pointless, meaningless, asinine celebrity! How fucking absurd is that!"

Johnny looks closely at Andy. He can see there are tears in his eyes. It's obvious to him that Andy is genuinely moved and upset by Joey's plight, but that's not new to Johnny, after all they've discussed the whole Joey issue before. He knows that Andy has feelings for the guy, but now he can see that he's maybe radically underestimated the depth of those feelings. He's still not jealous though, and it *is* a real shame about Joey. Andy's right, he is a nice guy. He understands now exactly how much Andy cares for Joey, he can see that he is way beyond just upset by events. He is in pain, deeply hurt and hurting. And that makes him furious. Absolutely fucking furious. He can't handle seeing his Andy in pain. Slowly but surely the rage is growing in his mind. It's an irresistible, powerful, hot rage, becoming so strong that it's beginning to possess him. He wants to hurt someone, he wants to break bones, wants to smash someone's face into pieces. He wants to kill. Somebody has to pay!

Nobody messes with him and Andy, nobody upsets the man he loves so much and gets away with it. It's clear to Johnny that somebody has to die. The rage inside tells him so. It's screaming for blood and for vengeance and Johnny knows with absolute certainty that it won't subside until it's placated with a human sacrifice, until it's given a human body, dead, broken and dripping blood.

As Andy talks and becomes even more visibly upset, Johnny can feel himself losing the thread of what's going on. He's worried that he is completely going to lose any connection to reality, like with the rentboy when he lost all track of who and where he was. That can't happen. Not now. Not here. He needs to be calm. His Andy needs him to be strong and supportive, not possessed by an uncontrollable fury. He jolts himself back to the real world by taking a deep breath and biting the inside of his bottom lip so hard that that the skin ruptures and bleeds, salty and metallic, into his mouth. The sudden pain of the bite works, almost like a small act of self-harm and the offering of his own blood is enough to quiet the rage within him...for now.

Andy's voice fades back in, "...so the dodgy doc will be there tonight. We're going to put an end of life care nurse in the house, she'll be there twenty four hours a day every day and I've told the doc to get whatever equipment is necessary to help ease things for Joey, and to give him lots of fucking drugs!" Andy pauses, looks down as though he can't, or doesn't want to, go on and says in a quiet voice, "and soon, with a little help from me, he'll be gone."

"Oh, Andy," says Johnny, moving closer and wrapping his big arms in a protective hug round his shoulders, "I feel for you, feller, I really do. I know you think a lot of Joey and that he's always been like a little mascot to you, I know you're gonna miss him."

"Yeh, I will, me and my fucking smartarse plan, this pretend cancer, all my own twisted, sick little scheme. God, I wish I'd kept my mouth shut and my smart ideas to myself!"

"Andy, that's silly, Joey dit'nt need to go long wiv your idea, did he? He made his own decisions."

"But don't you see, he *did* have to go along with it. It was that or kiss his career goodbye. And then when he saw how well it was going he thought he'd follow it through, all the way. So he starts to fucking poison himself….oh, Johnny, I'm so very sorry to dump all this on you!"

"But, mate, that's what I'm here for..."

"There's something else as well. Something I haven't told you yet. I'm in the shit with Charlie, I've told him he's not going to get to film his death scene with Joey again, and I introduced Janey's foetus eating into the conversation as leverage to get him to leave Joey alone. He wasn't amused. He's agreed to let Joey be, but he wants compensation."

"Shit, what does he want?"

"Six hundred thousand. In cash. By tomorrow afternoon."

"Fuck, even shitter."

Johnny is not happy. He doesn't like any of this. He's very worried about Andy now, owing Charlie Gold money, getting on the wrong side of him. That's bad. Christ, this is all a bit convoluted and surprising even by Andy's standards. Johnny may not be happy, but he knows what to do, as always he'll stand by the man he loves, "you do what you need to, feller, I'll be there, any help I can give, whateva you need, just ask."

"Thank you, all this crap, I don't know what to say, it's something that I seem to have got sucked into step by inexorable step. I'm tired of it, I wish it was all over."

"And it all *will* be over soon, just stay calm and hang on in there and do what you do
best, think and plan!"

"You're right, you're a real love, you know that? I'll get all this nastiness with Joey and Charlie out the way and then and then I'm going make sure that pig, Hunter, gets a good kick in the balls! He's the one I blame for all this, without him none of this would ever have happened"… oops, Andy's off again, this could take some time… "arrogant fucking, over- privileged, public school cunt. Those fucking people, so right on and politically correct, but put some poor working class lad in front of them and it's open season. Go on, go for it, say whatever you want about the ignorant prole, belittle him, patronise him, hold his life up to fucking ridicule, he's nothing more than a stupid, uneducated oik, breeding uncontrollably, a drain on the welfare state and he deserves whatever he fucking gets! And that's exactly what Hunter did that night Joey blabbed his mouth off. He goaded him, needled him, took the piss until he got what he wanted: Joey saying something stupid! It's alright for the likes of Hunter, mummy and daddy both worked in the media, all his Oxford mates work in the media and, surprise sur-fucking-prise Hunter gets a job in the media and quickly cruises his way into his own fucking TV show and all his school chums proclaim him "Britain's number one chat show host!" Oh, the entitlement! For fuck's sake, he's not even good at what he does, he's totally second rate! I tell you, no word of a lie, I could go down the fucking pub tonight and pick some random geezer who could a better job of interviewing somebody than Hunter! It pisses me right off, it's all been so easy for that guy! What does he know about Joey's life of and the kind of stuff he's had to go through?"

All through their conversation, Johnny has kept his arms wrapped around Andy. He can feel him shaking with anger. Johnny is angry is too. Who the fuck does Paul Hunter think he is? Does he know what he's done, does he know how much he's upset his man? The rage is back, and it's growing inside him, once again wild and barely controllable. "Yeh," continues Andy "at the end of the day, Joey is in this mess because of that cunt, Hunter. You know what, I'd like to put my hands round the bastard's neck and squeeze the life out of him!"

And that's it. Bingo!

Johnny's rage finds an opening, a focus, a way to expend itself. Andy's right. This whole thing is Hunter's fault. He did this. He pushed Joey to say something stupid. He was the start of all this with his snobbery and arrogance. Hunter is the one who bears the responsibility for hurting his Andy. A price must be paid, there must be sacrifice. Hunter must die. With this realisation the rage in Johnny calms. It is no longer shouting and screaming, it is purring, happy, gurgling contentedly at the thought of the murder to come

SHELLEY

Shelley is sitting in a nice little Italian place just off Kensington High Street. Just as she expected, she received a call from Jack this morning requesting a meeting to discuss the divorce and they'd agreed on this venue. She'd only been up a short while when Jack called and was in Anthea's luscious living room with the lady herself. They were both feeling fuzzy and still more than a bit wired from the large amounts of crack and champagne they'd consumed the night before to celebrate Shelley's stunning triumph over her soon to be ex-husband.

When Jack called he was in his Porsche and speeding down the M6 to London. To be honest, Shelley was a bit surprised that he should want to meet face to face, but didn't think much of it. He probably just wants to beg, to get himself a little bit off the hook that Shelley's got him on, but fuck him, she's already decided she's going to have him for every last fucking penny. He probably wants her to let him keep his little fag getaway: the house in Sitges. She knows he loves sneaking off there without her to get up to his dirty faggot, bum chum nonsense…well, tough luck, Jack, she's having the house in Cheshire *and* the house in Sitges. She's going to bleed him dry!

The only vague worry that Shelley had after the telephone call was that Jack didn't sound quite as, well, humble and defeated as he should. If anything he sounded a bit cocky. She gives this some thought then decides she's probably just a bit paranoid from last night's crack binge. After all Jack's got nothing to be cocky about, has he?

Shelley is sitting at a secluded table in the restaurant, but not that secluded that people can't see her, so she's a bit pissed off that no-one seems to be noticing her. Don't they realise who she is for fucks sake? Peasants! She tries some sexy pouting and hitching up her skirt a bit to show even more of her fabulous legs, but still nobody pays her any attention. What a bunch of total fucking arseholes! Bored, she looks through the restaurant menu. She considers ordering food but decides she's simply not hungry, she's too excited by the prospect of getting rid of Jack and because tonight she's going to The British Pop Awards ceremony. She knows she'll be seated at the best table in the show, right at the front, and she also knows that she's been nominated for something: she's sure it's Best British Female Singer. Huh! This time next year with that fag Jack out of the way and with her new American boyfriend, and her new glittering career in America, well, this time next year she'll be winning the Best International Female award. That fake old skank

Janey Jax needs to watch her back because Shelley is coming! Yep, just another year from now she'll be the major international star she deserves to be!

She spots Jack coming into the restaurant. About fucking time she thinks. She needs to make this meeting quick. She still needs to get back to Andrea's and start glamming herself for the awards show - make herself even more beautiful than she is already.

Jack speaks with a waiter, looks across the restaurant, spies Shelley, scowls, and walks purposefully towards her. When he gets to her table, Shelley does not stand up for a kiss or even offer to shake hands. Nor does Jack. He sits down. She looks at him directly and smiles, "Jack, darling, how are you, nice to see you, I guess you want to, like, talk about the divorce settlement. Sorry, but I is not changing my mind, innit. All that gay stuff you do, I is not having it no more and I want my twelve million quid to make up for all the years I been, like, humiliated by you. So if you're going try and talk me out of anything you're, like, wasting your time. Oh, and by the way I want the house in Sitges as well as the one in Cheshire, innit, and if I is not getting what I want then that dirty, queer little film of yours is going, like, straight to the papers! Now let's make this quick because I is going to an award ceremony, innit!"

Jack is quiet as Shelley talks, he's looking right at her, leaning away from her as though she smelt bad, with his arms crossed over his chest. This isn't right, by now he should be sweating, panicky and ready to beg but as

Shelley returns his glare she sees the bastard is calm, relaxed and...smiling. What the fuck is going on?

"Nice to see you too, Shelley," Jack picks up the menu, "I think I might have something light to eat, just a quick snack, what about you? You look like you need a good meal, you're looking a bit thin, kind of...unhealthy."

Shelley does not like his manner, does not like it one bit, with a face like a slapped arse she snaps, "I'll just have a half bottle of champagne, and make it, like, a really good one."

"A good bottle of champagne, eh? I think a cheap bottle would be better, don't you? A nasty, cheap bottle for a nasty, cheap, backstabbing slag!"

Shelley can't believe what she's hearing. "How dare you," she says, trying not raise her voice, "I'd rather be a backstabber than a fucking shit stabber, you fag bastard! I is real pissed off now, innit. Let's end this conversation, just tell me when I is going to get my money and, like, make sure you get it to me bloody quick because I is not ready to wait long! Oh, and I want you out of the house in Cheshire as of now, innit. And you just remember, I is being good to you, innit, because I is ready to play along with the blonde bimbo story but if you piss me off or don't do what I, like, want then the press and everyone is going to know that butch Jack Rigby is actually a sodding brown hatter, and that's your career gone, innit. Face it, I got you by the balls, Jack, so just tell me when I is, like, getting my divorce and my money!"

Hah, that's it, thinks Shelley, I've let him know who's boss here...and yet the bastard is *still* smiling!

"No, Shelley," Jack replies calmly.

"What do you mean "no," who do you think you is?"

"No, you *haven't* got me by the balls. I know what you've got on me, that dirty little film, and I know you paid Andrew Manning to set me up and, yes, last night I was shitting myself and I was ready to give you whatever you were going to ask for. But this morning another package was delivered to me. I've no idea who sent it, but stuck to it was a little note saying "from a friend." Interesting that, don't you think...no, no, don't talk, I'm sick of the sound of your fucking voice and I want to finish my story. So, where was I, oh yeh, the package, well I open it, have a look inside and what do I find? Pictures, Shelley, of you, Shelley...you with a fucking crack pipe in your face! You silly, silly bitch, you're back on the crack, just like the fucking cheap, two dime crack whore that you are! You can have your fucking divorce with pleasure, I'll be glad to be rid of you to be honest, can't stand the fucking sight of you and the sound of your voices makes me fucking ill. Truth is, Shelley, everything about you disgusts me and it always has. But, you cheap bitch, you leave this marriage with nothing more than you bought to it and *I'm* having the properties, not you, so I want *you* out of the Cheshire place! In fact, you know what I did this morning before I got in the car to come here? I got your entire collection of shitty, over-priced handbags, put them in a big pile in the garden and then, dearest, I poured petrol on them and burnt the fucking lot! So send somebody for your clothes by the end of the week or I'll burn those too!"

Jack delivers this all in a tone that is quiet and restrained, but underlain with hatred. Shelley is unsure what to say and for a few seconds she sits there looking at him with her mouth literally hanging open. He can't have burnt her handbags, surely not? They were like children to her, how can he have been so cruel!

This is not real, it's not right, it can't be happening to her, she's Shelley Bright, this is supposed to be the first day of her new, even more fantastic life and career. Jack's full of shit, he's lying, bluffing, trying to save himself.

"You're lying," snaps Shelley.

"Hush, keep it down, we don't want people hearing this conversation, do we? No, I'm not lying. I should've seen it myself ages ago, once a crack whore, always a crack whore. All that sneaking around you've been doing, all the days spent in London, the fact that you're so fucking thin. Anyway, if you don't believe me have a look at this, I think it'll more than prove my point. It's just one of the pictures I've got of you smoking crack…"

Jack reaches into the inside pocket of his jacket, pulls out a folded piece of paper and hands it to Shelley. Shelley takes it, she's not happy now, she does not feel good at all, things are just not going as she expected them to. Quickly she unfolds the piece of paper, one fold, two folds and there before her is a picture. It's grainy and obviously shot with a telephoto lens, but the girl in it is definitely Shelley, that's definitely a crack pipe she's holding, and that's definitely smoke she's inhaling from it. Shit!

Shelley's world implodes. She sees everything collapsing around her. The new career in America, the money, the houses, fuck, shit, wank! The turd burgling cunt has fucking got her! If this gets out, she's fucked. This would be the second time she'd been caught doing crack, this time she wouldn't get away with it. She can see the headlines already, SHELLEY, BACK ON THE CRACK and SHELLEY'S NEW CRACK SHAME and she knows that they would finish her!

Her panic is interrupted by Jack, he reaches into his pocket again and pulls out a tiny pen drive, he throws it on the table and tells Shelley, "here, I scanned all the pictures and put them on here for you, have a look for yourself when you get a chance. There's a good forty or so shots of you doing your junky thing, Anthea is in a few of them as well, you girls, eh?" Shelley reaches out, grabs the drive and in one quick movement shoves it and the now

refolded picture of her with the crack pipe into the open (Prada) handbag by her side. "You bastard," she says, "I'll finish you, I'll fucking finish you, I'll will find a way to make

you pay…"

"Yeah, yeah, whatever. But in the meantime let's just say that *you* agree to *my* divorce terms. By the way, you can keep the blond bimbo idea, I like that one! Right, I fancy some food. Shall I get that nasty, cheap champagne for you, *darling*?"

Shelley shoots Jack a look of pure and undiluted hatred, she grabs her handbag, stands up and storms out of the restaurant. Her head is spinning, there's a ringing in her ears, her stomach is churning over and over and there's the bitter taste of hatred in her mouth.

ANDREW

Sodium Pentobarbital. That's how you kill someone. Quickly. Smoothly. Painlessly. Just a small amount. It can be given as drink, it's quite alkali and doesn't taste good, but some sugar can be used to mask the taste. In just a couple of minutes the drinker will fall into a deep sleep, very soon after that the sodium pentobarbital will paralyse the respiratory system and death quickly follows.

Quick. Smooth. Painless. Can be given as a drink. Perfect. That's how I'm going to kill Joey. Whenever he decides the time is right I will finish him, quickly and painlessly. I've gleaned this info from the dodgy doc. I dragged him out of a dinner party yesterday evening (he was very grumpy about it, but it's always money first with our doc) to get round Joey's place and see what could be done for him in the way of palliative care. This morning before I came to the office, I popped into the doc's place for an update on his condition. He told me that a formidable amount of medical equipment, drugs, and a nurse had been installed at Joey's house that very morning, that he was in a very, very bad way.

God bless private healthcare! You, you poor sod, just an ordinary person, have to rely on the cold-hearted, bureaucratic incompetence of the NHS, I feel sorry for you, I really do, I mean, do you have any idea of how many people the NHS kills every year? The National Health Service? Bollocks, it should be the National Health Disgrace! The only thing that can be said for it is that it knocks the socks off a privatised system, which is what you'll be getting soon enough, anyway.

It was when I asked how to end a terminally ill patient's life in a humane fashion that the good doctor suggested sodium pentobarbital. He said he could have some biked round to my office that very morning. As always the doc asked no questions, just supplied what was needed.

That's why I'm sitting here, in my office, in Mayfair, staring at a very small brown bottle on my desk. I'm not one to philosophise much, but it strikes me odd that the contents of this one tiny bottle can kill someone so quickly: how thin and fragile is this line that we walk every day, between life and death, how easily a life can be extinguished. How simple it is to write the last words of the final chapter of the story of someone's life.

I told you I was going to do this. Kill Joey. I already offered you the chance to bail out some time back. You should have gone then. It's too late now, you're up to your neck in this. You're going to have to see it through and hope to God that we don't get caught.

Upon my instruction, Joey's management company broke the news yesterday that he has, tragically and unexpectedly, lost the fight against his "cancer." This morning it's all over the front pages and in all the news bulletins. Joey's management tell me the website and all Joey-related social media gone mad. Apparently there's an absolute "feeding frenzy" of advertisers wanting to jump on the bandwagon before he dies. Fucking ghouls. Also, Joey's got a very lucrative photo shoot booked with "Hiya" magazine, an AT HOME WITH DYING STAR AND HIS BEAUTIFUL CHILDREN feature. He'll be pleased by that, I suppose. I'm not sure how Mabel will react, though. At this point some kind of commotion breaks out downstairs. I hear voices, a male voice, indistinct, Griselda's deep voice, more distinct, loud and swearing, Kerry screaming, "boss, boss!"

Oh shit, what the fuck now! I run from the office and down the stairs to reception. Griselda has a young man pinned to the floor. She's sitting on his back shouting "when I say mister Manning won't see you I mean he won't see you and when I say piss off out of the building I mean fucking piss off, now are you gonna go or what?"

The guy on the floor is trying to speak but can't get a word in edgeways as Kerry is standing over him with a copy of Yellow Pages and intermittently smacking him over the head with it. Faithful and loyal, my girls!

"Okay, okay, enough...Griselda, let him get up and Kerry, stop hitting him!" Kerry desists with the Yellow Pages, and Griselda stands up, still maintaining her grip on the guy's arms so she pulls him up and ends standing behind him, holding him in an arm lock. "What's going on here, Griselda?"

"This guy comes into the office and says he needs to see you about Janey Jax. No one sees you without an appointment, boss, but he just goes on and on saying you'll want to see him and when I tell him to leave he refuses."

Janey Jax. Shit. You've not told anyone about Janey, have you? If you have that's bad news because it means you've involved yourself directly in the affairs of very dangerous people. People I told you to avoid. If you've said anything, anything at all, then you've put both our lives in danger.

I look at the guy that Griselda is holding in an arm lock. He's mid-twenties, unshaven, tall, thin, dressed in skinny jeans, a pair of silly pointy shoes, a shirt with something stupid written on it and a casual jacket. He has a ridiculous (and somewhat mussed up) blow-dried upwards hair style. I guess this is what passes as fashionable with young men nowadays. To me it looks fucking horrible and ugly. "Who are you?" I say to the mystery visitor, "and what on earth are you doing here?"

"I...I...we've not met before, I'm a freelance photographer and will you *please* call this bull-dyke, lezza bitch of me please!"

Griselda is displeased and jerks the guys arms suddenly up towards his shoulders, making him yelp in pain.

"Ow, get offa me!" he shouts.

"A photographer, well, you're right, we've not meet before, I don't want to meet you now *and* you've been rude about my staff so I'm *definitely* not going to see you. Griselda throw him out!"

Griselda starts to drag the guys towards the door, but at that point he shouts out, "Janey Jax, Janey Jax, I know about what...what...what she eats!"

"Griselda, stop!" My attention is suddenly focused on this annoying photographer. "What do you mean, what she eats?" I ask, hoping to God that he doesn't mean what I think he means. "Her special food," he says, "the special food that your other half picked up from the doctor in Harley Street."

Okay, for goodness sake, stop sniffling, I'll take your word for it, you haven't said anything, which is just as well for you. But this bastard does know something. It seems the cat is out of the bag, or should that be the foetus is out of the liquidiser? We could be so fucked.

Fuck shit bollocks wank cunting fucking arseholes.

I pale visibly and snap, "Griselda let him go!" I point at the guy and shout "you, upstairs and in my fucking office now!"

In my office, I gesture to the photographer to sit down. "Now then, what's all this nonsense about Janey Jax and "special food," all sounds a bit silly to me, and to be honest I don't really want to waste too much time with you, so just get straight to the point."

"Ahh, well, mister Manning, I'm afraid you are going to have to spend as much time with me as I decide, because, *mister* Manning, I've got you and Janey Jax over the proverbial barrel!"

"Okay, just spill it, stop fucking around, what have you got to say!" I've decided I've got potential big trouble here and I want to know exactly what is I'm dealing with and quickly.

"All right, mister Manning, actually I'll call you Andy from now on as I'm sure we're going to end up being good mates. It's like this, Andy. Couple of weeks back I got a lead from, let's say, a friend of a friend. Anyway this friend of a friend has a friend who works for your doctor friend, you know, the Harley street guy, and this friend lets it slip to my friend of a friend that your doctor has a nice side-line in doling out no questions asked prescriptions to various celebrities. Now I decide that's worth investigating, so I spend lots of time hanging around outside the doctor's surgery with my camera ready, you know, just waiting to see who goes in and out of the place. Then one day who do I see going in there? Why, it's your other half - Johnny, I think that's his name. Anyway, when he comes back out he's carrying this strange box made of Styrofoam. Hmm, that's odd I think to myself, what's he up to? I decide, on an impulse really, to follow. And that's what I do, follow him, all the way up to The Bishops Avenue. Then, *Andy*, imagine my surprise when your Johnny turns off into a big, big house, which I happen to know is the one Janey Jax is staying in. That's when I think, blimey, there's definitely a story here. So…I park up and grab me camera. I see there's lots of security at the front of the property and I decide to pop round the back and see what I can see. There's a wall all the way round the house, but it's not high and I'm pretty fit. I climb up on it easy. I don't see no security so I decide to go for it - I'm over the wall and in the garden. Still no security which definitely is well lapse, don't you think, Andy? This garden is a pap's paradise, lots of bushes, lots of cover. I settle myself down in a nice bit of shrubbery, all hidden away and comfy, and I scan the house through my telephoto lens and, to my surprise, I find myself seeing into the kitchen of the house and in the kitchen is Janey Jax herself and, well…see for yourself!"

At this point my new pap friend pulls a piece of folded paper out of his jacket pocket
and throws it on the desk.

I unfold and….

Jesus fucking Christ! He who lives by the telephoto lens dies by the telephoto lens! I suddenly remember how happy I was seeing those grainy shots of Shelley smoking crack, pleased at how much they were going to fuck up her plans. I even had images of Jack Brierley doing exactly what's just happened here, throwing a picture of Shelley smoking crack down in front of her. And now here's me, hoist on my own fucking petard...

The pictures on the piece of paper are a series of still photos. They go together in a time sequence. Janey Jax opening a box. Janey Jax holding up something biological and foetus like in one hand, looking at it. Janey Jax holding the foetus thing over a liquidiser. Putting it into a liquidiser. Switching on the liquidiser. Straining the liquid from the liquidiser. And drinking. The pictures are grainy, taken from the some distance, but there's no mistaking Janey and no mistaking what she's doing.

Your comments about sowing and reaping aren't appreciated, thank you very much, now shut up and get back in your box.

Oh fuck, I am so fucking fucked, my heart rate shoots up, my mouth is dry and I'm sure I've gone white as a sheet and I feel like I need the toilet.

The photographer talks on, and my hysteria grows, "you see, that's why I said Janey Jax's special food! I blew up one of those shots and I was pretty sure about what I was looking at so I did a bit of Google image searching. That thing she's dangling over the liquidiser, it's a human foetus, about fourteen weeks old, as an educated guess. Now that is sick and weird, don't you think? And why would Janey Jax want to drink a liquidised foetus anyway? To be honest I don't care, and I don't need to know because whatever her sick reasons are they don't change the fact that I'm sitting on the celebrity scoop of the century. What do you say to that, Andy?"

I say the only thing I can say in the circumstances, "how much do you want?"

"Ahh, well...*mate*, it's not as simple as that, you see it's not just a question of money. I'm guessing these pictures are worth at least a million quid, maybe a cupla mill even, but that's not what I want. You see I'm just a humble pap at the moment but I really, really want to be a journalist, a top journalist, and this is my chance to move my career on in that direction. What I want is some money, yes, but just three hundred grand in cash will do nicely. Then I want four tracks off Janey's upcoming album licenced to me, for no charge obviously, so I can sell them on as a freebie cover-mount to a Sunday paper of my choice. Also, I want an exclusive interview with Janey, and I want to be given the sole rights to film, photograph and report on her worldwide concerts. All quite simple, nothing complicated. I reckon that little package will give me an open door into any media organisation in this country. If you can deliver me that, Andy, which I know for sure you can because your obviously deeply involved in this whole affair, then you can have the pictures and we'll not say another word about Janey's perverted and disgusting eating habits."

"Have you told anybody else about this?" I ask.

"No" replies the photographer "this little beauty is all for me, my work, my glory, my money."

Okay, time to be calm, think this through. What I can ascertain about this guy's character that I can use against him? First off, he's a greedy little fuck, very greedy. He's got arguably the greatest celebrity scoop of the century but he's kept it to himself as he wants more than just a fat cheque. He wants to break himself as a reporter, using concessions from Janey that are actually worth far more even than the pictures he has. That shows he's greedy *and* ambitious. Ambition and greed I can use. Ambition and greed are good, they blind people to the obvious, make them do stupid things. From the way he's approached me I already know he's cocky and arrogant, that's good too, I can work with that, he'll over-estimate his own abilities to control the situation. And finally, he's stupid, very stupid. He knows Janey Jax is a big star, but he doesn't realise quite how big, or the amount of money that some very nasty people have invested in her career. And he's absolutely no idea how far they'll go to protect

her. Me, I know all too well. I have to deal with this troublesome little pap or Charlie Gold will kill me. Christ, I have to go and see the fat bastard today about the Joey fake death nonsense and the six hundred grand that I now owe him, talk about shit timing! What the fuck do I do!

I make a decision. I can work with this guy's greedy, stupid arrogance, and blind ambition. He's absolutely no idea how much danger he's placed himself in by coming to see me here today. "All right," I say, "I can swing that, I need a couple of days to get the money together, and I'm not handing three hundred thousand pounds over in the street so you'll have to come to my home. Let's say Wednesday night, about nine. I'll clear all the other stuff with Janey's people and get a contract drawn up...now fuck off, ask Griselda, the bull- dyke as you so rudely called her, for my address on the way out and I'll see you Wednesday. You come alone and if you breathe a word of this to anyone then the deal is off, you understand?"

"Perfectly, Andy, mate," says the smug little git.

After the photographers gone, I breathe deeply and calm myself. This is bad, but from adversity comes opportunity. The silly sod has kept all this to himself, so if *he* goes away the *problem* goes away.

Stalin said it originally. "No man, no problem."

Yes, I am contemplating what you think I'm contemplating. Deal with it. I never said that hanging around with me was for wimps, and I never said I was a nice guy and if you think I'm going to jeopardise everything I have for the sake of one ambitious photographer then you're very much mistaken. Kill. Don't kill. It's easy.

I call down to Griselda and tell her to get every piece of info on our photographer friend that she can, especially where he lives.

Just for a change of pace and to try and calm myself by doing something that I know I will enjoy, I put a call through to Shelley with the intention of telling her that, regretfully, pictures are circulating of her with a crack pipe. My fun is totally spoilt when I only get Shelley's voicemail, so I leave her a message to call me about "an important matter."

What am I going to say to Charlie, what am I going to say!? The panic I felt when saw the grainy pictures of Janey and the foetus is returning. I calm myself with the mantra "no man, no problem...no man, no problem."

What's the issue with you and this photographer? Why are you worrying about him? He's
nothing to you, you should be more concerned for me than him. Yes, you're right, what I'm thinking about isn't very nice but he's the one who's decided to play with the big boys, and he's going to have to accept the consequences of that. That's the way life is. You need to toughen up, snowflake. Show some fucking backbone!

THE PRODUCER

The Producer is on the phone. And he is not happy. He's talking with the editor of Britain's best-selling Sunday tabloid. That dumb cunt who was in his office the other day, the girl whose tits he spunked on. What was her name? Zandra, that was it, the slutty one. Stupid cow has only gone and taken her story to a newspaper! Who does she think she is? Like any paper is going to print something that he doesn't want printed!

It's a short conversation, the editor mentions that the girl says she was physically and sexually abused by The Producer. He's sure there's nothing in it, that probably she was just bitter and angry and couldn't take the constructive criticism that The Producer was giving her. Exactly so, says The Producer, the girl was a bit of a nut-job frankly, and by the way would the editor like to run an exclusive on his latest boy-band sensation next week? The editor says he would, that it's very kind of The Producer to offer, and obviously the girl is psychologically unbalanced and they'll not be running with anything she has to say.

The Producer hangs up, that's that sorted, silly bitch. He's still pissed off, though. Not that the girl went to the press *per se*. That kind of thing is not a problem to him.

He's pissed off that she should be so *ungrateful* as to go whingeing to the papers after he invited her to his office to give her, what was it the editor said, oh yeh, constructive advice. Ungrateful slut, skank, whore from hell!

Anyway, he's got more fun lined up today, so fuck her! Today is a different kind of Fun Day. The Producer doesn't just get off on sexually abusing the innocents he invites into his lair. Sometimes he finds it just as much fun to vary his routine, to leave the sex bit out and just go in for pure, unadulterated, blistering, nasty as fuck humiliation. Every now and then, instead of a pretty boy or girl a fucking ugly one (a "fugly") will find his or her way from the "reject" pile to the "see" pile, specifically to be invited in for a "roasting." The aim of "roasting" is to so humiliate and insult the victim that they are reduced to a quivering, crying wreck, their self-esteem should be left in tatters, any illusions they may have about their talent should be shattered and any hope they have for the future comprehensively extinguished. The victim should be made to feel like the worthless piece of shit that they are. The Producer remembers one girl who actually pissed herself with fear. That was a particularly good roasting, it gave him a stonking hard on and fuelled sadistic masturbatory fantasies for weeks afterwards.

That's why, today, he's invited Maggie to his office. Maggie is twenty-one and works in a call centre, but she want to be famous. He's seen and heard the material she sent in. Ironically, she's got a great a voice (not that he'll tell her that, obviously), but she's fat, drab and unattractive. All that adds up to a massive no-no in The Producer's mind. Fat and ugly people do not become famous, they shouldn't even have careers, period. After all, what is the point of ugly, fat people? The Producer doesn't know why they think they have a right to exist, let alone to think that they should have even the smallest chance of being famous! They must be punished for such ridiculous aspiration, taught a lesson they won't forget, be reminded that they are physically repulsive and useless.

The Producer's P.A. knocks softly on his office door, he calls her to "come," she opens the door and lets in Maggie. As Maggie walks into his office the door swings quietly shut behind her and The Producer presses that handy button under his desk that locks the door and closes the blinds.

"Hullo, Maggie, how are you?"

"I'm well, sir, very well, I'm so excited to be here, it's like a dream come true!"

"That's good, Maggie, love. Please, come forward, stop moving around so much, dear, and stand in the circle, there, in the carpet in front of my desk, that's it, good girl"

Maggie moves nervously forward. The Producer assesses her coolly. Seeing her in the flesh he's very, very angry with her. Up close and personal she looks even fatter and uglier than he thought. She is short, about five foot four, she has curly brown hair which is down to her shoulders and badly cut, she has a broad, flat face with small brown eyes, a big nose and narrow lips, she even has acne for fucks sake! Who the fuck does she think she is? Doesn't she understand that fame is for pretty people?

"Well now," says The Producer, "I've reviewed what you sent in to me and I've some comments to make, which I hope you will find enlightening."

"Thank you sir, any tips or advice you could give me...well...I'd be very grateful…"

"All right then, I'll bear your request for feedback in mind. First of all I'd like to ask you a question, do you think you can sing?"

"Well, yes, I do sir, I hope so, sir!"

"And do you think that being able to sing is something that can make you a star?"

"I guess it must help, sir..."

"Ah, well that's where you're wrong, dear. It's completely fucking irrelevant, none of my acts can sing, they just speak into a microphone and computer programming does the rest."

"And that little fact, Maggie, leaves you with a problem, because even if I were to say you had a great voice, which I'm not by the way, that still wouldn't be enough for you to succeed in this business. The most important factor would be how I chose to market you and at what audience I intend to aim you, and that's really determined by how good you look. Bearing that in mind I can now give you your feedback… unfortunately for you, Maggie, you don't look good at all. I'm afraid you're fat, far too fat. I'm sorry if you don't like what I'm telling you, but I'm a plain speaking man who says it how it is."

The Producer is pleased to see that Maggie's thin little lips are hanging open and that her face has gone red with embarrassment.

"But...but...but I could lose weight!"

"Oh sure, you *could* lose weight but there would be no point because as well as being fat I'm afraid that you're also very ugly. Very ugly indeed. Pig fucking ugly, in fact. You'd simply go from looking like a fat, ugly pig to looking like a thin, ugly pig!" The Producer laughs at his own little joke, and continues: "in fact, Maggie, you know what, I'm really fucking annoyed that you've come here today, you're totally wasting my time...I mean look at the state of you, you've even got fucking spots for Christ sake!"

"B-b-but...but...you...you a-a-asked me to come" stammers Maggie, who is now crying.

"Shut up, woman, don't bloody interrupt me...now where was I? Oh yes...you've wasted my time today. I mean for fucks sake, take a look in the mirror, girl! You're an obese, piggy, minger, a fucking charity shag, you're so fucking ugly that you'd be the fucking booby prize in a fucking "let's see who can pull the dog" competition. Do you really, really think anybody would pay good money to see you, a performing pig with spots, a bad haircut and saggy tits on stage? You're fucking deluded, utterly deluded. I mean, what the fuck do you think you have to offer? Look at you, you're a sad excuse for a woman, you're as ugly as warthog with smallpox and fat as an obese elephant on a junk food diet! The idea of you ever being famous is ridiculous, fucking ridiculous and the upshot of your delusions is that I, a busy and important man, end up having to waste time on people like you, a fat, ugly, piggy-faced, acne-ridden, drab, no hope, pathetic skank! You, Maggie, are a troll with tits."

The Producer gets up from his desk and walks over to the circle in the carpet where Maggie, now quaking and crying loudly, is standing. "Now have you got the message, girl, has it drilled through your thick skull to that pea-sized lump of turd that you call a brain? You haven't got a chance of making it, not a chance. Listen to me, you're too fat and too ugly to be famous. It ain't going to happen. Not now, not ever, so go back to your sad little job in your sad little call centre and maybe one day you'll marry a sad little man who's just as ugly as you and together you'll breed a deformed brood of sad, no-hope, gut bucket, disgusting looking baby trolls who'll grow up to be as useless and troll fucking ugly as their parents!"

The Producer is standing just a couple of inches from Maggie, leaning over her, his spit flecks her hair as he rants. He has a hard on. Not because he finds Maggie attractive, obviously not and God forbid, but because he has power over. He has humiliated, destroyed her. He can almost smell her fear, her embarrassment, her pain. He grabs Maggie's shoulders, spins her round and shouts in her face, "now get out of my sight you ridiculous, worthless, repulsive, tub of lard!" He pushes her roughly towards the door of his office.

Maggie is distraught, she can't believe this has happened. Poor girl, her dream has turned into a nightmare. She tries to get out of the office, yanking at the door handle, banging her fists against the door, screaming and crying. But the door is still locked and as The Producer watches her frantic and unsuccessful attempts to leave his office, he becomes increasingly aroused by her distress.

He puts a hand down to his crotch and feels his throbbing erection. He decides he's had enough fun with Maggie and presses his special button to open the office door, Maggie runs out, screaming and hysterical.

The Producer sits back at his desk and laughs and laughs. Oh, what fun he has had! When he's finished laughing, he replays Maggie's roasting back through his mind and masturbates enthusiastically, as he feels an orgasm approaching he stands and walks, still wanking, over to the circle in his office carpet and shoots a heavy load of sperm directly on to it.

JOHNNY

Johnny's on his bike, cruising through the traffic, on his way to Paul Hunter's London home in Notting Hill. In the pannier on the back of his bike is a black rucksack. In the rucksack are a hammer, four flat-headed, six inch masonry nails, a length of thick, flat electrical flex tied into a noose, a bottle of poppers, a big, chunky .45 revolver (Andy doesn't know he has this, it was a present from his Essex mates), a pair of women's stockings and a pair of woman's knickers. The rucksack also contains some hardcore she male porn mags ("Breasty Chicks with Big Dicks," "Bareback She Male Sperm Whores," "She Male Cock Creampie Orgy", that kind of stuff). Johnny got everything ready in the outhouse in the garden of his and Andy's place earlier today. Everything has either been cleaned and very thoroughly wiped down or newly-bought. Nothing has been touched without gloves. Johnny has those same gloves on now, he'll keep them on until the night's work is done.

Getting an invite round to Hunter's house had been easy. Andy, after a bit of subtle prompting, had told him all about Hunter, about how he'd made himself a small fortune by exploiting his contacts with his public school chums in the City and the financial press to engage in some sneaky insider trading. Nothing really major, but still of dubious legality and certainly more than enough to cause him a degree of discomfort should it become common knowledge.

Johnny put a call through this morning to Hunter's PA and said that he wished to talk to "Mister Hunter" regarding his financial dealings with a certain company. Within the hour a distinctly flustered Hunter returned Johnny's call. Johnny explained to him that he wanted to discuss with him, on behalf of Andy, certain mutually beneficial arrangements concerning information relating to Hunter's financial affairs. He suggested it was very urgent and that they'd need to meet discretely and preferably that very same night. As expected, a worried Hunter took the bait and suggested that Johnny visit him in his Notting Hill home, yes, he could do it tonight, and, yes, his wife and kids were at the house in the Cotswolds so there'd be no question of anyone else hearing their conversation.

And that was it, easy as that, and now here's Johnny speeding down the Westway on route to Hunter's home. The rage inside him is very noisy now, it wants its vengeance, it wants its sacrifice. Johnny knows on an instinctive, primeval level that if he doesn't give the rage the blood that it craves then it will build up in him until it explodes and carries him away with it, with consequences he doesn't care to even think about.

Johnny reaches Notting Hill. For the sake of caution he chooses not to park near Hunter's house, which is in Ledbury Road, but a few streets away in nearby Colville Gardens. He parks up, takes his black rucksack out of the bike's pannier and slings it over his shoulder, then walks down Colville Terrace. It's night now and the streets are not well lit, that makes Johnny feel more secure.

In a few short minutes he's standing outside Hunter's house. He's impressed. A big nineteen century five story townhouse. Gotta be worth six, six and a half mill, thinks Johnny, but Johnny knows what Hunter's chat show contract is worth so whilst he's impressed, he's not surprised.

Johnny checks for CCTV covering the entrance to the house. There isn't any, that's good, one potential complication less. He walks up to the door of the house and rings the bell. Almost immediately Hunter answers the door. He's big man, but out of shape, heavily padded with flesh and with a good head of hair arranged in a large and loose, flicked back quiff. He has the all the bearing and arrogance of his class.

"You're Johnny, I take it. I've not met you before but I know Andy and I know of your reputation, you're Andy's pet guard dog and enforcer aren't you?" Oh dear, thinks Johnny, this guy is pissing me off already, "well, mate," he replies "I wouldn't describe myself that way but you feel free if you wanna think of me like that, don't bother me either way. Now can I come in or what?"

"Certainly," says Hunter standing away from the door and waving Johnny through "just go up those stairs, then into the first room on the right - my study."

Johnny enters the house into a wide hall and mounts a set of richly carpeted stairs. He bounds up two steps at a time, Hunter follows along somewhat more slowly. Hunter's study is all thick curtains (drawn Johnny's pleased to see), dark wood and comfortable looking leather armchairs. The only reference Johnny can come up with to explain the decor is that it's like something from that programme that used to be on the tele years back, what was it? "Brideshead Revisted," that was it, some wanky old bollocks about fucked in the head posh twats.

Without asking, Johnny settles himself into one of the leather armchairs, placing his rucksack between his legs. Hunter sits in an opposite and identical chair. "Now," he says, "Johnny, if I may call you that, exactly what is this all about?"

"Well, Paul, me old mate, if I may call *you* that, to be honest I haven't bin entirely straight wiv you. I'm not really here about your finances, couldn't give a shit meself, mate, though you have been a naughty boy. You public school lads, eh, all stick together dontcha? I'm here on another matter, something completely different"

A frown crosses Hunter's face and he steeples his hands, touching his lips with the tips of his fingers and says, "I see, and may I ask what that might be then?"

"Well, you see I watched that interview on catch up this afty, you know, that one what you did wiv Joey Camps and I was kinda wondering where the fuck you get off wiv being such a tosser. I mean Joey's a nice lad, he's done well for himself but he's not an educated guy and he ain't that bright and in that interview you just push him and push him. It's like you *wanna* make him say something stupid. I didn't think that was very nice, Paul, cos it were like you were bullying him, using all the benefits of that public school education what you've had to basically take the piss outta someone who's just ain't nowhere near your intellectual equal. Then when he says that the Queen is a cunt, yeh, you looked shocked but there's something else there too, you looked chuffed, you've just needled some lad into fucking his career and you're getting off on it. You, Paul, are a bully and an arsehole."

There's a pause.

Hunter looks at Johnny over the top of his steepled hands, with his head angled slightly downwards. For all the world he looks like a school master examining a particularly recalcitrant schoolboy and says, "firstly, I didn't make Joey shoot his mouth off, he did that all on his own and secondly, who the hell are you to speak to me like this and if you're not here to discuss my, erm, financial affairs, I suggest you leave now."

"All right, take it easy, just listen up a mo' and I'll explain everything. What I'm here about is young Joey. You see, there's more stuff going on wiv that kid than you know. Andy is well pissed off wiv the way you treated him, he holds you, like, responsible for what's happened to the kid and he wants you to apologise on your next show for what you did, for pushing him too far." Actually, Andy doesn't even know Johnny is here tonight, but a bit of lying is necessary to get Hunter to play ball.

"I see, that's quite a big ask. Perhaps you'd like to tell me how anything I did led to him getting cancer and why I would I even think about apologising to that talentless idiot?"

"Well, I suppose I *could* tell people about your sleazy share deals if you didn't, but you see Andy, right, he tells me that you'd get off wiv all the financial stuff. Sure, it'd be temporarily very embarrassing for you, but at the end of the day, you'd be fine cos all your public school bum chums would rally round and help you and all your cheating would soon be forgiven and forgotten. Honestly, you people, eh? You lot are everywhere! Politics, law, banking, media, anywhere there's an easy living to be made. Andy, now he tells me that you people are a, what's the word he uses, oh yeh, "self-referential" group. What he means is that you all help each other out, all say how good you all are, how such and such is just right for such and such a job and how much you deserve the silly money that you all get paid. That's what my

Andy says, and he's a clever guy so I believe him. Andy also says the only way to get to people like you is to humiliate you, he says you lot are so puffed up wiv your own self-importance that that's your weak spot, your pride. So, Paul, that's what this is all about. I'm here to make sure that you *do* apologise to Joey, cos you're going to give me something that would be so embarrassing and humiliating for you if it got out that you won't dare not do."

"You're completely mad. I don't have any skeletons in my closet, and, as you yourself admit, the matter of my financial affairs just isn't going to cut it. So, whatever you may have in mind, Johnny, is simply not going to happen. To be quite frank, that idiot Joey can get stuffed. He's no more than a jumped up piece of working class trash who doesn't know how to behave himself and he dropped *himself* in the shit because he's too stupid to control what comes out of his mouth. Whilst I may be sorry that subsequent to appearing on my show he developed cancer, all his other troubles are of his own making. This conversation is over, you deluded freak, now get out of my house!"

"Sorry, Paul, that's where you're wrong, see, because you're gonna do exactly what I tell you to do."

Johnny reaches down, unzips his rucksack and pulls out his gleaming, large and very threatening .45 revolver. He aims it at Hunter's face.

"Shit, fuck, shit!" says Hunter, scrabbling about in his chair, a look of shock on his fat face. "Yeh, Paul, shit and fuck is about right, now you just sit there and I'm gonna tell you what's gonna happen."

"Okay, Johnny, okay...we can sort this out, I've got money, lots of money, in a safe, upstairs, you can take it all, Johnny...just put the gun down, we can do a deal..."

"Sorry, mate, no deals and I don't need your money. What you have to do now is exactly what I tell you to do. It's simple, remember what I said about humiliation, well I'm here to get some *very* humiliating pictures of you, and when that's done I'll be outta here. I'm not gonna hurt you in any way, long as you do what you're told. Once you've apologised to Joey on your show, well, then I'll give you the photos won't I, and that'll be the matter over and done wiv. On the other hand if you kick off or don't do what I ask I'm gonna put a bullet in your brain and, as it happens, I don't fucking like you, so best not give me any excuses."

Johnny can feel Hunter's panic now and it excites him, he can feel the rage building, taking him over.

"Johnny, please, stay calm, tell me what you want from me!" Hunter is sweating, pale-faced.

"You ever heard of scarfing, Paul?" The posh way of saying it is "autoerotic asphyxiation." What happens is people put something round their neck - like erm, a noose - and have a wank. Then they pull this thing round their neck real tight just when they're gonna shoot their load and it gives them this really intense orgasm. Weird thing to do, kinda dirty and pervy, ain't it? Anyway, that's what's you're gonna do. You're gonna do some scarfing and I'm gonna photograph it. Now just to make it *extra* embarrassing when you do your scarfing you're gonna do it wearing ladies stockings an' knickers and you're gonna be surrounded by she male sex mags, wiv a bottle of poppers up your nose. I think that would be what you call humiliating, don't you?"

"You're mad, fucking mad, I'm not doing it!"

That's a direct challenge to the rage, and the rage doesn't like it and it explodes inside Johnny, he almost loses the plot and before he's even aware of it he's across the room, standing next to Hunter and pushing the gun up against his head, holding it between his eyebrows. "Perhaps I've not made it clear enough," he says in a menacing voice "the deal here is that you do what I say and you get to live, if you don't....I leave you dead on the floor. It's up to you. You decide - but decide quick cos I'm losing patience wiv you!"

"Okay, okay, I'll do it, I'll fucking do it!...but give me your word you won't hurt me..."

"I told you already, I just want the pictures. You gimme them and you have my word I won't even touch you."

Pale, shaking and compliant, a terrified Hunter asks what it is he is supposed to do.

Johnny looks round the room, spies a leather foot-stool. Perfect he thinks.

He grabs his rucksack and takes out the hammer and large masonry nails, and the short length of flat, thick electrical cable he has knotted into a noose. He hands them to Hunter and directs him to pick up the nearby foot-stool, place it in the open doorway to the study, and stand on it. When Hunter is standing on the foot-stool, Johnny tells him to nail the electrical flex into the doorway, two nails about six inches above the top of the door frame, another two into the doorframe itself. Johnny informs Hunter that he'll shoot him there and then if there's any funny business with the hammer.

As Hunter hammers, Johnny takes the she male mags out of his rucksack and places them, open, on the floor near the doorway. Hunter is confused, desperate and clumsy with fear so it takes longer than Johnny would like for him to hammer all the nails through the electrical flex, but finally he's finished. Johnny orders him to toss the hammer on the floor and get down off the foot-stool. He tells Hunter to remove all his clothes. Red with embarrassment, Hunter undresses. He is so scared that he doesn't even bat an eyelid when Johnny tosses him the women's stockings and knickers, instructing him to unpack them and put them on but pulled up only as far as his knees. Johnny notices, with an inner smile, that Hunter has a very small penis.

When Hunter has complied with this request Johnny tells him to get back onto the stool and place the noose around his neck. He obeys meekly.

Johnny takes the final prop from his rucksack. The bottle of poppers. He opens it, drops the cap to the floor, holding a finger over the top of the now open bottle. "Right, feller," he says, "I think we're about ready now, don't you?"

"Please tell me this is nearly over, Johnny...it's too much, too much, you promise not to hurt me, I'm doing what you asked, aren't I?"

There is a wheedling, plaintive tone to Hunter's voice, it irritates him, but the jobs nearly done now, no point losing his temper. "Don't you worry yourself," he replies, "I just need you on that stool wiv the flex round your neck for two minutes while I snap some pictures and then it's all done. You be careful now cos this scarfing lark is well dangerous and people have been known to accidentally kill themselves while doing it, don't want no accidents now do we!"

Hunters nods an "okay."

"Good on you, feller, nearly done now, now take this," he hands the bottle of poppers to Hunter. "Unscrew the top and give them a good sniff...careful though, it's amyl nitrite and it'll make you a bit woozy. Don't wantcha falling off that stool, not wiv a noose round your neck an' all!"

Hunter sniffs the poppers cautiously, and as the amyl nitrite causes his blood pressure to plummet, he wobbles precariously on the footstool.

Hunter's head clears of the poppers, and he has a sudden and startling insight. Johnny has not taken his gloves off since arriving at his house, and what about the pictures he supposed to be taking, he doesn't even have a camera! Where's the camera, where's the fucking camera!?

"Johnny, what's going on," he says "why aren't you taking any pictures?"

Ooops…the penny's dropped, thinks Johnny, it's time. He strides over to Hunter on his foot-stool.

"You know when I said I wouldn't hurt you, Paul?" he says. "I was fucking lying!"

With that Johnny kicks the footstool away. Hunter drops, only a few inches, but enough to make the electrical flex around his neck tighten and cut off his breathing. His hands shoot up to the noose, they claw uselessly, trying to loosen it, his legs kick, his eyes bulge, his face goes red then blue, he tries to scream but has no breath, he pisses himself, and then his bowels give way. The room is filled with the smell of shit and piss which mixes with the strong aroma of poppers.

Johnny watches all this transfixed, the rage inside him is released and it screams and laughs inside his head, made ecstatic by the sight of a man dying.

It takes Hunter a surprisingly long time to die on the end of that noose, the body still twitching some minutes later. When Hunter stops moving completely, and Johnny is satisfied that he is dead, he re-positions the footstool nearer the body picks up his rucksack, and quietly leaves the room and then the house.

As if he had never been there.

JOEY

Joey stirs from a deep sleep. Truth is, he spends more time now asleep than awake, and when he wakes he wishes he hadn't because that's when it hits him. In those first few waking moments it strikes him like a sledgehammer, the fact that his life is all but over. He is lying in this bed waiting to die. That thought fills him with despair. He wants to be left to sleep for ever.

He looks around him, still foggy from sleep. He takes in the Philippina nurse who seems to be constantly fussing around him, and the mass of medical equipment, which he guesses is all that's keeping him alive. There is a fluid drip going into his arm, feeding him the salts and sugars he needs (he finds it impossible to eat, managing only to drink a small amount of water), his penis is cathered, the urine collecting in a bag by the side of the bed, and tubes run from his wrist into a dialysis machine pumping the blood out of his body, cleansing and replacing it, taking the place of his now defunct kidneys. Another machine monitors his breathing and heart rate.

The Philippina nurse asks him if he has pain, does he needs morphine? He is tempted to say "yes" and drift back into sleep but declines. The nurse is a sweet girl, solicitous and gentle, and between her and his mum and the kids he is never alone. Even his da is here now and a regular and welcome presence in Joey's world, which has shrunk to the size of this one bedroom.

At first Joey was reluctant to have the twins in the room, he wasn't sure they should be seeing him so ill, that it might scare them, but now he's glad of their visits. They are the highlight of his day. They sit on the bed, they stroke his face, hold his hand, plant gentle kisses on his cheeks which are like fluttery, little pieces of heaven. He'll need to have a conversation with them, though. *That* conversation, the "daddy is going to die" conversation. He's no idea as yet exactly how he's going to have that conversation, or what he's going to say. How do you discuss death with a pair of kiddies? But he knows he has to talk to them: to just slip away without any saying anything would be wrong and he's not going to take the easy way out and leave all explanations to his ma, he loves the twins too much to do that.

He guesses from the level of light coming in the window that it must now be late afternoon. The morning had been very difficult, with the crew from "Hiya" coming round to do their "at home" feature. Lots of pictures, lots of silly questions and he'd had to get ma, da and the twins upstairs to be in the pictures, too. Ma was not happy but accepted it, Joey having explained that it was good money and absolutely the last public appearance he would make. Literally. The last. Ever.

When Joey's in one of his short waking periods he finds himself thinking a lot, drifting back to his past and wondering, well, was that it? Was that his life? Was that all he could do, all he could have been? All that fame, all that money but ultimately a complete fuck-up. A man who's had to poison himself to death so that he can go out on a high, so that he can at least leave his kids some kind of useful legacy. What the fuck has it all been about then, this life thing?

So often, his thoughts come back to the twins, has he really done the right thing? They've already lost their mother, now he's taking their dad away. Oh, the twin's mum, poor doomed Katy. He did love Katy, but maybe not enough. Should he have tried to love her more? Could he have done more to get her into rehab, or been more of a shoulder to lean on? But when all is said and done, he realises that he's not to blame for Katy's overdose and death. Nope. The problem with Katy was that there was a hole at the centre of that girl so deep that nothing was ever going to fill it. No amount of love or support would have helped and celebrity certainly didn't, couldn't, fill the void in Katy's soul. Poor, poor girl. Why was she like that? Joey didn't know then, and he doesn't know now. She was just fucked up. Sometimes life is just like that, it gives you a lot but then, for the hell of it, adds a big dollop of shit on top. Life can be blindly, inexplicably, unfathomably and maliciously cruel.

The pain is back now. A burning, intense stab of agony from the base of his spine up through his body and into his brain. His eyes close, he moans and the Philippina nurse stirs. He considers again accepting her offer of morphine, but then, thankfully, the pain decides to relinquish its grip, for now, and Joey is able to think again, this time about Andy. He has to say that, whatever his reasons, the guy has proved to be a great friend. It might not even be for the right reasons, but Joey doesn't care. He is very grateful for his help, and that standing in for Charlie Gold's money, that was well above the call of duty. And Andy will be the guy that finally brings this whole sorry story to an end. Thank fuck for Andy!

Joey hopes fervently that the end will be soon.

ANDREW

After the hideous, blackmailing paparazzo bastard leaves my office, I spend some minutes composing myself. I need to be calm and I need to carry on business as usual. I follow up on a matter Johnny bought to my attention, that of Jimmy Morley, he of the famous daytime television show. He's made a living out of demeaning the poor and ignorant and exploiting their difficult and emotionally troubled lives. But this great moral arbiter, this saint of our times, has only gone and dipped his dicky in some eighteen year old girl's lady bits and got her pregnant. What's worse is that she was a participant in one of Jimmy's shows. Oh dear, dirty, stupid old git! I telephone Jimmy, get straight to the point, tell him there's nothing to worry about. Griselda has already sounded the girl out, she just wants cash, a *large* sum of, then she'll have an abortion and she'll keep her mouth shut, bish bosh, like it never happened. Jimmy just needs to get the money to her (through ourselves with appropriate commission and expenses, obviously). We'll get the girl to sign a killer contract that'll frighten her into never opening her mouth about the matter (drawn up by Hersham, Poulter, Gaston Solicitors, who are very expensive, very effective and who, like Jimmy, enjoy nothing more than bullying and terrifying the poor and the ignorant), and then she'll get her money. Half when she signs, the other half after the abortion.

Now you know all this stuff about Jimmy, you'll not be able to watch his show in the quite the same way as before, will you? I do apologise if I've spoilt it for you, but I'm afraid the truth about Jimmy is that he really isn't a modern day saint or wise-man, rather he's a piece of human detritus, a real bottom feeder (literally, but that's another Jimmy story I'll maybe tell you another day).

That particular matter sorted, I'm free to leave the office for my appointment with Charlie Gold. I scoop up my bottle of sodium pentobarbital (which has remained, unnoticed, on my desk throughout my discussion with the pap), drop it in the inside pocket of my jacket and leave - bidding the girls a good day on my way out.

Yes, you're right, it's probably good that the photographer didn't notice the bottle. I doubt he would have known what sodium pentobarbital was (you certainly wouldn't have known if I hadn't told you, I mean, it's hardly the kind of thing that you come across every day, is it?) but you can't be too careful, especially in the matter of killing people.

The Bishops Avenue is a bit far from the West End even for me to walk, so having made my way up to Oxford Street, I hail a cab and jump in. The cabby does an expert U-turn and heads down Oxford Street, turning left at the end into Tottenham Court Road. I know I've quite a long trip ahead of me (Tottenham Court Road, up to Camden Town via Hampstead Road, then to Kentish Town to pick up Fortress Road, to Junction Road, into Archway Road then left on the Great North Road into The Bishops Avenue), so I have time to think and decide exactly how I'm going to handle Charlie.

Tell me, if you were me, what would you do? I bet you wouldn't tell Charlie that a pap has blown Janey's foetus eating habit, I bet you would try and get it all sorted out quickly and quietly without telling Charlie a thing. Given that he's a murderous bastard that would probably be a reasonably good idea. But you know what, you aren't me, you don't have my "chutzpah." And you don't owe him six hundred thousand quid. You don't know what "chutzpah" is? Oh, good grief, go and Google it

I'm going to tell Charlie all about the journalist and then, as they say in the circles in which he moves, make him an offer that he can't refuse.

Sooner than I was expecting, the cab pulls into The Bishops Avenue and comes to a stop outside Janey's place. It really *is* a fucking mansion, that woman has got money to burn!

Take a good look, this is how some people live. Amazing isn't it? One poor sod who's never done anyone but himself any harm, spends his nights sleeping in a shop doorway whilst someone else, someone like Janey, who is so fucking depraved that she eats human foetuses… well, she has at it all, she has everything. It was ever thus, I suppose. Depressing though, isn't it?

I pay the driver, giving him a nice tip, and get out of the cab. I approach the gates to the house and, as if by magic, an unfeasibly large and aggressive-looking security guard appears and asks me my business. Mister Manning for Charlie Gold, I tell him. He consults a walkie talkie and I'm cleared for entry, the gates swing open. Oh well, into the lion's den I go!

I walk up a long driveway to the house, then climb a large, sweeping and impressive set of stairs. As I'm doing so Charlie comes out of the house to greet me. He is wearing another one of his tent-like suits, this one is deep navy blue. The dark colour should make him look slimmer but that particular little fashion tip doesn't work with someone as fat as Charlie: he still looks like a dyspeptic and grossly overweight toad.

Don't forget the rules: when Charlie's around you hide, keep out of the way, I don't need any more blood on my hands.

"Andy," Charlie says with his usual transparent insincerity, "great to see you!" his multi-chins wobble as he holds out a meaty hand for me to shake.

"Hi, yeh, good to see you too. I guess we've a lot to talk about, shall we go inside and get straight down to it?"

"Sure, good idea, you just follow me."

And that's what I do. Follow Charlie as he waddles down long, plushly carpeted corridors before turning off into a large study, richly and grotesquely furnished in that Louis the Thirteenth style favoured only by very rich people with absolutely no taste whatsoever.

Charlie gestures me to a chair, "sit yourself down, you wanna drink?"

"No thanks, I'm fine, all good. How's Janey by the way?"

"Shit, she's in a lousy mood, she's had a pair of lower ribs removed and she says she's in a lotta pain, but, hey, she has to keep that hour-glass figure of hers."

"Blimey, lower ribs removed....erm, okay, seems a bit extreme to me but I guess you don't look as good as Janey without some sacrifice."

"Exactly."

"Right then, Charlie, all the stuff we have to discuss...where would you like to start?" I sit, feeling a more than a little bit nervous and Charlie (the chair killer) lowers himself into a large and horribly upholstered sofa that creaks ominously as it strains under his vast bulk.

"Okay, first thing on the agenda...it kinda concerns me that you ain't got a bag with you, so you got my six hundred grand or what?"

"Well, actually, no, I don't have your money I'm afraid."

Charlie looks at me with his mouth slightly open and his piggy eyes seem to swell and I swear his face is turning a rich shade of puce. I can tell he's struggling to hold his temper, not something he's very good at it, and in a few seconds the struggle is lost.

"Waddaya mean you don't have my fucking money you? Are you shitting me, you cocksucking bastard?!"

Charlie's a bit a pissed off to say the least, I reply calmly and quietly, hoping to sooth him a bit, "I'm afraid something rather awkward has come up that slightly changes matters."

"Jeezus Christ, "something rather awk-waard," you bloody English, why d'you all have to go and speak like fags, what the fuck you on about, Andy?"

I see no point skating round the issue so I get straight to the point.

"It's Janey and the foetus. She's been papped, I got a guy with pics of Janey and a foetus." Charlie face has gone from a deep puce to one of almost blinding white.

"Jeezus, shit...how the fuck has this happened? You'd better have a real good explanation because right now I am really not liking you, not at all!"

"Seems some pap was staking out the doc's place regarding another matter entirely, by chance he saw Johnny coming out with a package and decides to follow him here, he got in the grounds, took the pictures and, well, we are where we are."

"He followed Johnny here, and Johnny noticed nothing? What a fucking idiot! This is not looking good for you, Andy - you are in deep shit. I'll be honest, right now I'm thinking about killing you so you need come up with a reason why I shouldn't, and quickly."

The look in Charlie's eyes as he says this looks like what I'm suddenly sure the gateway to hell looks like. I'm left with no doubt that he means exactly what he says and I feel an icy chill running down my spine. No time to bottle it now, though.

Don't you dare bug out on me now, I need some moral support here!

"Okay, I hear you, but first of all you need to understand that this is not Johnny's fault or mine...it's yours."

"What the fuck, who the fuck you think you are? How fucking dare you!"

Charlie's Technicolor face is back in puce mode.

"Charlie, I think you're slipping a bit, getting on maybe, losing your edge. First there was that business of the fake death scene with Joey, that was just crass and stupid. And now this disaster. You need to be honest with yourself here, the reason the pap has the pictures of Janey is because there wasn't enough security around this mansion. Security is down to you, it's your job to safeguard your clients' interests. You should've anticipated the possibility of something like this happening. I mean letting Janey liquidize a foetus near an uncovered window...whoa, that's amateurville."

Charlie is now looking at me with his mouth fully open, he is having difficulty processing what I have just said. I don't think anyone has spoken to him like this. Ever. No-one alive anyway. Suddenly he's up on his feet and with a degree of agility surprising in one so fat, he's reached inside his jacket and pulled out a little snub-noised revolver (which I can't help noticing is, rather fetchingly, gold-plated) and he's holding it a couple of centimetres from my face. Jesus, fuck, where did that come from!

"You dumb little fuck, you fag bastard, you think you can speak to *me* like this? I'm gonna take this gun away from your face and I'm gonna sit back down and you are gonna tell me how you're gonna deal with this and if I don't like what you say then, so help me, I'm going to blow a big fucking hole in your head!"

Okay, that's fine, not a problem, that was the reaction I was expecting: I'm shitting myself but I'm still alive, that's the main thing, still in with a chance of sorting all this out. You stay calm, Charlie's not going to kill me because my little attack on him may have pissed him off but it's shown him I have balls and now I'm going to convince him that he needs me and my balls. Just keep hiding behind that chair, he can't see you there, keep it that way. Charlie may need me but he definitely doesn't need you.

"Charlie, let's take this nice and easy, eh? I appreciate you're pissed off, but killing me isn't going to help. In fact, I'm the only one that can help you with this mess. The pap with the pictures, yeh, it's obvious, he has to die. Look, the thing is he's a greedy fool, he hasn't told anyone but me what he has on Janey because he thinks he can get even more for himself than just a fabulous wedge. He, err, wants an interview with Janey, uhmm, tracks from the new album as giveaways, exclusive coverage of her tour, three hundred thou in cash..."

Oops, Charlie's face has gone puce yet again, definitely time to move the conversation on!

"The important point here is that he trusts me to deliver what he's asked for. I have a meeting with him at my house on Wednesday night and he thinks he's going to pick up the money and that he'll be signing a contract for all the other ridiculous shit he's asked for, but in reality he's not going to get anything. The little shit will be leaving my house as a corpse"

Charlie is looking somewhat mollified, I think talk of people dying is, to him, like a dummy to a baby. Now's the time to hit him with the killer blow.

"All I want for cleaning up this issue for you, Charlie, is that my six hundred grand debt is written off."

Charlie hears this and burst into hearty (but, I'm sure, ironic) laughter.

"Get outta here, six hundred grand, oh, I'm fucking laughing...why don't I just kill you and get one of my guys to do the job?"

"Because, presumably, you'd have to get someone in from the States, unless you want to trust it to some amateur, and that takes time. Also…if you start hitting people over here then your associates are going to figure out there's maybe some kind of issue around Janey. You don't want them thinking stuff and getting nervous. And, most of all, you simply don't have the time to fuck around with this. We need to squash this pap as soon as possible, and if I do the job you know it'll be done well and done right. Remember, it's my neck that's on the line here as well, I'm into all this foetus shit deep, just as much as you are, I need this guy gone too. I appreciate you're angry and that you don't want to lose money, but I'm the best option you have right now. In fact I'm the only sensible option you have right now."

Charlie stares at me long and hard. He is thinking and I can almost smell the rubber burning. "Okay," he says, "here's what we do. You're a smartass, cheeky bastard but, yeh, you're probably right to say that I need this matter cleared up without my business partners knowing, so I'm gonna go for your deal. If you fuck this up though, Andy, there will be severe consequences and you know what they will be. Don't let that happen, don't let things get to the point where there's no reason for me to let carry you on living. I want this guy and his fucking pictures gone and gone quick. Now fuck off and do it, and do it right."

I decide not to make any smart remarks about it being a "pleasure to do business" or "I knew you'd see sense." I know that I've pushed my luck as far as it can go, so I stand and excuse myself, turn my back on Charlie and leave the room, navigating my way back through the ridiculously plush corridors. I want to get out of that house as quickly as possible.

It's not until I'm down the driveway and out of the gates of Janey's mansion that the enormity of what I've just done strikes me. Suddenly I feel sick and dizzy. I bend over, supporting myself with my hands on my knees and taking great gasps of air. Fuck, that was close, not many (not any!) people get to push Charlie Gold that far and walk away alive!

A bit further down The Bishops Avenue, I stop a passing black cab. I throw myself in the back and ask to be taken to Primrose Hill. I take a few moments to reflect upon what I've just committed myself to do. By the end of this week I'll have been responsible for two deaths. First Joey, and how do I feel about that? I'm not sure. I know that I'm only doing what he has asked me to do, that, as Johnny said, he chose this course of action and I know that what I am going to do for him will be done for the best motives, out of love and compassion. I know all that. But, still, I can't help feeling guilty that I am, thanks to my cancer scam, responsible for Joey's death. And the pap? How do I feel about having that scalping little fuck killed? No problem at all. I'm nothing if not practical. There was never a chance in hell that Charlie would have agreed to give the guy what he wanted, and if he sold those pictures I'd be in a whole shitload of trouble: there's no such thing as bad publicity *except* being involved in foetus eating. Oh, and Charlie would kill me, too. Let's not forget that particular small, but crucial, detail.

I don't really have a choice but to kill the pap, it's his life or my career and my life. No contest. Why get all sulky about it? The guy has to die, end of story. Don't you see that to get on in life you have to do bad things. It's like what I was saying about Janey before, all that stuff you got taught as a kid about being nice to people, about being a good person. It's cuntola, it's all cuntola. Life does not reward good people, it shits all over them. The good die young, miserable and poor but bad men flourish and prosper and are happy. It's sad, it's horrible and, God knows, I wish it wasn't so, but that's the way things are. Christ, you have got a strop on now, haven't you? I'm sorry if you don't like what I'm saying, but I'm afraid it's the truth. Tell you what, if you want to go now, then go, I'm getting bored of pussy-footing around your precious sensibilities anyway. Come with me, don't come with me. Your choice.

The only one thing that worries me about the whole pap issue is that I'm going to have to ask Johnny to do the deed. I freely admit that I'm too squeamish. I mean giving Joey a fatal poison I can deal with, but the sheer physicality of killing someone who's standing there in front of me, someone who definitely doesn't want to die...that's more than I can handle. And how will Johnny react? I know he has a physical and violent side to his nature, but will he really be prepared to kill somebody?

Aha, you're still here! You're going to carry on with our little tale. I'm glad. You can be a bit of a pain in the ass but I've grown quite fond of you and your wide-eyed naiveté. Mind you, I knew you would stick around. I knew, because you've got that dark place inside you, you just haven't fully embraced it yet. Right you, pull yourself together. We've things to do, places to go and people to kill.

JOHNNY

Walking back from Paul Hunter's to his bike, Johnny was buzzing. He felt elated. The rage in him satisfied and happy, at least for now. He'd taught that Hunter a real lesson, showed him what a total fuck he was. The bastard deserved to hang, upsetting his Andy like that and driving that poor kid Joey to his death! He thinks how funny it'll be when somebody discovers Hunter's body. Him hanging there, tongue protruding and eyes bulging, noose around his neck, surrounded by she male porno and reeking of piss, shit and poppers! He can't wait to see what the papers have to say about that. After all, they do love a nice juicy celebrity scandal, particularly if it involves drugs, sex and death!

Johnny decides that the only way to round off a night this good is to indulge in some rampant, dirty, no holes barred sex. He gets on his bike and points it in the direction of the sleazy gay fleshpots of Vauxhall.

Some hours later he's done the bars and the clubs, he's slaked his lust and is on his way back to Primrose Hill. If anything he's even jollier than he was before, having had some marvellously dirty sex, and in a cheerfully reflective mode.

He's never killed anyone before, battered some people quite badly, but never killed. How does he feel about it? Good, to be truthful. Good. Hunter was a shit of a man who deserved everything he got, a man who sailed effortlessly (and talentlessly) into his position on a river of privilege.

And then suddenly a blinding flash of insight and he sees his calling! He knows what all the anger, all the rage is about! He is an avenger! He's spent many years in the world of celebrity, he's seen how these people behave. Okay, one or two of them are perfectly decent sorts, but most are nasty, back stabbing, heartless, vain and utterly self-obsessed or are self-satisfied, smug, over-privileged tossers like Hunter. It's for those kind of celebrities that Johnny is here. He's here to punish their bad behaviour, to cull the worst from the sewer of celebrity by utilising the ultimate sanction: death.

He is judge, jury and executioner. He is an avenging angel!

He can see it all now. What he did with that rentboy, nearly throttling him, that was bad, the guy was really just an innocent, a bit player in the carnival of freaks that is celebrity. But Hunter, yeh, that was good, he needed to be culled. He shall remember this night as a glorious one, the night he was magically reborn!

Johnny's now at ease with the rage. He thought it was a bad thing, that perhaps he was losing his mind, but now he knows it has a purpose, that it's calling him to do Holy Work. He's a man with a mission and he will not fail his calling.

When Johnny gets back to the house in Primrose Hill, he's surprised (it being well after three in the morning) to find Andy in the living room, lying back on one of the sofas, drinking a large glass of red wine. He's looking uneasy and troubled.

Johnny walks over to Andy, "hullo, sweetheart, how you doing?" he says. Andy reaches out his hand to Johnny, and Johnny clasps it in his own. "You're looking troubled, mate...shift up will you, lemme sit down, tell me what's on your mind." Johnny eases himself on to the sofa as Andy shuffles up to make room for him.

"Johnny," says Andy, "we've got a problem, a big problem."

"Ahh, I knew it, could tell from the look on your face, I knew something were wrong. What's going on?"

"It's Janey and this foetus thing, it's all gone a bit pear-shaped. Some cunting arsehole fucking photographer cunt has gone and blown the gaff. That day you picked up the foetus from the dodgy doc's office, this photographer followed you and to cut a long story short he's got photos of Janey shoving a foetus into a liquidizer."

"Shit! That's bad, real bad. This is my fault, I should have bin checking what were going on behind me. I'm so sorry!"

"Johnny...it's not your fault at all, the pap was watching the dodgy docs for a completely different reason. He got the fucking pictures of Janey by chance because he was able to get into and stroll happily around the grounds of that mansion of hers. Fucking Charlie fucked up badly with the security!"

"The pap's asked for a whole load of stuff that Charlie's never going to give. That'll leave him with only one option, which is to sell the photos and then we're all in the shit. I've said I'll clear up the mess for Charlie. If I don't he says he'll kill me."

"All right, so it's obvious," answers Johnny, "you need to shut the pap up in some way. What you got in mind?"

"It's him or me, so there's only one choice here, oh Christ, this is a hard thing to say…I…"

"Just tell me, whatever it is, it's fine with me."

"I need the guy dead! Will you do it for me, Johnny? Get rid of this bastard photographer?"

Johnny thinks for a moment. He's surprised Andy has asked him to kill someone, but he can see Andy's point. Charlie Gold is a vicious, dangerous bastard, not a man to fall foul of. In Johnny's judgement Gold's threats to kill are real. Would killing the pap fit in with his new role as an avenger? The journalist is no celeb, but he's still part of the celebrity world, and surely another aspect of his role as an avenging angel is to keep his beloved Andy safe? Yep, it all fits. He'll kill the pap with pleasure, just another part of his sacred mission.

"Okay, Andy, no problem, the pap has to go. How do you want me to do him?" Andy puts down his wine glass, turns, throws his arms round Johnny, kisses him and says, "thank God, I knew you'd help me, you always do. You're everything to me, Johnny, you know that? Everything!"

"Oh, stop being so bloody gay," laughs Johnny, playfully pushing Andy away "just tell me how we're gonna do this and when."

"Wednesday, Wednesday night, he's coming here, it's Rosa's bingo night so we'll have the place to ourselves..."

And so on a quiet night, in a beautiful house, in upmarket Primrose Hill, two men in love plan a murder.

<u>KERRY</u>

After running out of *that* man's office, Kerry fled deeper into the anonymity of Soho, seeking shelter and safety in aloneness. She sits now in one of those soulless chain coffee shops. On her own. Seat by the window. Hunched over a large mug of the brown, bland hot drink that passes for coffee in these places, steaming like a warm cup of piss on the table in front of her.

She is appalled with herself. She is jittery. She is shaking with shame and anger. How could she have been so utterly stupid as to have her own secret dreams of stardom when she works in the world of celebrity? She knows, better than most, that it is a world of fakes and freaks, trickery, lies, abusers and cheats. But no, despite that fact, despite the fact that she's got a great, well-paid, interesting job and has lovely workmates, despite all that she has her secret, stupid bloody dream of being a singer.

And because of that, she ends up in that office. With that man. That pig. Dirty, disgusting, pig. Invited in to "discuss her career." For fucks sake, how fucking naïve. She should have known something was wrong when he started going on about how she was older than his usual type of girl, but so pretty and so fresh-faced and reached under his desk and pressed something that closed the door and blinds of his office. Then he started coming out with all that shit about trust and commitment and he asked her to take her top off. When she wouldn't do it the dirty old fuck became abusive, stood up, came up to her, put his face in hers, mouthing obscenities and stuck his hand between her legs.

That was her more than enough for Kerry. She kneed the bastard in the balls. Hard. He fell to the floor, huffing and puffing in pain, and she aimed a quick kick to his face and was pleased to hear a satisfying crunch as his nose broke under the impact of her foot. From there she was right on her toes, round the back of the guy's desk, found the cheeky little button he'd pressed to lock the office door, pushed it, door opens, she jumps over the prostate figure of the revolting fuck and she's out of the office and out of the building.

Christ. What does she do now? She wants to punish the dirty, nasty bastard. A knee in the balls and a busted nose isn't enough. She wants to screw him over, see him broken, destroyed, maybe even dead - not just for her but for all the other people that she is absolutely sure he's done this to before. But how? She knows the way fame and wealth work, knows there is no point going to the Old Bill or the media. Like that'll get her anywhere! This guy is far too rich and influential to be troubled by minor nonsense like press and police.

What on earth is she going to do? She needs to talk to someone about this, if not to get revenge then at least for her own sanity. Kerry pauses in her thoughts and stares down at her rapidly cooling mug of coffee-type drink. She looks up, and catches sight of an old tramp shuffling around the coffee bar, he's going from table to table, asking for money, getting nothing but refusals in the form of stunted shrugs and a half-mumbled "no, no." The tramp looks up from his latest unsuccessful prospect and his and Kerry's eyes meet. He is a ragged, dirty, rumpled man but, God, the eyes! To Kerry his eyes burn with an incredible intensity of intelligence and compassion. They are spellbinding. She can't understand why no one else has noticed them, why they should dismiss so readily a man who so obviously shines from his soul. The tramp smiles at Kerry, looking at her as though she's the exact person he's just popped into the coffee shop to meet. He heads straight for her table and in seconds, he is standing by her. He smells bad, of sweat and dirty clothes, but Kerry hardly notices, she is entranced by those eyes, waves of understanding and love seem to flow from them and she feels warm and comforted, as if someone has woven a net beneath her to catch her should she fall. She is convinced that she is in the company of an angel. A dirty, smelly, ragged angel, but an angel nevertheless. The tramp/angel opens his mouth and says to her to tell Johnny, Johnny will know what to do. Johnny will make everything right. And with that he turns away, walks out of the coffee bar and vanishes instantly into the crowds of Soho.

As if he had never been there.

Kerry is confused. She's calm and happy, her strange visitor has definitely improved her mood, but she's confused. Why did she think that the tramp was angel? After all, the idea of an angel disguised as a tramp walking through the streets of Soho is just silly…isn't it? But why did he know about Johnny? *How* did he know about Johnny? And why does she know as a matter of absolute certainty that she *is* going to tell Johnny exactly what that dirty, rich, famous, abusive piece of shit did to her?

SHELLEY

When Shelley left the restaurant, she was blind with fury. She stormed out into the street, hardly able to believe that her so lucrative divorce from Jack scheme had gone so horribly wrong. Okay, she was still going to get her divorce, but bugger all else. And Jack had been so fucking smug about it! Cheap champagne for a cheap tart! How fucking dare he! This just can't be happening!

And he burnt her handbags! Shelley is heartbroken, how could he do something so cruel? They were her babies, she loved those handbags more than anything in the world!

Shelley is so angry and disorientated that for a few moments out there in the street she's unsure of where she actually is. She even forgets she has her car and driver parked and waiting for her in a nearby street. She needs to get away from here. Away from Jack. Away from the restaurant. Away from the common people in the street, these horrible, ugly, ordinary no-hopers.

Acting almost from instinct rather than any rational plan, she flags down a black cab, shouts "Holland Park" through the front window and without waiting for a response from the cab driver, climbs in the back.

As the driver pulls away Shelley notices him looking at her in his mirror, oh shit, a fucking fan, that's the last thing I need right at this moment!

"'Ere" says the driver, "you're that Shelley Bright aintcha, blimey, just wait 'til I tell my girls I had that Shelley Bright in the back of my cab, they love you they do, you're their idol..."

The cabby witters on as he drives about how great Shelley is, how much his girls love her. Normally this kind of stuff is music to Shelley's ears, but today it is all just so much la-de-fucking-dah. Shelley tunes out the cabby and nods and says "lovely" and "thanks" at appropriate points in the cabby's monologue, acting on well-practiced celebrity autopilot.

Who the fuck got photos of her smoking crack and who got them to Jack? Why? Who wants to fuck her up? Suddenly Shelley feels very, very paranoid and wants to be out of this cab and back at Anthea's place as quickly as possible. She needs to be in safe, familiar surroundings and she knows there'll be some crack at Anthea's place, or at least some coke. Christ, she needs a fucking hit!

After what seems like an eternity the cab finally arrives back at Anthea's. She jumps out, reaches into her Prada handbag (the last of her precious and beloved babies), pulls out a handful of notes and presses them into the cabby's hand without even asking what the fare is or waiting for change. As she flees to Anthea's house she can hear the cab driver shouting, "thanks for the big tip, darlin' I'll tell me girls you said 'ullo!"

Once inside, she slams the big front door behind her, locks it with the deadlock, draws the bolt and collapses on to her hands and knees, breathing heavily. She's in a total state. She needs drugs and she needs them now. Christ, one fucking afternoon, one meeting, a few minutes with Jack and all her plans for her beautiful, big divorce pay-out and her new career in America are out of the window. Who did this to her, who took those photos?

She puts a call through to Anthea (who's out shopping, as usual). She tells her the whole sad story, crying. Anthea says it's all terrible (darling), makes all the right noises, but something in her voice tells Shelley that Anthea's just not that interested, that she wants to get back to buying stuff. She does at least agree with Shelley's desire for a quick pharmaceutical crutch. Anthea tells Shelly that they finished all the crack last night (bad), but that there's some coke and diazepam in her bedroom (good), at the back of her knicker draw and the house is awash with booze (super). She tells Shelley to help herself. Knock yourself out, girl, she says.

A couple of hours later and Shelley is coked up to the eyeballs and swigging neat brandy. She's downstairs, hiding in the living room. This time she's drawn the curtains and she's going to leave them that way, not getting caught out like that again, no way!

She feels slightly less worse now that she's had a drugs and alcohol top-up, but she's still not feeling warm and fuzzy, rather her bitter disappointment has morphed into a hard and bitter anger.

She knows who's stitched her up. It's that fucking Andy, he's the one behind those pictures and he's the one who got them to Jack. She knew it was him as soon as she listened to his message on her answerphone. She knows what the "important matter" is. Fucking gay, shit stabbing, bastards! Queers sticking together, that's what this is. Bum boys watching each others' arses. The pink fucking mafia, the secret botherhood of the fucking velvet and sequins glove. She's going to kill them, kill them both. That's it. She'll find someone, someone who's ready to kill for money, and put an end to their miserable, worthless, turd burgling lives. Her anger swells and swells, becoming more and more absorbing and soon she is pacing around and around Anthea's large and opulent living room, talking to herself and saying again and again, "I'll fucking kill them, I'll fucking kill them, dirty fucking bummers, I'll fucking kill them, both of them." She pauses only occasionally in her rant to throw more brandy down her throat or snort another line of coke. She finally sits down, relaxing back a bit into Anthea's comfortable sofa. But she can't settle. She moves and leans forward across an exquisite coffee table. She picks up the bag of coke that's lying there and uses her Amex Centurion card to cut yet another couple of fat lines. Just a couple more, they'll help to keep her on top of the situation, help her to think of a way out of this mess.

As she finishes snorting the second of the two fat lines she's just cut, something horrible dawns on Shelley. She's completely forgotten about the British Pop Awards! Shit, she's due there in a couple of hours! But, all the drugs and booze...is she in a fit state to go? Maybe she should just swerve it? No. No way. She knows for definite that she's been nominated for an award, so why should she let fucking Andy and fucking Jack spoil that for her as well? She's going, she is just *so* going!

That said, she can't go like this. She's had a shit load of coke, she feels very jittery and spaced, not even the brandies she has had have smoothed that out, and the paranoia she was feeling earlier has made a comeback, if anything stronger now than before. She needs to bring herself back to ground a bit more. She needs something to calm her, something on top of the brandy that she fully intends to carry on drinking. Of course! There's diazepam in Anthea's room...that'll work, that'll hit the spot. She'll have a bit more brandy, a diazepam or two and a nice hot bath. That'll sort her out!

Fifteen minutes later and Shelley has ransacked the knicker draw for the diazepam, and is lying in a beautiful hot bath in the en-suite of the room she uses when staying with Anthea. She wasn't sure how many diazepam to take so she took four. When they didn't work immediately she panicked and took a couple more. Happily, the extra diazepams, the hot bath and still more brandy have together achieved a marvellous result. Where before her head was full of noise, full of anger, hatred and disappointment it is now full of an agreeable, dozy, smooth warmth. She likes these diazepams! She's bought the box with her and put it on the side of the bath. She decides to take a couple more for luck, swilling them back with the last of the brandy.

Yes, mmm, that's nice, she feels so comfy now, so warm, she's not worried about anything anymore, she's lovely and sleepy, yes she could almost fall asleep here in the bath, that would be so wonderful.

Dimly Shelley is aware of a clunking noise. Somewhere at some level in her mind she knows that this is the sound of the heavy tumbler she was drinking brandy from hitting the floor. Even more dimly she's aware that this has happened because it has slipped from her grasp.

Shit, now she *is* falling asleep. Shouldn't do that in the bath, Shelley. But what the hell. Why not. It's so nice, so comforting and maybe when she wakes up all this Jack and Andy and pictures stuff will have been nothing more than a bad dream.

Slowly Shelley's body, now in a deep drugs, alcohol and warm water induced sleep, slides down the bath. Her head begins to slip beneath the bath water, up to her chin, then over her beautiful cupid's bow lips, then over her nose, that famous, finely structured nose that is neither too big nor too small.

Somewhere inside Shelley's brain and nervous systems, frantic messages are going out...hold your breath! Jump out of the bath! Wake up! But both are so addled with coke, diazepam and brandy that they are unable to co-ordinate and with every breath she takes water, not air, enters her lungs.

Shelley understands that she's done something very stupid, something with absolutely fatal consequences. She's never going to make that awards ceremony. She'll never conquer the American market. She'll not even see another day. With this chilling thought Shelley no longer feels warm and comfortable, she feels a terrible regret and a horrible sense of unending and devastating loss. She realises that she is going to die and that in her life she's never loved anybody but herself and her handbags, and nobody has ever loved her. Jack never loved her. Her fans don't love her, they love the dream of escape from their ordinary lives that she represents, not her. Shelley never even loved her family, she never got on with them, and she dropped them like a hot brick when she became famous, too embarrassing and working class. Shelley sees her life flashing by her. She sees that she has lived it all wrong. She'll never have it again, she'll never be able to fix it. It's gone. Over. And just before Shelley slips into an endless oblivion of nothingness the sense of regret is painful and overwhelming and she feels very small, very cold and very alone.

Shelley lies dead in the bath. Under the water. A beautiful but unloved corpse.

ANDREW

The day me and Johnny are going to kill the pap, I wake up with a tremendous hangover. It's early but Johnny (Christ, he must feel even worse than me!) is already up and gone, he has a busy day ahead and has to start it with a visit to some acquaintances of his in Essex.

Yesterday night, with the murder of the photographer all planned and the event itself looming, we decided, for the sake of some justifiable light relief, to visit a club in Lisle Street, in China Town. It's gay, obviously, a mixed crowd of boys and girls, but predominantly young. It's small and always busy.

You should have come with us, it was fun. All that nonsense you spouted about being scared to come because if you went to the toilets there somebody would feel you up. What a load of crap. Anyway, you should be so lucky - have you looked in the mirror recently? You're not all that, you know.

We called a cab and whilst we were waiting we opened a nice, chilled bottle of Dom Perignon. The cab arrived quickly so we took the champagne with us, finishing it on the journey down to the West End. Johnny was in a fantastic mood, didn't seem to be remotely bothered by the fact that he was going to take another man's life the next day. Still, I guess that's my Johnny, always keeps up a cheerful front. I'm sure he's struggling with this deep down, he's just not showing it so as not to upset me. I mean murder is a big deal for anyone, unless they're a complete psychopath.

When we arrive at the club it's already late. It's busy, we're definitely the oldest people there. I order beer for me and Johnny, probably not a good idea to mix it with the champagne we've just drunk, but what the hell!

Whilst I wait for our drinks I let the atmosphere of the club sink in. It's hot, sweaty, there's a mass of people, pissed or on drugs, or both. People shout to be heard over the thump of the dance music, they laugh, smile, all around me is life and energy. And all this on a work night, too! This is why I love being a gay: the irresponsibility, the lack of necessity to conform, the constant fun-filled search for the next drink, the next line, the next shag, the living life for the sake of living life, the camp, frothy, lightweight nonsense of it all.

Honestly, don't be so po-faced, I'm not 'making light of a serious issue'. That's the way I feel about being gay, is all. Anyway, I'm the gay one here, not you. Well, I say that....

An hour or so later and me and Johnny have been knocking back the beer and we're both pretty pissed. A group of young lads push past us, with smiles and apologies, to get to the bar. In my over sentimental drunken state, I'm moved by their beauty and (comparative) innocence. I hope they stay young and fresh, I hope they keep their youthful and simple delight with life, I hope they don't choose to chase fame or celebrity. I share an anecdote with Johnny about a friend of mine who's into quite rough sex. I once had to take him to the Whittington hospital because he had a billiard ball up his arse, his partner had shoved it up there as part of some strange sex game. It got stuck in his rectum and he had to have it surgically removed. Johnny finds this hilarious and at one point is actually on the floor laughing. Later, the gaggle of youngsters who pushed by us to get the bar adopt us. They can't quite believe that we're as old as we are yet still out there in the clubs. They, and we, joke about our age, it's all light-hearted and fun. At one point one of the lads gives me his smart phone and asks me to take a picture of him with Johnny and his mates. I demonstrate my fundamental incompetence with technology, and my advanced years, by taking the picture with the phone held the wrong way round, succeeding in photographing only my hand. The lads find this very funny.

Another hour later and me and Johnny are even more pissed and we find ourselves on the dance floor, dancing some kind of crazed "embarrassing uncle at the wedding reception" type of dance. I'm sure I look ridiculous, an old geezer in his forties, throwing himself around as though he were still young. But I'm gay, I'm pissed, and most of all I'm very, very rich, so I don't give a fucking damn.

Eventually we leave the club at four in the morning, we go to the nearest mini-cab office to get a car back home, arriving back in Primrose Hill in good spirits and very drunk.

You see how much fun you missed? All because you make assumptions. No, you did make assumptions. You assumed that gay people are so sexually rampant and out of control that they wouldn't be able to resist touching up a piece of (allegedly) straight meat in the toilets. But you do that a lot, don't you? Make assumptions. You make assumptions about me, about other people, even about yourself. Here's a tip. Don't do it. Base your ideas about a person only on what your head and heart tell you to be true, never assume anything about them, people are not black and white, they're a very complex shade of grey and making assumptions about any one individual can have fatal consequences. You should trust what I'm saying here, I'm like Joan Crawford on this one: I've been to that particular rodeo before.

But that was then and this is now. It's 7.30 in the morning, I've had maybe three hours of sleep, I feel like cuntola and not even one of Rosa's wonderful breakfasts is going to shift my cuntingly bad hangover. For fuck's sake, I really don't need to feel like this today, I've got an awful lot on my plate at the moment. Like having one man (snot-nosed pap) murdered and mercy killing (beautiful Joey) another.

How's that for a fucking workload, don't get that in a standard 9 to 5 job, do you?

And then it all gets suddenly worse. Rosa comes in with the morning's papers. "Meester Manning," she says " I know you have bad hungovered but is important you see papers, not is good news I'm thinking..."

Rosa dumps a pile of newspapers on the table in front of me, no, indeed, not is good news. Suddenly my breakfast and even my hangover are forgotten. I rifle quickly through the papers, as if to confirm myself that what I am seeing is true: ENGLAND'S SWEETHEART IS DEAD, SHELLEY BRIGHT FOUND DEAD IN BATH, MYSTERIOUS DEATH OF SHELLEY BRIGHT, SHELLEY TOPS HERSELF IN TUB, SHELLEY SUICIDE RIDDLE, SHELLEY: SHE'LL SING NO MORE, SHELLEY DRUGS & BOOZE HORROR DEATH. Shit! Shelley, dead, poor cow. All the papers describe Shelley as being found dead in a bath at 'multi million pound home of ex Lady's Night singer'. Some allude to drugs, others to suicide. Quickly I make a call to one of my tame coppers to get the inside track on what's happened. I get straight through to him (probably thinks I'm going to put money his way, greedy fuck) and he tells me that, yes, although they're are still waiting for a toxicology report, they're pretty sure its drink and drugs related, they're thinking more accidental overdose than suicide.

Poor bloody Shelley. I'm guessing that yesterday Jack told her about the pictures of her that 'a friend' had sent him. Christ, I knew that she'd be pissed off, but this, this is way over the top. God, death does seem to be hanging around me today! Poor, poor Shelley, I never liked the girl (loathed her, to be honest) but I would never have wished this upon her.

No, you can't say that, it's simply not fair to say that I have Shelley's blood on my hands. Her death is simply an example of the law of unintended consequence. Forgive me for saying this, but you're becoming a bit of a liability and a real pain in the arse. You're always whingeing and criticising. But you're still here, aren't you? If you were really upset by what I do then you'd have left already. Dare I suggest that you're spouting a proper load of old cuntola and that you're probably a bit of a hypocrite?

JOHNNY

Johnny was up and away early. Now he's zipping round the M25 at a steady ninety miles per hour. He had masses to drink last night and has had very little sleep, but here on his beloved Kawasaki, the wind speeding over his body, he feels exhilarated and deliriously happy. Last night out with Andy was a blast! That story of the guy with the billiard ball stuck up his ass, loved it! And Andy asking him to kill for him, well, what better expression could there be of Andy's trust in him? And what a fabulously good omen for his new role as an avenging angel. Johnny sees it as a sign, an affirmation. If there is a God then Johnny knows that he is doing God's work. He is on the side of the angels and the rage in him is quiet. It is happy. It is singing softly to itself. It knows Johnny is where he belongs, a prodigal son, returned to his family.

Johnny's destination is Hornchurch. He is going there to meet some proper geezers. He called them as soon as he and Andy had put together a plan for killing the slimy pap. What a fucking toe-rag, blackmailing his Andy, who the fuck does he think he is? Dead meat that's what he is.

The boys in Hornchurch are Essex are old school gangsters. They're into drugs, cybercrime, extortion, murder, armed robbery or any other way to turn a quick and illegal buck. They are tough, bound by their own code of honour and, long as you treat them straight, utterly trustworthy. Fuck with them, and they'll kill you. Johnny's used them before for some of the jobs he's done for Andy, but nothing on this scale. Johnny knows that they won't have a problem with what he wants. He'll need to pay, but they'll do the work, efficiently, quickly and without questions.

His visit is to firm up details and to make a large cash payment on account. He needs the Essex boys to help him shift the body once the job is done and to properly and securely dispose of it, and he needs a guy to help him remove any electronic equipment and media from the photographer's flat immediately after he's been killed. Andy thought that would be a sensible precaution just in case the little shit kept any copies or back-ups of the pictures. According to Griselda (and Griselda's info is never duff) he lives alone in a one bed flat in Shoreditch, so that shouldn't be a difficult job.

As Johnny hits a surprisingly quite stretch of motorway, he guns the bike's engine over the one hundred mark and considers how he's going to kill the photographer. Initially he thought he'd just bash the little cunt's brains out with a claw-hammer (he's got a nice heavy one somewhere in his tool-kit), but now he thinks that that would be, well, messy, and not very stylish. What he needs as an avenger is a signature method of killing, to leave a sign to those who can sense this kind thing (Johnny immediately thinks of Charlie Gold), that this killing was carried out with style and panache, that it was done up close and personal. And it needs to be something that's not too quick. Something that's frightening and painful. After all the avenging angel's victims are going to be grossly fucked up and nasty celebrities or sleazy, chiselling bags of shit like the pap. They don't deserve a quick death. Suddenly an image of Paul Hunter, face blue and grotesquely distorted, swinging in a doorway in his Notting Hill home, comes to Johnny's mind and he knows what his particular style of killing will be. Strangulation. Perfect. It's slow, horrifying and it's something that he will have do close-up. He'll be able to feel the bastards kicking and struggling. He'll be able to look in their eyes as they draw their last breath, watch their eyes glaze over, feel the soft whoosh as their damned souls leave their corrupted bodies.

Strangulation. Perfect, lovely job. Now, where did he put that electrical flex?

JOEY

Joey has bedsores. Two, one on each heel of his feet. Fuck they're painful. The nice Philipina nurse has filled two latex gloves up with water and tied them off, placing one under each of Joey's heels. This seems to give some relief from the sores, trouble is he can now feel another one developing on his right buttock. Yet another thing to add to the symphony of pain and discomfort that is his body. His dying body. The pain is particularly bad at the moment as he's forgone his morning shot of morphine. He wants to keep a clear head as Andy's coming to visit him, he hopes to put the finishing arrangements in place for his last goodbye. He wants to leave now and go on his final journey, escape all this bloody pain.

This thought gets him thinking about death: what will it be like? Will it be painful? Will he be any more scared than he is already? Is detaching from the earthly world and moving to the next (whatever that might be, if anything at all) a smooth and easy process? Or is it difficult, painful and traumatic? Even though Joey knows he is close to dying, he still can't imagine what it's like, that intangible space between life and death. He tries to envision crossing it but comes up with nothing except a feeling of disbelief: his brain simply can't compute the possibility of it, of him dying, of going from a state of existence to non-existence.

From downstairs comes the sound of a doorbell, of a door being opened, and muffled chatter, his ma talking to Andy, then footsteps as Andy mounts the stairs up to Joey's room.

Andy strides in, looking confident, smiling, "Joey, love, how are you," he says and then turns to the Philipina nurse, politely asking her to leave the room so that he can talk to his "client."

After the nurse leaves the room, closing the door behind her, Andy sits on the side of Joey's bed and takes one of his hands, squeezing it firmly between his own, "oh, my poor, poor Joey," he says, "you look bad…"

"Mate, you don't know the 'alf of it, I got pain from me head to me toes, I got bedsores, I can 'ardly move and I can't bloody remember the last time I weren't lyin' 'ere in this fuckin' bed…please tell me we can finish this…I just can't do it no more."

"It's sorted, it's all sorted, all in place and we can do it tomorrow," Andy squeezes Joey's hand even tighter, looks intently into his eyes and continues, "I don't want you to worry about a thing, not a thing. I've got something from the doc. It's something you can drink, it's quick, easy, you'll just fall asleep and drift away, much better than that lousy plan you had to gobble down paracetomol, you silly sod!"

"Thanks, fuck, thanks, but exactly 'ow we gonna do it, like?"

"Ahh, I have a plan, and there'll be no cameras, no public viewing of your demise and I've already covered the money Charlie was going to give you. It's coming from offshore so it'll take three or four more days to get to your bank, you're okay with that? You trust me or you want to delay this whole thing until you can see the cash in your account?"

Joey thinks momentarily if he can trust Andy, has he really transferred the money? Stupid, of course he has, look at how Andy's stuck with him, this is the man who's going to help him take his own life, and if you can't trust someone who's prepared to do that for you, who can you trust?

"I trust you, Andy, totally. I want it t'be tomorrow....enough is enough...'ow quick will I go after I drink this stuff, like?"

"You'll be asleep in two or three minutes and gone in five, tops."

"I'm okay wi' me ma and pa bein' 'ere when we do it, I want them to be able t'say ta ra, like...but I don't want the twins 'ere, don't want 'em seeing their dad die..."

"Don't worry, not a problem, your parents will be here, and I'm pretty sure your mum would agree with you about the twins so you don't need to stress on that one. This is how things are going to play out, Joey. This afternoon the doc will come to see you, he'll pretend to examine you and afterwards he'll tell your mum and dad that you're critical, that you could go anytime. What that's about is preparing the ground for tomorrow evening when I'll be here to, er, well…to do the job. All you need to do on your part is make sure there's a glass of water by your bedside before I arrive. When I'm here with you I'll send the nurse out of the room, so we can talk about, I dunno, business, I'll put the doc's special "drink" in your glass and then you have a health crisis of some sort and I'll call up your parents. Once they're with us you ask me for some water from the glass by your bed, I pass it to you, you drink and, sweetheart, you'll have just enough time to say your goodbyes before you slip away."

"That sounds perfect, Andy, scary, but perfect."

"Good, I'm glad, I hope I've made things a bit easier for you, I really do…Joey, I want you to know that I'm going to miss you very much. I've always held you in a special place in my thoughts and I'm proud to be able to help, and proud to be able to give you a dignified death instead of that horrible crap Charlie Gold had planned for you." Are those tears that Joey sees filming up Andy's eyes? Surely not thinks Joey, not Andy, not cool, calm, coldly calculating Andy. But when he turns his face away from him and surreptitiously runs a sleeve across his eyes Joey realizes, yes, it *was* tears. He knows Andy's always fancied him, but he had no idea quite *how* much. "Andy," Joey says, breaking the moment, "I know you don't want me to say it but I really am dead grateful, you bin very good to me, you bin a rock."

Andy smiles, surprisingly he puts a hand on Joey's head and ruffles what's left of his once beautiful blond hair, "and you, my friend," he says "are one very brave young man."

After Andy leaves, Joey spends some time thinking about what an absolute star the guy has been. He said he'd sort everything out and that's exactly what he's done. He's so glad that he got Andy on board with all this, he's proven to be one hundred per cent reliable and supportive. Andy, thinks Joey, is the only honest and reliable person he has ever met in the world of celebrity.

ANDREW

As I leave Joey's room I feel kind of sad, a bit empty. Had a bit of a moment there, teared up. Truth be told it was because I was feeling a bit a rotten. Poor old Joey, he's lying there feeling like, well, death and he's thinking he can rely on me to sort everything out. He's put total trust in me. And up to a point he's right to do so. I'll be here tomorrow with the sodium pentobarbital, I'll give him the drink that'll end it for him, I'll make sure his parents are there, I'll facilitate his going and his goodbyes. The only thing I won't do is transfer that two million quid. I've already done a lot for Joey, I'm really going out on a limb for him, and I've got a pretty good idea of Joey's finances. He's stashed away more than enough to ensure his kids a very comfortable life, that last HIYA photoshoot alone was worth four hundred grand, for fucks sake. Anyway, Joey will be dead before my "transfer" doesn't get to his account, so who's to know?

You're off again, back on that moral high horse. I'm not interested in your opinions on this subject and you have no right to call me a twat. I never told you I was a nice person, like I said before, I am what am. Listen, I'll try and help you to understand this, here are some more little factoids which you should try and comprehend: nobody is entirely good and nobody is entirely bad.

Good people do bad things, and bad people do good things. That's the way life is. Get over it.

Mabel gets me at the foot of the stairs. I give her a big hug, I tell her I'm so concerned about Joey and his deteriorating health that I've asked the doc to come and visit him later in the day. I'm saying nothing that she isn't thinking herself and she hugs me and cries quietly into my shoulder. I hold her for a very long minute or two then kiss her goodbye and say lots of supposedly reassuring words that are nice but fundamentally empty. Once again, the paucity of language in the face of loss.

As I'm walking down Glenilla Road, away from Joey's, a black Range Rover with tinted windows pulls up suddenly besides me. Two guys jump out the front, big guys, white, buzz cut hair, black suits that don't seem quite able to restrain the muscles beneath them. Good looking in a cruel kind of a way, definite air of casually catastrophic violence about them. One of the guys opens the passenger door of the Range Rover and out steps, the one, the only, Charlie Cunting Arsehole Fucking Gold. Jesus, will I never be rid of this fat cunt? Charlie stands in the middle of the pavement, a one man road block, a black-suited thug either side of him. "Andy," he says, "meet Stanislav and Vlado, I mentioned to one of my Russian friends that I needed a bit more security and he assigned these two guys to me. They're Croatian, cut their teeth in the war in Bosnia. He keeps them on a retainer here in London for when he needs work of a certain nature undertaken. I guess you know what kind of work that is?"

"I can guess, Charlie, but why don't you go ahead and tell me anyway?"

"Ah, well, you see Stan and Vlad specialise in dealing with awkward situations, and I kind of thought it would be a good idea to keep our eyes on you today, see what you're up to. I thought we could hang out outside your place tonight, just to make sure that photographer doesn't come out alive. Course, if he does…then I know we all got a big problem and that's where Stan and Vlad come in."

Charlie's eyes narrow, he looks at me coldly, a sneer on his face, and pokes me in the chest with a Cumberland sausage size finger, "Stan and Vlad are here for if you fuck up, they'll kill the photographer and then they'll fucking kill you, am I making myself clear? I don't wanna use these guys because then I'll have questions to answer to my partners, but make no mistake, I will if I need to."

"Please, you really don't need to worry, everything's on track, the job will be done tonight as planned."

"I hope so, I kinda like you, you got real balls, and I'd hate to have to rub you out, so I hope everything goes down like it should..." Charlie pauses and waves away the two thugs "hey, fellers, piss off and sit in the car will you."

Vlad and Stan exchange a glance, look very disappointed that they're not going to get to hurt anyone and return to the car as requested.

"Hey, Andy, I was maybe a bit rude there, but you know, those guys were here and, hey, I've got an image to maintain, you know what I mean?"

"Not at all, quite understandable."

"Jesus Christ, "quite understandable," there you go again with that funny English talk, cracks me up, it really does, anyway, what was I saying...oh, yeh...assuming all goes well tonight then I need you to speed up the next foetus delivery. Janey says she's feeling a bit run down since she had the ribs removed and she wants a new foetus quick, you got 'til next week."

"For fucks sake, isn't there enough going on?"

"Hey, I'm only doin' what the lady says and it's not like you're in a great position to negotiate here."

"Okay," I say through gritted teeth, "I'll sort it."

"Knew you would, you're one of the good guys, and, hey, don't forget, me and my fellers will be watching tonight!" Charlie waddles back to the Range Rover, his huge bulk wobbling with every step, like some kind of huge, grotesque, super-sized human jelly.

Just before getting in the car Charlie has one more thing to say, "Andy, if you do fuck it up tonight I will kill you, but I want you to know that I won't enjoy it as much as I usually enjoy killing someone, it will only be a matter of business, you understand that, don't you?"

And with this comforting little gem he's away in the Range Rover with his two Croatian assassins.

Blimey, that was a bit scary, but nothing I didn't expect to be honest, just Charlie doing his job and putting the frighteners on. Making sure I keep up my end of the bargain. Have to say though, if that was Charlie liking me, then I'd hate to see what Charlie "not liking" me is! With friends like that and all that shit, I guess.

I arrive back at my house after the short walk from Glenilla Road. Rosa's in the kitchen, bustling around. Just to make sure that she'll definitely be out tonight I ask her if she's still going to bingo, she confirms that she is. Good. Johnny should be back from his trip to Essex soon, and then, once Rosa's gone off bingoing, we can get everything in place for our murder.

Feeling that it's all coming into place, and feeling I can maybe relax a little, I switch on the tele to catch up with what's happening in the world. And…cuntola! Would you believe it, the news channels are full of one thing: Paul Hunter is dead! Seems his wife discovered his body in their Notting Hill home. Police say they are not looking for anyone in connection with his death. What on earth has happened here? Curious, I put a call through to the same tame copper who gave me the low-down on Shelley's death. He tells me the Old Bill think it's all accidental. A kind of "when good wanks go bad" scenario, something to do with self-strangulation. Poor old wifey found his body hanging in a doorway, wearing ladies knickers and tights and surrounded by she male porn mags, poor cow. Bloody public schoolboys, all that fiddling around with each other in the dorms always leaves them with one dodgy sexual hang-up or other.

I'm glad Hunter's dead. If it wasn't for him Joey wouldn't be lying in that bed, dying. And he was a really smug cunt. I can't wait to see the papers tomorrow when all the self-strangulation and she male shit comes out, not to mention the knickers and tights! The tabloids are going to go into a frenzy! Hunter's reputation is going to be completely trashed, I can just see the headlines now, CHAT SHOW HOSTS TRANNY SEX SECRETS, CHAT SHOW KING'S PERVY DEATH , KING OF CHAT FOUND DEAD IN KNICKERS AND TIGHTS, TRAGIC HUNTER'S TRANNY TORMENT. Love it, just what the bastard deserved!

Now, come on, be fair, not even you can begrudge me being happy about Hunter's death. I mean, look at Joey, look at what Hunter did to him. The man was a grade A arsehole. The world is a better place for him no longer being around. And look at this in a wider context. Hunter's death is a message of hope for us all. It tells us that, every now and then, every once in a while, people really, really do get what they deserve from life.

JOEY

"Hey, kids, 'ow you doing...come on, scoot up here on the bed by me side, good boys, that's it, make sure you don't get tangled up in all them tubes and wires, good lads. I've asked your gran to bring you t' see me cos I want to tell you both summat."

"Dad, what do all these wires and machines do?"

"Well, your dad's not very well, an' all these thing they're kind of like...medicine."

"And will they help you get better, dad? You've been here for ages and ages and you still don't look well."

"Ahh, that's what I want to talk to you about, you see, oh...this is so difficult...you see daddy is very, very ill an' he's not going to get better. I'm going to be going away, boys, I'm going to die."

"What's dying, dad?"

"Well, it's when your body stops working but I don't want you to worry cos your body is like...it's like...a shell, an' in the shell there's the real you an' the real you isn't a body it's summat else, It's like an energy, like a...ermm....let's say a ghost but a very good ghost."

"Does that mean you won't be here anymore?"

"My body won't be 'ere no more, but that's not important. The real me...me ghost...that'll be staying with you. You won't be able to see me or 'ear me, but I'll always be in your memory an' your 'eart, you'll always carry me with you, an' I'll always be watching over you..."

"But will we ever *see* you again?"

"Well, lads, you know, we will see each other again, yes, cos, you see, time is one big circle and the bodies we 'ave, well they come an' go, but your ghost, that's like, indestructible, erm,…it can't be broken….an' your ghost travels round this circle of time again an' again, forever in fact, an' as it travels round the circle it lives lots of lives in different bodies but it always remember the people it loved in other lives, an' them people remember that they loved you too, so the ghosts, well, they're always seekin' out each other as they go round the circle an' 'cos ghosts are magic they always manage to meet...an' we love each other, don't we? That means that we *know* we'll all meet together again cos this circle, right, is very, very big and when you lads 'ave finished livin' this life you're livin' now you'll both be off travellin' round the circle livin' other lives an' our ghosts'll be together again over an' over. One thing to remember, though, we'll not always meet as sons an' fathers, we could be, like, friends, or one of you might end up bein' *my* dad or we could all be girls, an', well none of that'll matter cos, like I said the body bit of us is just a shell, and the bit that matters, our ghosts, will know that they're back with the people they love."

"So, you're going away, but not all away and not forever?"

"That's right, my loves, I'll always be inside you in your 'earts an' I'll stay there 'til we meet again....somewhere on that circle, remember?"

"It's horrid that you have to go, dad, but at least you're not all gone."

"Yes, not all gone...that's right...but while I am away kids, your gran an' granddad, they'll be your new ma an' da so I want you to promise to be good to them an' I want you to work hard at school, be nice to people an' you must promise to never, never try to be famous like your dad. An' most of all...always remember that I love you."

After the twins leave, Joey reflects on his "circle of life" idea. He'd only come up with it half an hour before talking to the twins, he'd needed something vaguely comforting to tell them about his death, and the "circle" was where his thoughts had landed. He thinks it's a pretty good philosophy, actually, at least as good as believing in religion or leprechauns.

THE MURDER

So, where shall we begin our grim tale of murder? Let's start it with the victim, the man who will be dead less than an hour from now. Let's dignify him with a name. The man previously known in these pages only as "the pap" or "the photographer" is actually called Cameron James. Cameron is twenty-six years old, an otherwise ordinary lad from an ordinary middle-class family, he studied journalism at Uni, but he fucked it up and left with nothing. Too much boozing, too many girls, not enough studying. He fell into his present paparazzi career through the encouragement of a family friend, and he likes it. It's connected to journalism (which is what he really, really wants to do), it gives him independence and provides him with an (until now) modest living.

That day he followed Johnny to Janey Jax's rented mansion and got those pics of her liquidizing a foetus, he knew he'd struck gold. It wasn't just the monetary value of the photos. Cameron also knew that if he played his cards right, then the photos could also get him that job as a journalist that he wanted so badly.

Cameron has come to Primrose Hill tonight to see Andy on the tube. The Mini had just been a hire job, he thought it might come in useful for his surveillance of the doc's place, and has he been proven right or what! When he gets out of the tube at Chalk Farm, he's feeling triumphant. He is only a few minutes distance from three hundred thousand in cash, and a shitload of Janey Jax exclusives. Wow! He is smokin'! He's hit the fucking mother lode!

He doesn't get what the big deal with that Andrew Manning geezer is, doesn't see why he has such a fearsome reputation. He rolled him over no problem. Just showed him the photos of Janey and that was it. He got what he wanted. He thought the guy was a bit of a muppet, to be honest. In fact Manning is such a fucking mug that he thinks that tonight's events are going to be an end to things. Stupid old bastard. What he doesn't realise is that, yeh, he'll get a memory card containing the Janey pictures tonight, but Cameron, Cameron is smarter than that. The memory card that he'll give Andy is just a copy. He'll keep the original one for himself and then, after a decent interval of a few months, after Janey's tour has come and gone and he's got what he wants from her, he'll dig out and sell the pictures to the highest bidder. That should be another million quid, maybe even two million, in his pocket…yeah, the biggest celebrity scandal ever!

Cameron thinks he's been really, really smart. He's convinced he's fucked over Andy and Janey not once, but twice. He goes happy and deluded to his death. Had he been maybe a bit older, maybe a bit more experienced, maybe a bit less blinded by dreams and greed then he might have realized that it's normal in this world for youth, hope and ambition to be crushed by age, experience and cynicism.

Let's leave Cameron for now, let him continue his short, damned walk from the tube station to Andy's house unmolested. Dead man walking. Let's go to Chalcot Square. It's night time, it's quiet, curtains are drawn, people getting on with their lives, nothing unusual there. Except perhaps the black Range Rover in which sit two very large men and one very obese man. And perhaps the white van parked a few doors down from Andy's house looks a bit out of place amongst the high-end motors of the residents?

Inside Andy's house, all is far from normal. Two men are putting the finishing touches to a plan for murder. Rosa is out at bingo, and Andy and Johnny are in the kitchen. This will be the scene of the murder (after all the kitchen is the heart of every home). Luckily, the kitchen is on the ground floor of Andy's house, easier to move the body after the deed is done. Johnny has repositioned the kitchen table. It's now in a position such that when Andy sits down he'll be facing the kitchen door, but Cameron will be sitting with his back to it. Andy has a large briefcase. The briefcase that should contain three hundred thousand pounds in cash. In reality it contains assorted paperback books. Andy has also placed some very impressive looking contracts on the table, standard stuff he's run off his laptop, not relating in any way to anything that Cameron thinks he's going to be signing. The briefcase, the "contracts" are all just props, there to lure Cameron into a false sense of security, to grab his attention whilst Johnny sneaks up behind him and slips a length of knotted electrical flex around his neck and throttles the life out of him.

"We ready?" says Andy.

"Yep, good to go," replies Johnny. And at that point the doorbell sounds. It's Cameron, come for his date with destiny.

Andy checks the video intercom, sees Cameron at the door and goes to let him in, walking slowly so that Johnny has time to hide himself in the downstairs loo.

Andy opens the door to Cameron, hopes he's had a good journey, exchanges comments about the weather, come in, do come in, just go down the hall, first door on the left, that's it. Settle down at the table there, all ready for you. All the time Andy is making small talk, he's aware of his heart pounding in his chest. He's scared at the thought of what's to come, doesn't know how he's going to react. It's a struggle for him to keep his voice even, to not give away the stress he's feeling but he's hyper aware how important it is to seem normal. Nothing out of the ordinary going on here, no, not at all. Move along, now.

With Cameron seated at the table, his back to the kitchen door, Andy asks him his name, claiming that he's forgotten since their last meeting. In fact he already knows Cameron's name, address, age, marital status, national insurance number and credit history - all thanks to the investigations of Griselda. He's just making more small talk, making sure Cameron is nice and relaxed and unsuspecting.

"It's Cameron, Cameron Jackson, Andy."

Andy wishes that this arrogant git would stop calling him "Andy" like they were bessie mates or something. Oh, what the hell - he'll be dead soon.

"I see, I see, thanks for that, I thought I'd better ask as, obviously, we'll need all your details to fill in these contracts. I explained to Janey's people the nature of the, er, photos you have of her and, as you've probably guessed, they're very keen that they should not be made public. So, you're going to get everything that we've discussed, everything you've asked for. It all adds up to quite a package, I must say. You're a very lucky young man."

"Thank you, I knew you guys would see sense, and let me assure you once I've got the cash and we've signed those contracts, the pictures of Janey will be yours to destroy, and you'll never hear from me again."

"Super, where shall we start with this, then?"

"Let's start with the cash...just so you know I'm acting in good faith, here..." at this point Cameron reaches into the pocket of his jeans and takes out a small memory card (the same sort found in any modern digital camera), "...are the pictures." He holds the memory card aloft.

"That's perfect, but before we proceed I need to ask you two questions, that okay?"

Cameron looks at Andy across the table and smiles, he knows he has the guy now. He's pulled off a fucking blinder, he's going to leave this house a rich man.

"No problem, Andy, me old mate, shoot..."

"Have you told anyone else about these pictures?" asks Andy, peering directly into Cameron's eyes. Cameron answers no, holding Andy's gaze. Good, thinks Andy, the boy really is an arrogant and greedy fool, he *has* kept all this to himself. Andy knew he would.

"And that memory card...that's it, there are no copies of the pictures?"

Again Cameron answers no, but this time his body shifts slightly to one side and his eyes don't hold Andy's entirely, they flick momentarily up and to the right. Cunt, thinks Andy, the little cunting arsehole, he's made copies. Still, no matter, that was half expected and can be dealt with in the clean-up after the little shit is dead.

"Alright then, Cameron, thank you for your confidentiality in this matter, I guess we can proceed with things now."

Proceed with things now. That's Johnny's cue. Johnny hears it and pads silently out of the downstairs loo, bringing a knotted length of electrical flex with him (cut from the same spool as the length that was used to hang Paul Hunter). He positions himself by the open doorway to the kitchen, where Andy and Cameron are still talking.

"So, I guess you'd like to see the cash, then?" says Andy.

"Yep, lovely," says Cameron.

Andy reaches down to the left of his seat, picks up a large, black briefcase and says. "the money is in here, have a look and you'll see it's all there."

Then events in our murder tale start to move very fast.

The money is in here. Johnny's final cue.

Cameron takes the briefcase from Andy and puts it on the table in front of him. Andy is looking at Cameron, but can see in his peripheral vision Johnny advancing quickly and quietly on Cameron's back. He makes sure he holds his gaze steady so as not to give anything away. Cameron clicks open the catches on the briefcase. Smiling, he opens it. He sees inside, sees it contains only paperback books, "what the fuck…" he shouts, no longer smiling, he's

angry but the anger is quickly superseded as a chilling thought dawns: he's been very stupid and has landed himself in a whole world of trouble.

And then Johnny is there, standing behind Cameron, slipping the knotted flex around his neck, he pushes his knee into the back of Cameron's chair and he's pulling back on the flex, using the knot at each end for greater grip, pulling backward with all his strength.

Cameron is trying to shout or scream, but nothing comes out of his mouth except a gurgling noise, he looks absolutely terrified. Andy has to jump back from the table to avoid Cameron's wildly thrashing legs. Cameron's face goes blue. His eyes bulge. His tongue protrudes. Life is slowly being throttled out of him.

ANDREW

As Cameron opened the briefcase, I was aware of Johnny coming up behind him. I see a length of electrical flex in his hands and notice, bizarrely, that he is wearing no shoes, just socks. All the better to sneak up on you with, says a decidedly hysterical voice in my head.

Then Cameron shouts "what the fuck" and Johnny slips the flex round his neck and pulls it tight. And just for a moment I see something in Johnny's eyes that I don't like: a look of triumph and glee - like he's enjoying himself - but then I think, no, that's just me. It's the stress of the moment. I know Johnny can be a bit rough, but there's no way in the world he would get any sort of pleasure from killing someone.

Cameron's really struggling now. I have to jump back from the table to avoid his legs which are kicking out everywhere. He's making strange gurgling noises, his face has gone blue. The kicking becomes less frequent and less frenzied, then stops. He's unconscious, open-eyed and drooling. I can't take this anymore. I run to the kitchen sink and puke. The puking stops, I look back over my shoulder to see that Johnny is still pulling on the flex around Cameron's neck, a look of ferocious concentration on his face. I have to puke again: this time I miss the sink, projectile spewing half-digested food over the kitchen floor.

When I'm entirely sure that that my vomiting has completely subsided, I turn round to face the horror show in my kitchen. Cameron is now most definitely dead and his open eyes are horrified, bulging, absent, empty. In my mind I imagine that they're looking at me, accusingly, judging me as a murderer.

"Johnny," I say, "you can let go now, it's done, he's finished," but Johnny doesn't seem to hear me. He's still pulling back on the flex, giving it an extra tug every now and then, making Cameron's head jerk as if in a grotesque puppet show. "Johnny, please, enough, stop now."

Finally Johnny relaxes the flex and lets it drop. He steps away from Cameron's body which slumps forward, the head clunking against the table. Johnny looks odd. Like he's been away somewhere else, or that he's just realised what he's done. Poor sod, he's just killed a man. He's probably in shock. I walk up to him and give him a hug and whisper "thank you" into his ear. As I hold myself close to him there's something in his trousers, hard, pressing against me. If I didn't know better I'd say he had a massive hard on. No, of course not, it'll be his mobile phone.

Now the job is done, the pap, Cameron, dead, I ask myself again how I feel. I thought I'd be okay with this, that it would be just a bit of necessary problem solving. But in fact I feel bloody awful – that's the honest answer. Watching Cameron die in front of my eyes was not a pleasant experience. I wish the guy hadn't been so stupid, so fucking arrogant as to think he could screw money and advantage out of somebody like Janey Jax and expect no blow-back. Silly, silly fool. I honestly feel sorry for the guy. Momentarily, for some reason, I think of his parents. They'll never see their son again. That makes me feel worse. I mustn't think like this; it was him or me, and that's that. And if I feel bad, shit, I should give a thought for Johnny. He's the one who had to do this awful thing. He must be in pieces.

Don't look at me like that. I did what I had to do to save myself. That guy was dead from the moment he told me about the pictures of Janey. Anyway, you stayed to watch it all, didn't you? You didn't need to, you could have simply walked away. But, no, you were there, hiding behind my big American fridge, popping your head round the side and drinking it all in. Me, I'm sorry the guy is dead, I regret it. But you. You. I saw the look in your eyes as he was slowly choking to death. You were fascinated, you were loving it, you were getting off on it. That's right, I saw you touching yourself down there. Something scaly and ugly and elemental and very old slithered out of that dark place in your mind, didn't it? The question for you now is can you push that creature back into the dark, or is it free to roam around your head for ever?

JOHNNY

As Johnny strangled Cameron he felt transcendent. The rage in him was singing with ecstasy and his mind and body soared to another place entirely, delighting in the struggles and strangled screams of the pap as the life was choked out of him. He's aware that he's revelling in the supreme intimacy of one human taking another's life. He has a stonking hard on. Suddenly he can hear Andy's voice coming from, it seems, somewhere very far away saying, "Johnny, please, enough, stop now." Johnny returns to the world. He stops pulling and tugging on the flex, lets it drop and steps back from the now very dead Cameron. Christ, that was fucking tremendous. He loved it! Another dead bad guy, another victory for the avenging angel!

Now he needs to get on with the rest of the job. But before he can Andy has crossed the kitchen and is hugging him, thanking him. Johnny hopes he doesn't notice his hard on. "No worries, Andy," says Johnny, "I've only done what needed to be done, that guy coulda screwed us good and proper, coulda got you killed...now you go wait in the hall and lemme get on wiv sorting this mess out."

Once Andy's gone, Johnny gets down to his work. He fetches a mop and bucket and clears up the puke from the floor. He opens the kitchen windows to dilute its smell and to disperse the miasma of death. Then he makes a call, and a man in the white van parked just a few doors from the house answers. "Melvin," says Johnny, "get round here wiv that box, I'm ready to go!"

While he waits for Melvin, Johnny pulls Cameron body to the floor and goes through his pockets until he finds what are obviously the keys to his flat, that's good, he'll need them for the next stage of "operation dead pap." He notices that Cameron has what looks like a memory card clutched in his hand, he guesses instantly that it'll be the one from his camera, the one with the pictures of Janey and the foetus. He knows that it should go with the body for destruction but the rage inside him tells him that this is something that might come in useful for the future. He should keep it. He slips it into his pocket.

ANDREW

It's the day after the night before. I'm up, breakfasted and dressed, upstairs in my room - answering a few emails on my iPad before I go to the office. I still feel bloody awful about Cameron, but it was a necessary evil, and that's that. Johnny, bless him, is still asleep. Last night was a very late one for him. For me too - I couldn't possibly even think about sleep until my Johnny got back from Essex and let me know that all had gone well. I consider waking him as it's getting late, but his part in the whole pap affair was entirely more, well, physical, than mine so I guess he deserves a rest. Again I find myself thinking about how he's going to cope with killing someone. I make a mental note that we should sit down and have a talk about the whole thing, but that'll have to wait: got a bloody busy day today. Soon as I'm done here, I have a meeting with Tom Clayton's manager. Tom Clayton, the world's favourite action movie star, a real man's man, tough as they come and butch as fuck. Allegedly. Trouble is, Tom is a screaming nancy. Yep. That's right, girls. That super handsome, masculine film star so beloved of the ladies likes, no loves, cock. Black cocks, white cocks, small cocks, big cocks, fat cocks, thin cocks. He loves them all! The man is a committed and insatiable arse bandit and cock gobbler. All that keeps his cock love out of the press is that, besides being an all-out penis addict, he's also an all-out litigator. I know exactly what Tom's manager wants. Tom's coming to Britain to shoot scenes for some new action epic or other and, whilst he's here, he'll be wanting to be supplied with an almost continuous flow of high end, discreet male hookers. I know because I've already done this for Tom in the past. It's not work that pays very much, but it's good for my profile (I always let it be known I'm doing work for Tom Clayton, though obviously not what the work is, I leave that as something to be gossiped about), so I'll do it gladly.

Does that info about Tom Clayton disappoint you? Sorry about that. That's just the way things are sometimes. There are so few things in this world that one can depend upon. Muse, feet of clay and all that.

And then, how will I be spending the rest of my day? With Joey, that's how. Giving him the drink that'll end his life and involving myself in yet another death. I do hope all this dying stuff is just a passing thing. I don't like thinking that I'm somehow trailing the Grim Reaper behind me wherever I go. My poor sweet Joey. This is going to be a *very* difficult day. I really will be so sorry to see him go. Anyway...can't think about that too much, it's just another job to be done. Which reminds me. I need the sodium pentobarbital. I root through the contents of my bedside cabinet draw and it's there, at the back, hidden away. I slip it into the inside pocket of my Armani jacket. Momentarily, that amuses me: I am an Angel of Death dressed in Armani. Ha bloody ha.

And then the fucking doorbell rings. Fuck! I don't need any interruptions in today's schedule. Who the cunting arsehole bollocks is that? Hopefully it's just someone like the postie and Rosa can sort it out. But then I hear Rosa coming up the stairs and I'm disabused of that happy notion. Rosa knocks on my bedroom door. "Come in!" I call. Rosa head pops round the door.

"Meester Manning is very important person" she says with a tone of excitement in her voice, "is very, very fat man and that singer lady, is big star, Janey something...the one that look too young, I think she has work done on face..."

Shit. Charlie Gold and Janey Jax, what the fuck are they doing here? Maybe something's gone wrong with my pap extermination plan? Oh fuck! "Thank you, Rosa," I say, "I'm coming straight down. Maybe you could just wait up here until our guests have gone?" Don't want no witnesses to this conversation, not even Rosa.

Oh, you're all excited I see. I guess that's because Janey is here and you're about to see one of the biggest stars in the world up close and personal. Don't get too excited, this visit could mean trouble for me. And trouble for me is trouble for you. I'll make sure it is.

I go downstairs. Walking slowly, carefully, deliberately, trying to stay calm. And there they are, the two of them, standing in my hall. Large as life and an order of magnitude as ugly. I pause three or four steps up away from them, unsure quite what to say. Charlie looks as unfeasibly fat as ever, and Janey looks fucking gorgeous. The foetus diet obviously suits her. In my state of mild panic I get the silly urge to shout at Charlie, FOR FUCKS SAKE, YOU STUPIDLY FAT BASTARD - STOP EATING, JUST *STOP* FUCKING EATING! I decide that would be a bad idea. instead I say "Charlie, Janey, such a pleasure, so nice to see you both. won't you come through to the sitting room?"

"Thanks, Andy," replies Charlie, "but we're good here - it's just a quick visit. Janey wanted to thank you personally for sorting out that awkward business with the photographer."

"Shit…" I blurt out, surprised that he's discussed this matter with Janey, "you told her about that…?"

"Me and Janey don't have no secrets Andy, and hey, stop hanging round up the stairs like that, Christ, you're making me nervous! come down here where we can see you."

I descend as instructed. As I approach Charlie, Janey steps forward. She is beautiful. Her hair is dyed deep black and immaculately cut. Her face is pale, her complexion flawless and her lips coated in deep red lipstick. She exudes a kind of glamour that I can only describe as…vampiric. She leans in towards me, puts one hand on my shoulder and gives me a kiss on the cheek. This close up I can see all is *not* perfect with Janey. There's something stretched and too tight about the skin round her eyes, the lips seemed pulled up towards the ears. Rosa's right, she *has* had work done. Strangely, as she kisses me, there is no warmth in the touch of her lips, rather an iciness that seems to paralyse my cheek and then creep down my spine. And her breath, her breath is disgusting. It smells of dead things. Janey's presence is totally weirding me out, what the fuck is that all about?

"Andrew," she breathes, in that deep, husky, sexy and oh so famous voice, "like Charlie says, I'm grateful to you for dealing with the photographer, I have your assurance that the matter is completely finished with?"

Now that I know Charlie and Janey are not here because there has been some unforeseen problem with my plan to get rid of Cameron, I'm confident when I answer: "absolutely, Janey. The guy was a loner, he hadn't discussed the pictures with anybody. He had kept copies, but we cleared everything out of his flat and destroyed it all, so, yeh, problem sorted."

"And there'll be no come back?"

"No, nothing, zip, nada...all done and dusted."

And at this point, I think Janey will just nod her approval and leave. Instead she steps right up to me and suddenly the bitch reaches down, grabs me by the balls and squeezes. Fuck it hurts! "Andrew," she says "whilst I thank you for your efforts in clearing up what was a potentially," she pauses, searching for the correct word..."*harmful* mess I have to say that some of the blame lies with you, or at least with your partner, and I will not, not, not…" with every "not" she gives my bollocks an extra hard squeeze "…tolerate any more fuck ups! Oh, and don't forget that I want another foetus next week. Don't screw that up, or Christ help you!"

And as I'm gasping in pain, that malicious bastard Charlie is looking on, chuckling. Enjoying every second of my agony, big, smug smile on his fat face. "Good, we understand each other then, Andrew?" finishes Janey, and at this point, her head tilts back. She lets go of my balls (thank fuck) and stares right into my eyes. Her glare is very cold and deep and kind of black, she pulls her lips upwards in a grim smile, baring her teeth and I can't help but notice that she has unusually long, sharp looking incisors.

And with that, it's over, Janey spins on her heel, walks imperiously back down the hallway, flicks a backward wave at me, opens the front door and lets herself out of my house, closely followed by Charlie who still has an ear to ear to grin on his face and is still chuckling quietly to himself. As the door opens I see that the two Croatian assassins, Stan and Vlad, are waiting outside to escort Janey the short distance from my door to their car.

And I'm left standing there, clutching my balls, still huffing and puffing with pain. Fuck. That was weird. Two things strike me. The first is that the relationship between Charlie and Janey is even closer than I thought. They obviously really don't have *any* secrets from each other. The second is how strange and scary Janey was.

I've mentioned before that I believe she's a psychotic, heartless, money-grabbing bitch. But this meeting was something in another league. She freaked me out so badly. That coldness when she kissed my cheek, that pale skin and dark hair, the distant eyes. The teeth. I keep coming back to the word "vampiric." For a moment I imagine what the world would be like if vampires really did exist and walked, unknown, amongst us mortal being. But that's just silly. Isn't it?

Oh, and by the way, I'm so glad that you found the sight of Janey squeezing my bollocks so very amusing, it's good to know who my friends are!

JOHNNY

The morning after the murder, Johnny had a lie in. It had been a bloody late night. The murder was quick. It was the cleaning up afterwards that had taken time. Soon as the job was done and the pap dead, Johnny had called Melv, who'd been waiting in his van just up the road. Melv came to the house with a very large, flat-pack cardboard box and a roll of gaffer tape. Together they opened out the box, applied lots of tape to the sides and bottom and, voila, they had a super-economy style coffin for Cameron's body. Body goes into box, Melv and Johnny pick it up carefully, supporting the bottom so that Cameron's corpse doesn't crash through, and under Andy's directions, they start manoeuvring the box and body out of the kitchen into the hallway.

And when they're in the hall what should fucking happen except that Rosa only goes and comes back early from her bingo! She lets herself in with her key and catches the three of them in the hallway with a humongous great bloody box and guilty expressions. "Hullo, boys," she says "I did good at bingo, I won five hundred pound so I return to quit while ahead...that's a big box , can I help to you, perhaps?"

Johnny doesn't know what the fuck to say. Fortunately Andy is there quick with a vaguely plausible excuse: "we're fine thanks, Rosa," he says, "just some, erm, old files of mine that I'm sending off for, er, incineration. You can't be too careful about client confidentiality after all!"

Unfortunately they all look suspect as hell. Plausible excuse or not, Johnny doesn't believe that Rosa, who's a shrewd old bird, is buying Andy's excuse. Consequently he's relieved when Rosa says, "ahh, files, yes, heavy files I see, to be destroyed. Well, is not my business. I from Georgia and in Georgia we are all blind. So - now I see nothing and I go to my room, good night, boys." And with that she squeezes past the guilty trio and is gone. Thank fuck for Rosa and her discretion!

As he and Melv were lugging the box-cum-coffin the short distance to Melvin's van, Johnny's pleased that the Square is quiet. No-one around. Except that he spots a big, black Range Rover. He can make out three people sitting quietly in it: two big guys and one very fat guy. Andy had already pre-warned him that Charlie Gold and his Eastern European muscle might well be keeping an eye on tonight's events and he's one hundred percent sure that that's exactly who he is seeing. He makes no comment and carries on regardless. Let them see, let them see Cameron dead and disposed of. Sure enough that black Range Rover would prove to be a constant companion to and observer of the night's events.

Once Cameron's body was loaded into the back of the van, he and Melv set off for Shoreditch, to Cameron's flat. Once there, they use Cameron's keys and let themselves in proceeding, quickly and quietly, to remove every piece of camera and electronic equipment and media, all Cameron's clothes and anything that looks like Cameron may have had some kind of personal connection to. They're quiet and thorough. By the time they've finished it simply looks like Cameron has come back to his flat, removed all his belongings and buggered off some place else.

From Shoreditch, the next stop was Essex. A scrap yard to be precise. The scrap yard belongs to one of the Essex geezers Johnny had met with earlier that day. There, with the assistance of more of Johnny's Essex mates, they feed Cameron's body, box and all (and everything they collected from his flat) into a large furnace. By morning, all that will remain of Cameron and his possessions is a handful of ashes. Job done. No man, no problem

By the time Melv dropped Johnny back at Chalcot Square, it had been early in the morning. Hence the lie in. Upon waking, Johnny had run the details of the murder through his mind. He remembered how Cameron had kicked and struggled as he throttled him. It made him feel giddy with happiness. With this second murder he has crossed a threshold and has truly arrived, he is now special, a taker of life: judge, jury and executioner. A true avenging angel. All these thoughts of murder and struggle give him a hard on and Johnny thinks (as he often does) about a quick wank, but is disturbed by the sound of the doorbell. He hears Rosa open the front door. She comes upstairs, speaks to Andy and then he hears Andy going downstairs. Out of curiosity he gets up, opens the bedroom door and sticks his head into the hallway. Now he can hear the conversation downstairs. He realises it's Charlie Gold and Janey Jax. Fuck, what are they doing here? He hears Charlie, then the low tones of Janey. Then he hears Andy gasping in pain and Charlie chuckling to himself. They are hurting his Andy! How fucking dare they! He wants to run to Andy's aid, to kick Charlie in the balls and then stamp on his head, to grab Janey by the hair and smash her face into the wall until her nose and jaw break into little pieces...but the rage inside counsels him. No it says, not now. Wait. Their time will come. Johnny knows the rage is, as always, right and wise. The conversation downstairs has come to an end. Andy is obviously okay, though maybe in some pain, and Johnny can hear Charlie and Janey leaving the house.

He retreats to the bedroom. He is furious at Charlie and Janey, he sits on his bed and pounds the mattress with his fists. How dare they, how fucking dare they treat Andy like that, he should kill them both, end their fucking lives bloodily and painfully. Charlie deserves to die because he's already threatened Andy's life, Janey deserves to die because she's a nasty, foetus-munching freak!

Again the rage says no, you need to wait, they are surrounded by people and well-protected. Develop your skills as an avenger. Hone them to perfection with easier targets - learn your craft Johnny, says the rage, learn your craft. The rage's words of advice calm Johnny. He stops banging the mattress with his fists, takes a deep breath and says to himself, yes, Charlie and Janey will die, but not yet. In the meantime there will be no shortage of potential victims for his avenging angel, after all, if you want to find out about celebrities who are acting in a truly disgusting and punishable way, then there's no better person to be living with than Andy!

ANDREW

I'm in a taxi on my way back to Primrose Hill. I rushed through my meeting with Tom Clayton's manager and, as I expected, he just wants me to procure rent for Tom. What is it with these stars of stage, screen and sport that they still feel the need to hide in the closet? I mean, I understand why they do. I understand, for example, that if Jack Brierley came out as a gay his career in football would be over. I understand that Tom Clayton feels he has his tough guy image to protect (what, gays can't be tough? Meet my Johnny), yes, yes, I get all that. But why don't *they* understand the general principle here? Them refusing to come out condemns the next generation of gay stars to hiding in the closet as well. Surely they can see that - surely they can see the need for a bit of backbone, a bit of self-sacrifice? If enough of them come out then eventually no-one will need to hide away anymore and the whole sad, pathetic charade of gay stars (and politicians and priests and the next door neighbour et cetera et cetera) hiding their real lives away from the public, and themselves, would end. Oh silly me, of course, I forgot, backbone and self-sacrifice, that's another two things celebs don't do.

I wish this fucking cab would hurry up. I need to be back in Chalcot Square. And then I'll go to Joey's place yet and do the deed. But first I have to see Johnny. At this precise moment I'm having a medium-scale psychological meltdown. It's all this killing stuff, that fucking photographer, Joey, the whole fucking thing. I've made Johnny into a killer, I'm going to become a killer. I can't stand it, it's all too much. Before I go and see Joey I must to speak to Johnny. I want to apologise to him and I need his strength, his forgiveness, his approval. I need him to tell me I'm doing the right thing.

Thank God for Johnny, I mean you don't give me any support do you? You just sit around on your fat arse throwing digs at me and being a mealy-mouthed hypocrite - and look at how you laughed when Janey was crushing my bollocks! I have to say that I think you're becoming a bit of a freeloader. I'm really not convinced that this relationship has legs. To be frank, the more time I spend with you, the more I'm not sure about you.

After what seems like an age and a half the cab arrives in Chalcot Square. I toss a crumpled up twenty quid note at the driver and dash up to my front door, put the keys in the lock, open the door and run in past a surprised Rosa, shouting "Johnny, Johnny!" To my relief Johnny's there and I hear him greeting me from the sitting room. I head straight to him.

And Johnny's just sitting on the sofa. Just there. Just like that. Calm as anything. He looks like a particularly contented Buddha. God I need this guys' strength.

I sit myself on the sofa next to Johnny and turn towards him, "Johnny, I need to talk to you, everything that's going on, I feel like I'm slipping under with it

Fuck…I've done bloody dodgy things over the years, but all this, that photographer, that bloody Janey Jax, and now Joey, it's just all too, too much..."

"Take it easy," says Johnny, putting a hand up to my face and holding it gently there. "Everything's gonna be fine, you'll see, you're gonna come through all this, you're one tough bastard and whatever happens I'll be there to help you out."

"But look what I've done to you! I've turned you into a fucking killer - can you ever forgive me?"

"Mate, you're being silly, that bloody pap got what he deserved, if we hadn't done him Charlie would've done us. I didn't enjoy doing it, course not, but we had no choice. My conscience is clear about him and so yours should be too. You're a practical bloke you know he had to die, you just need to think it through and keep your cool. And all that shit we're doing for Janey wiv the foetuses, it is what it is, it's the job we're in. All right, it's a bit nastier than even we're used to, but it's just a job and in a little while that Janey, well, she'll be gone won't she? She and that Charlie…they won't be around no more and it all be over."

Mmmm. Charlie and Janey will be gone? Not around anymore? Doesn't that all sound a bit final to you? Kind of a bit more affirmative than just they've gone back to the States. What's Johnny actually saying here? Strange…

Johnny's words calm me. He's right. This is the job we do - the pap left us with no choice and Johnny obviously doesn't hate or resent me for asking him to kill Cameron, which is a tremendous relief. I give him a big hug and say "thank you, thank you, Johnny, you really are my rock! Listen, while we're talking about this stuff, I've just got one other thing to tell you about. I'm going to Joey's place this afternoon. I'm going to help him do that thing we talked about, you know…end it…and I'm just not sure I can do it…"

"Why not, Andy?"

"Because, well, is it really, really the right thing to do?"

"You don't need to even think about that. Of course it's the right thing. That boy is done wiv life, he wants to die so you're only helping him do what he wants to do. Imagine the pain he must be in now, he wants to be free of that and whateva you do or don't do, he's gonna kill himself. Without your help, state he's in he'd probably cock it up and die in horrible pain. What you gotta remember here is that taking a life can sometimes be as beautiful as creating a life."

"Hmm, that's quite sweet, and quite philosophical. You're full of surprises, aren't you!"

"Yeh, well, whateva, but you get me dontcha, Andy? You ain't doing a bad thing here, you're just helping Joey, easing his way."

See, that's how a proper supportive person acts, you should try and learn from my Johnny. Perhaps then you'd have a few more friends than you do.

And he *is* supportive. It's amazing how much sitting down and talking to someone you love and who loves you can help, to feel their support, their understanding, to gain their insight. Already I can feel that my meltdown has been averted. I feel refreshed, calm and strong again. I give Johnny another hug and then he asks a funny thing: "so how you gonna do it then, how you gonna do Joey?"

"Ahh, it's this stuff I got off the dodgy doc, sodium pentobarbital it's called. It's a barbiturate apparently, whatever that is. I give it Joey to drink and within a few minutes he's gone - he'll just go to sleep and not wake up."

"Wassit called again?"

"Sodium pentobarbital"

"Oh, ok , sod-i-um pen-to-barbi-tal," Johnny says the words slowly, moving his lips in an exaggerated fashion. (*Almost like he's making an effort to fix them in his mind. Strange…again…*)

After thanking Johnny again for his understanding and support, I'm good to go, to do the Joey job. Before leaving I pop into the kitchen - take out my little brown bottle of sodium pentobarbital, open it, and carefully feed in a couple of spoonful's of sugar. I put the top back on and shake. And that's it. Death delivered to your door.

JOEY

Joey is woken early that morning by the Philipina nurse fussing around. Making sure all his wires and tubes are in the proper place he presumes. Actually, is "woken" the right word? Does he really fall asleep and wake up nowadays, or does he just drift in and out of consciousness? Joey's not sure but he thinks probably the latter.

Yesterday was a big day for Joey, he's surprised that he got through it. Saying goodbye to his kids, Christ that was hard. He'd had pretty much a repeat conversation with his ma and da later on. He told them that he felt that he didn't have long left (a message that Joey knew Andy's dodgy doctor would reinforce to them). His mum kept saying, "don't be silly, Joey lad, you'll get through this," but he could see from her eyes that she didn't believe it, and she could see from his that he didn't believe it either.

As he explained his (recently made up) philosophy of time as great circle, with spirits racing around it and meeting again and again as different people but always instinctively recognising each other…well…he could see it seemed odd to his parents. At times they looked at him as though he was delirious, but he got over his central message to them. Then he explained that the twins would be their responsibility, that there was plenty of money coming their way after he died. Most of all he told them he loved them dearly and he was grateful beyond words for everything they had ever done for him, that he was immensely proud that they were his parents. He wonders what they'd think should they ever find out the reason for his illness, not cancer, but his own self-administered poison. They must never know that. Joey is grateful that only Andy knows the full story behind his condition. His secrets are safe with Andy.

Having checked all his various tubes and wires, the nurse helps Joey, on his request, to move position in his bed. From lain flat to sitting up. Joey has very little strength and the poor girl has to push and pull mostly on her own. Joey's grateful that, though only a small woman, she seems to have surprising strength. Together, they get him into a sitting up in bed position. The nurse plumps up pillows behind his back and puts one behind his head. She asks him if he needs anything else - does he need the bed pan? No thanks (there's nothing in him to shit out), but could she open the curtains and maybe get him a small glass of water? Thank you.

The nurse opens the curtains, and daylight streams in. Joey thinks it must be a beautiful day outside. The realisation hits him like a physical blow. Shit. This is it. It's a beautiful day and it's this day that I'll leave this world. Today is the day I die. I'll not see any more beautiful days. I'll not see any more days, full stop. Joey is hit with a huge sense of loss. You know what? Despite all the shit, all the grief and all the cunts and haters it really is a beautiful, beautiful world. With this thought, the nurse returns, bearing his glass of water. She holds the glass to his lips and helps him take a few small sips. He asks her to leave it by his bed.

Joey slips back into sleep/unconsciousness and he dreams. He dreams a gorgeous dream. If his dream were a film it would be in widescreen, Technicolor, 3D, high definition, the whole shooting match. He dreams he is with the twins. His ma and da are there too and Andy and three of his oldest friends from his Doncaster days: Liz, Helen and Susan. They're all at Blackpool Pleasure Beach. There's nobody else there - it's empty. Fantastic! The whole thing open just for them! And Joey's body is well again. It's young, healthy, vital, it is whole.

In the dream everybody is having a great time. They eat candyfloss and donuts, the twins go mad in the arcades - piling a stream of coins (that just keep spewing from the machines like magic) into the slotties and video games. Then they hit the rides. There are no queues, nothing to pay, they just walk on. They do the Dodgems, laughing hysterically as they bump into each other; enjoying twirling on the Teacups ride; whizzing through the air in the old Hiram Maxim flying machines; screaming in wonder as they take a ride through time in the River Caves; pretending to get scared on the ghost train. Then after more donuts and candyfloss it's time for the grand finale: the Big Dipper. They squeeze close up together in one giant dream-sized Big Dipper car and they're off, racing along the track. Normally Joey hates this kind of thing, but this dream Big Dipper is special. It's fast but smooth and, surrounded by such happy friends and family, Joey feels totally safe and secure. The Dipper speeds along - slows as it whizzes round a sharp bend - then begins to climb a hill that seems to go on forever. It soars high up above the Pleasure Beach, way up above Blackpool, and looking to his left and right Joey can see far beyond the town and right out to sea. All the other rides become small and toy town in size. Now the hill is so high that the view is like that from a plane. The Dipper is pushing up higher and higher into the sky and as Joey looks down and beneath him he can see big, fluffy pink clouds that look like the candyfloss he has just eaten. Then huge objects appear above Joey's head: vast, snowflake-like constructions made of sparkling, clear ice, desperately beautiful and delicate and filled with a brilliant and warming, white inner light and Joey knows that they are stars. He is amazed, fascinated. They are so beautiful that they move him almost to tears. Then, as if it had decided it could go no further up, the Big Dipper car begins to descend, travelling down a huge and straight slope that seems to go on and on and on. It charges down, faster and faster. The wind whistles through Joey's hair, he feels an exhilarating freedom, everyone is loving it, Joey is loving it. But then he feels himself detach from the car, sucked out by the wind caused by its downward plunge. He's not scared, though, not worried. This sudden detachment seems like the most natural thing in the world. He flaps his arms and, just he as knew would happen, he can fly. He flies after the Dipper car for a while, but he can't keep up with its breakneck speed and he sees his family and friends are waving back at him from the car and shouting. They are smiling, they are saying "goodbye, Joey, we love you." Joey calls after them, "I love you too," and stops trying to follow. He knows where he must go now. Feeling light and happy he begins to fly upward, back up to those beautiful, snowflake shaped stars.

Suddenly, Joey's dream vanishes. He is awake, disturbed by some bizarre burning pain in his chest. He's pissed off, that was a lovely dream. If only he could have stayed there! The ever present nurse has seen him stirring and ask if he's alright, "I'm fine, love," he says but grimaces in pain. The nurse notices and asks if he would like morphine. He thinks about accepting, but this is his last day, he doesn't want to spend any more of it asleep or in that warm morphine haze, so he answers in the negative and asks the nurse if she has the time and she replies, "it's just gone three o'clock , sir"

"Please, don't call me "sir" anymore, it's Joey, and you, what's your name?"

"Amor, sir...Joey."

"Amor, that's a lovely name. Amor, I want to thank you for all the 'elp you've given me, you're a great nurse an' you 'ave a very sweet nature."

Amor beams from ear to ear and says "thank you, Joey, you're a kind man, a good man."

"Now then, enough of all this compliment swapping," says Joey trying to set a light tone, "'elp me sit back up will you?"

After some mutual huffing, puffing, pulling and pushing, Joey is back in a more upright position. Shit, he thinks, Andy will be here anytime now. He checks the glass of water is still

by his bed. Yes, it is, good. So this it. The end. He has less than an hour to live. Fuck. He's not scared though, that dream he had has been strangely reassuring. He's ready to go, happy to go, to be honest. Glad to escape the pain and discomfit that's been the main feature of his life for so long now. Sorry to leave everyone, of course, but, following his new philosophy of life and death, hopeful that it won't be for ever. Joey is about as prepared to die as any man can be.

There's a quiet knock at his bedroom door. Slowly it opens and first one head pops round, then another and another. Fuck. It's just like his fucking dream! It's Liz, Helen and Sue. "My girls!" cries Joey in delight, "come in, come in, it's so good to see you!"

The girls move as one, they come to Joey in his bed. Liz sits one side, Helen and Sue sit on the other. They're all touches and greetings, kissing Joey's cheeks, holding his hands, running their hands through his once thick hair. "Your mam called us last night, Joey," says Sue, "she told us you'd love to see us and so here we are."

"You mean," says Joey "that she told you you'd best get down 'ere quick like, before I go."

"Well, she said you weren't good, but you're going to pull through this, Joey," says Liz.

"Liz, girls, its good of you to say that but truth is I'm dyin', but I'm ready, I don't want no tears or sympathy so you three pull ya selves together...anyway, tell me, you musta left Doncaster bloody early to get 'ere for now, how's things up there, then?"

And so it goes. Joey spends a delightful forty minutes chatting away to his three old friends. He's always loved these girls, they were his best friends at school (he never really got on with other boys, he can see now that that wasn't a failing on his part: he just pissed them off because he was too bloody good-looking). They remained friends after school, and when Joey became famous. They were always there for him - a shoulder to cry on when things were bad, a source of mostly good advice and someone to share his success with. They were never envious of that success, never asked for more than he could give. They were always true friends.

And then, sadly, this sweet little chat has to end. Andy has arrived. He's standing in the open door of Joey's bed room. Looks very smart, thinks Joey. He likes Andy's suit, Armani he guesses. Joey waves Andy forward, saying, "Andy, come in, these are friends of mine from Doncaster, Liz, Helen and Sue. Girls, this is Andy. 'e's a friend an' 'e kinda 'elps me out wi' me, er, legal stuff." Andy and the girls exchange handshakes and greetings. Joey can tell that Andy's a bit stressed and seems a bit hurried. He's moving a bit funny too, like somebody had kicked him in the balls. Joey senses Andy needs his attention so he says, "girls, Amor, can me an' Andy 'ave bit of privacy for a few minutes? There's some stuff I'ave to talk about wi' 'im, business, that sorta nonsense." Of course, nod the girls and the nurse and they make their way out of his room, Andy following and closing the door behind them.

"Joey," says Andy looking nervous, rubbing his hands together and smiling rather fixedly as he does so, "how are you and are you ready for this? Christ, sorry, that's a stupid question but I...I just don't really know what to say, I've never helped anyone top themselves before!"

"That's okay, Andy, it's fine, don't worry, I ain't never topped meself before so I don't know what to say either!"

"And you're sure that this is what you want, that this is what you really, really want?"

"Absolutely sure, yeh. I'm exhausted, I just can't fight to keep meself alive anymore...just one thing, though...it won't 'urt will it, Andy?"

"I have the doc's word that this stuff he's given me will be painless, and he might be dodgy as fuck but he does know his stuff when it comes to drugs."

"Good, good," nods Joey.

"Joey, can I ask you a question?"

"Anythin' mate."

"Are you scared?"

"I'm shittin' meself to be honest, 'ave been for days now, it's a big thing to get yer 'ead round. I'll be like, 'ere one minute an' gone the next. To be 'onest, though, that ain't been the 'ardest bit of all this, not even the pain 'asn't been the 'ardest bit. It's leaving people behind, that's what 'urts. Leaving me friends, me ma an' da, an' especially the kids...that's the killer, the kids, I don't know 'ow many times I've asked meself if I'm doin' right by 'em, leavin' 'em wi' out a da, like...."

"They'll be well looked after, Joey, and they'll have your money behind them."

"I know, I know, an' that's the answer I always come back to in me 'ead. They're better off wi'out me around bein' a total fuck up."

"You were never a fuck up. Sometimes shit just happens."

"That nice of you to say, Andy, but we both know it ain't quite true, 'preciate the sentiment though...an'...when I said about leavin' friends behind...I meant you, too."

Andy clasps his hands in front of him and looks down, like a little boy in trouble and says in a genuinely sad voice, "thank you, that means a lot."

"No worries, I seen a different side to you in all this. Even after all these years of dealing wi' fucked up celebs like me, there's still something carin' in you, even after all this time you still got an 'eart. You make sure you don't let any other fuckers in this business know that or they'll screw you. Keep it well 'idden, eh, mate?"

Andy smiles and laughs, "don't worry, Joey, I learnt that years back, heart stays well hidden, I promise!"

"Right, well, that's that done, ain't got much else to say now except 'ow we goin' to do this, Andy?"

"Okay, it'll have to be quick, hold on a mo'." Andy moves rapidly, he takes the glass from besides Joey's bed, dashes into the en-suite, pours out the water and returns with a now empty glass. From his jacket pocket Joey sees him remove a small brown bottle containing an amount of liquid, he opens it, pours the liquid into the glass, puts it back besides Joey's bed. Andy takes one of Joey's hands, "this, Joey, is what you need to drink. I've put sugar in it but it still won't taste nice so swallow it quick. At best you'll have a couple of minutes to say your goodbyes, and then that's it..." Andy shrugs, continues, "what I'm going to do now is I'm going to call downstairs - say there's something wrong with you and get everybody to come up here. You ready for this?"

"'appen I am...but let's do it now or I might change me mind!"

Andy leans forward, takes Joey's head in his hands and tilts it upwards, planting a soft, warm kiss on his lips and says, "goodnight, little Joey. My sweet, sweet friend..." Joey nods sadly. There's no more to be said.

Joey watches Andy carefully. He's in his last minutes - he wants to take everything in. He sees Andy turn away from him, cross the room, open the door and shout out in a loud voice "quick, quick, there's something wrong with Joey, get up here!"

Andy retreats back to Joey's side, ready to pass Joey the glass (glass of death, thinks Joey). Joey is aware of a commotion downstairs, lots of noise on the stairs and then people gathering in his room; his mum, his dad, Amor, Helen, Liz and Sue and Andy is saying, "he had some kind of fit, it didn't look good!" Amor begins reflexively checking all the medical equipment he's wired up to.

"Joey, love, what is it?" his mum says, dashing to his side.

"There's summat wrong, Ma, I'm feelin' so weak..them twins wi' the nanny, yeh?"

"That's right son.. you want me to get 'em?"

"No thanks, ma, I've said me goodbyes to me little loves. I never wanted 'em to see me die an' I think that's what's happening ma. I think I might be dying…"

"No, Joey, no, don't say that!"

"Ma!" says Joey insistently, grasping her hands, "really, I think this is it..."

Joey's mum starts to cry, Joey feels her pain and it almost overwhelms him and for a short, panicked moment he thinks about backing out but thinks no, he's come this far, this is it.

"Andy." he says, "I got a terrible thirst...gimme a drink will you, mate."

Joey watches intently as Andy picks up the glass of death, leans over him and holds it to his lips. Here we go, he thinks. He pauses, he feels fear, he feels more panic, he feels a sense of total disbelief. But still he drinks.

"Thanks, Andy," he says. "Ma, da, I love you both more than I can say - look after them lads, give 'em plenty of love."

"I'll love 'em like they were you, son" replies Joey's mum.

Joey's already feeling tired and he decides he needs to be quick.

"Da...you look after ma, girls, look at you three, what do you like, 'ave a drink for me every time you go out. Don't forget me. Amor, thanks for lookin' after me, you're a love, and Andy, you're a real mate..."

Now Joey's feeling not just tired, but heavy. He knows things are beginning to slip away. He takes a look round the room and it's a sad little tableaux. His da's at the foot of the bed trying to be a proper northern bloke by attempting not to cry. Amor is in the background, biting her bottom lip, her eyes sad. Liz, Helen and Sue are standing side by side, arms over each other's shoulders - standing like footballers in a defensive line out. They're all crying, tears smudging their makeup. Andy's standing to one side of him, a hand on his shoulder and his ma is at his other side, sitting on his bed, crying and holding his hand. Joey takes a deep, deep breath, wanting to taste life one more time, looks to the window. Sunlight is streaming in. It's still a beautiful day. It's still a beautiful life. Fatigue overwhelms him. He feels very warm and there is a rushing noise in his ears like water going down a plug-hole. The last thing he hears is his mum whispering in his ear, "son, I love the very bones of you." He has a wonderful understanding that he has always loved and been loved. That besides love, nothing else is worth a damn. And with that final realisation, his life is borne away on a smooth and happy tide.

ANDREW (AND YOU)

When Joey asked me for a drink, I picked up the glass with the deadly liquid in it and held it up to his lips, tilting it forward to help him drink. He winced at the taste but swallowed it down. As he drank his eyes looked up at mine. They seemed to contain, in equal measures, terror and relief.

After the drink was downed, things happened very quickly. Almost immediately a tiredness, a resignation, seemed to overcome Joey. He said his goodbyes to everybody in the room and everyone, including me, began to cry. I saw Joey look round the room intently, like he knew this was the last thing his eyes would ever see and wanted to fix the scene in his mind. And then his eyes closed. I saw Joey's mum put her mouth to her son's ear and whisper something and very soon after that the machine measuring Joey's heartbeat screeched in alarm. Amor advanced towards Joey's bed, perhaps intending to try and bring him back. I caught her eyes with mine, I silently shook my head conveying the message "no, leave him," she paused and nodded back to me and stopped where she was. And then it was all grief, Joey's dad covering his face with his hands, sobbing, his mum lying across Joey's body letting out a low and continuous moan and the Doncaster girls huddled together, united in tears.

And me. Me, I couldn't stand it. Too much sadness, too much pain. I fled from Joey's room. Before I know it, I'm down the stairs heading towards the front door of the house, but that's not a good idea: there's too many paps out front. Don't want them seeing me like this. I turn on my heel and instead make for the back of house and out into the garden. The garden is sunlit and quiet. At the back, under the shade of a chestnut tree, there's a table and chairs, which I head straight towards. I sit and hold my head in my hands. My Joey, poor, sweet Joey. Dead. Gone.

I feel bloody awful, devastated. There's a question screaming out in my head. The question is "who really killed Joey Camps?" I know the answer, and it's not a happy one. Celebrity killed Joey because he had come to define himself so much as a "celebrity" that he couldn't even contemplate the idea that one day he might just screw it all up and lose his blessed, stupid, pointless celebrity fucking status. He simply couldn't envisage having any other life other than that of a star. Did I kill Joey because my (highly successful) cancer plan showed him how much public sympathy can be gained from a 'strategic' illness? No, it was Joey that changed the rules of our little 'cancer' game. Did I kill Joey because I held a poisoned chalice to his lips? No. It was Joey who chose to drink.

But if we accept that celebrity killed Joey then, by extension, I killed Joey. I killed Joey because I'm part of the whole machinery of celebrity.

And you, you're looking smug again. Well you've no reason to be. You killed Joey too because you're as much part of that machinery as I am. Every time you bought a celebrity magazine, you killed Joey. Every time you watched a chat show or voted in the latest reality TV extravaganza, you killed Joey. Every time you read a sleazy tabloid exposé, you killed Joey. Every time you dreamt of your own fifteen minutes in the spotlight, you killed Joey.

We're both culpable. Me and you, together, we killed Joey.

THE ENDINGS

You want a nice, neat ending for this story, don't you? You want one that you can simply file and forget. I'm afraid that's not going to happen. This story is a story of peoples' lives and as such it can't have just one ending. Because that's not the way life is. You see, no matter how lightly we try to step through this world, we always leave footprints in the Souls of Others. Your story will end one day, sooner or later you will die. And when you die, your story will have ended to you in one particular way. But for those who love or hate you, or who are just indifferent to you? They'll have different views of how your story was played out. For them the tale of your life will end in a way unique to their own experience of you: to one person the end of your life will be a cause for sorrow, to another, a cause of delight or a complete irrelevance. Our lives are made up of many differing threads, we are different things to different people, we are different people at different times. There are many different faces to a single Soul. It's not possible to weave all the diverse strands of a life together to create one single narrative, or to create one definitive ending.

What follows, then, are the endings for this story as I see them. You may see things differently. You may decide my endings are wrong. That I've misread or misunderstood the story in some way - or maybe I've been feeding you lie after lie? If you believe any of those things, if you really do see me as unreliable witness to events, then, please, write your own endings. They will be as real, or as illusory, as mine, and I'd be delighted to read them.

Joey once remarked that Andy had a heart. Events were to prove him correct. Some days after Joey's death Andy still felt awful about it all. He couldn't quite put his finger on why. Okay, yes, there was the whole involvement in the machinery of celebrity thing, but his unease was something more than that, something deeper. Then one day it struck him why he felt so bad. Blindingly bloody obvious, really. Andy had promised Joey that he would pay him two million quid for the aborted Charlie Gold live on TV death scene. And he hadn't - but he'd let Joey die with the impression that he had. What a complete and utter tosser! How could he do that to Joey?

The very next day Andy transferred the money to Joey's estate. Now Andy felt ready to move on and he plunged himself back into his work dealing with the dysfunctional and at times plain weird problems that his celebrity clients brought to his doorstep.

After two killings Johnny felt like a new man. He now had a true role and function in life: an angel of death, an avenger. He sometimes speculated how he'd ended up as a murderer. He came to the conclusion that it was too many years in the world of celebrity. Celebrity cheapens everything. It takes human experience and packages it up to sell as simplistic and sensational sound bites and headlines. If human existence and emotion become so cheapened and commoditized, so too does human life. At least that's how Johnny sees it. He is a product of the environment he lives and works in. That's his justification.

Johnny already has his next victims lined up. He's decided that Charlie Gold and Janey Jax have to die – for treating Andy badly and just for being so plain fucking sick and weird. They are pretty big targets, though, so Johnny appreciates that he'll have to wait until the time is right. He has the memory card with the images of Janey drinking a liquidised foetus safely stored away. He knows it'll come in useful. In the meantime, he's got another badly behaving celeb lined up and ready to do: a particularly rich and famous entertainment industry figure. Poor Kerry, embarrassed and humiliated, had come to him with a story of a visit she'd made to the guy's office and the disgusting way in which he'd treated her. Johnny is very fond of Kerry so he was well pissed off with what she told him. His mood was furthered soured when he probed Andy for more info on the guy: word is that the guy is a predatory sex beast who exploits the young wannabe stars he invites to his office to "talk" about their careers. He dangles the carrot of fame in their faces but gives them nothing back but sexual abuse and humiliation. Exactly Kerry's experience. Bastard. He will definitely be Johnny's next kill. He's thinking very large dildo with razorblades embedded in it.

What can be said about Joey? After all, he's dead. But what a beautiful death. Quietly, calmly, surrounded by friends and family. Even the media was kind. Joey was a Lovely Young Man who Struggled Bravely against Cancer. There was much sympathy for his family and particularly the twins. The entire Queen as a rancid old cunt incident was entirely forgotten and forgiven. Joey got what he wanted - he went out on top and was fondly remembered.

The twins moved up to Doncaster with their grandparents, richly provided for by Joey's will (Joey also, in a tribute to the man he was, left a substantial chunk of money to Amor). And if they sometimes missed their dad intensely, they were always comforted by the fact that somewhere and somehow, around that circle of time, they and their dad would meet again.

Shelley is also dead. Gone. Slipped out of the public consciousness: Shelley who? Nobody gives a flying fuck that she's no longer alive - not even Anthea who's far too busy shopping to spare a thought for Shelley. And, anyway, she's found a new Best Drugs Buddy.

Shelley's death was not pleasant. It was cold and lonely, full of regret. If she had been able to see the press reaction the next day she wouldn't have been any happier. There was no more "England's Sweetheart," it was all about the drugs, all about Shelley as a sad and lonely drug addict. A women who, as it turned out, had no real friends and, as various witnesses (real and pretend) slithered out of the woodwork, the true extent of Shelley's drug habit became known. Shelley is remembered nowadays, in as much as people still speak of her, as "that junkie singer that drowned in the bath."

After not being able to contact her husband, Paul Hunter's wife decided to visit the Notting Hill house to find out exactly what was going on. Upon entering the property, she was struck by the smell. Rich, pungent, putrid. She, literally, followed her nose upstairs.

When she saw Paul's body hanging in a doorway, blue in colour and grotesquely swollen, her initial reaction was to scream. But as she took in the she male porn mags and the ladies' knickers and stockings she began to laugh and laugh, so much so that she had to sit down to get her breath. Paul was philanderous bastard. She'd had to put up with affair after affair from him. He was patronising, occasionally cruel, mean with money, small-dicked and shit in bed. She only stayed with him for the sake of the kids. And now he was dead, and in the most bizarre and humiliating of circumstances. Good. Fantastic. He'd got what he deserved and she was delighted to see the back of him. She hopes he'll rot in hell.

There would be no dignity in death for Paul Hunter. When details of how Paul died were leaked to the media there was a feeding frenzy: she male mags, knickers and stockings, poppers, scarfing…it all came out. Paul's reputation was utterly trashed. Had he been alive, he would have died of shame.

After several days without any contact from their son, Cameron Jackson's parents reported him to the police as a missing person. Eventually, as part of the enquiry into Cameron's disappearance, the police would break into his flat. They found nothing suspicious there. Indeed, everything was very neat and tidy. Cameron's clothes had gone and there were no computers, laptops or cameras that you would have associated with Cameron's career. It looked like Cameron had simply packed up his stuff, upped and left.

And that, in fact, was what the police would come to conclude. There was nothing suspicious in Cameron's disappearance. He was just another one of the hundreds of people every year who walk out on their lives. Just another person who chose, for good reasons or bad, simply to disappear and begin a new life in a new town.

The missing person investigation was quietly shelved and the police informed Cameron's parents that they considered the case closed..

Charlie and Janey were fine. People like them always are. The only slight fly in the ointment as far as Janey was concerned was that the foetuses were just not hitting the spot anymore. She felt that she needed something bigger, more substantial. A small child, perhaps. She would raise the subject with Charlie. Charlie would know what to do, he could lay his hands on anything. He lives to serve her.

And you. Did you learn anything? About life? About love? About celebrity? Maybe you did, maybe you didn't. Learn. Don't learn. I don't care either way. It's not my role to teach you stuff. I just put the facts (or are they the facts?) before you and let you make your own decisions. I learnt things about you. More than you would think, in fact I know all that there is to know about you and your dark places. It's all stored away in my head. One day I'll maybe use what I know. You didn't learn anything about me, did you? Am I a work of fiction? A composite character? A real person? Or am I just a pathological liar spouting a load of old cuntola? I did tell you on a number of occasions that I would always surprise you. And I have - all this time together and you've still no idea who I am or what makes me tick, no idea whether I'm a good man or a bad man. That pleases me because that's as it should be. That means I'm doing my job properly.

Let's say our goodbyes now. I wish I could say it has been a pleasure to meet you, but I'm not sure it has. To be honest, I've grown to dislike you. You really pissed on your chips, as far as I was concerned, when Joey died. It was like Cameron all over again. You were just there watching and enjoying. A brave young man died, and to you it was just a show: no involvement beyond looking, no emotion beyond cheap voyeuristic thrills. No connection, no empathy. Just entertainment. All that time we spent together and you never really appreciated how much Joey meant to me. One final word before we part ways. Everything you've seen, everything you've heard, keep it to yourself. A lot of people, including me, could be damaged if you don't keep your mouth shut. Breathe a word to anyone and I'll be sure to see to it that our paths cross again, some lonely place, some dark night when you're least expecting it.

Thank you…

…for reading 'Dying to be Famous', I hope very much you enjoyed it! If you did, could I trouble you to leave a positive review for the book - if you do, I'll put a good word in for you with Andrew.

After all, you never know when you might need his help…

If you'd like to contact the author (that'll be me!) directly with thoughts, comments or just plain old ranting, please feel free to email me at reallyreallynovel@gmail.com

Made in the USA
Middletown, DE
18 February 2019